COSIMA
Unfortunate
STEALS A STAR

LAURA NOAKES

Illustrated by Flavia Sorrentino

HarperCollins *Children's Books*

First published in the United Kingdom by
HarperCollins *Children's Books* in 2023
HarperCollins *Children's Books* is a division of HarperCollins*Publishers* Ltd
1 London Bridge Street
London SE1 9GF

www.harpercollins.co.uk

HarperCollins*Publishers*
Macken House, 39/40 Mayor Street Upper
Dublin 1, D01 C9W8, Ireland

1

ISBN 978–0–00–857905–0

A CIP catalogue record for this title is available from the British Library.

Typeset in Weiss Std 11pt/18pt by Sorrel Packham

Printed and bound in the UK using 100% renewable electricity
at CPI Group (UK) Ltd

To my parents, Jackie and Tim, for always believing in me. To my husband, Connor, for being at my side through everything. And for every disabled child who doesn't feel seen – your story matters.

Cosima

Pearl

Mary

Diya

Miss Stain

Mr Stain

Aggie

Lord Fitzroy

Miles

THE LONDON GAZETTE

13th November 1899   Price 2d

MISS DOE STRIKES AGAIN – LIES OF A FACTORY BOSS

*London's pluckiest and most mysterious girl reporter has once
again proved that energy rightly applied and directed will
accomplish anything. The young Miss Doe has used her derring-
do to expose the shoddy treatment of matchbox makers and secure
better wages and treatment for the women and children.
Read the full story only in next week's* Gazette.

Lord Francis Fitzroy,
WORLD-FAMOUS EXPLORER, proudly presents:
THE EMPIRE EXHIBITION
HELD AT THE TREASURE PALACE, EXHIBITION ROAD

*Gaze at wonders from around the world. EXOTIC ANIMALS
never seen before on our shores, ANCIENT FOSSILS of long-ago
creatures, SPARKLING JEWELS discovered in our great British
colonies, WHIRRING INVENTIONS that will marvel onlookers.*

Opening Friday 20th November

*And see the JEWEL IN THE CROWN,
the symbol of British might throughout the globe:*

THE STAR DIAMOND TIARA
Admission – ONE SHILLING; from 10 a.m. till 9 p.m.

*Vagrants, foreigners and degenerates discouraged from visiting.
Read all about it on PAGE 2 of today's* Gazette

MEETING OF THE INSTITUTE –
PLEA FOR CURE FOR DEFECTIVES

*Under the auspices of The Institute, a meeting of interested
parties was held yesterday on the subject of what to do with
the permanently defective. Members resolved to hold their next
meeting at the Treasure Palace next Saturday evening.*

CHAPTER ONE

Cosima pressed her face against the frost-covered window of the ground floor of the Home for Unfortunate Girls, her breath fogging up the glass. She could just about make out a shadowed figure striding purposefully towards the front door. Muffled sounds drifted through the flimsy walls, and Cos caught the *swoosh* as Miss Stain welcomed in the mysterious guest from the snowstorm outside. The well-to-do ladies Miss Stain had invited round for tea weren't due for hours yet.

Footsteps thundered towards the schoolroom.

'Mr Stain is coming,' Cos hissed to the others. 'Hide everything!'

As fast as she possibly could Cos creaked herself upright, her joints performing a cacophony of painful clicks. Activity buzzed through the schoolroom as maps were torn down from the wall, contraband items hidden hastily under loose floorboards, and Diya shoved her half-finished invention into the cupboard.

Cos grabbed her walking stick, made from an old broom Diya had found in the back of a cobweb-covered cupboard, and limped across the groaning floor. She sat with a thud on a cramped school desk just as a peephole embedded in the door opened.

A beady eye peered inside, glaring at the children. Cos tried to look as innocent as possible as Miss Stain's brother, the

equally awful Mr Stain, surveyed the room, counting under his breath to make sure all were present and accounted for.

Cos glanced around at her friends. All were dressed in identical uniforms and hunched over desks, staring glumly at the old rope they were unpicking.

'Number one, back to work!' Mr Stain barked at Cos. 'Miss Stain wants each of you to unpick three pounds of rope by tonight.'

Huffing, Cos grabbed the rope coiled upon the desk and began picking apart the fibres.

Number one, she thought mutinously, *is not my name.*

She glowered at the wonkily sewn 'number one' on her uniform. When a child arrived at the Home for Unfortunate Girls, they were immediately assigned a number. Most children were prised from their families when they were older, and their disabilities had become unignorable. But Cos, who had arrived at the home when she was a baby, was number one.

That fact clogged in Cos's throat like the almost inedible gruel the Stains fed their charges. She swallowed it away and a hopeful fluttering soared in her belly. One day she would uncover her past. Not *if*, but *when*.

Mr Stain finally slammed the peephole shut, and Cos immediately let the rope fall from her hands.

She stood up, wobbling a little as she leaned into her stick. 'Afternoon tea with their ladyships doesn't start for hours, the baker's dropped off the goods and now an unexpected visitor has distracted Miss Stain,' Cos whispered, as soon as Mr Stain's footsteps faded into nothingness. 'It's the only time today when she won't have her hawk-eyed gaze on the kitchen door. This is our chance!'

There was a murmur of agreement from some of the girls,

14

but others still stared resolutely at their rope.

Cos sighed. They'd given up. She couldn't blame them. But Cos was a firm believer that a mouthful of cake had healing properties, and she was determined to cheer her friends up. She turned to the three girls nearest to her: her best friends in the home.

'I'll need a crack team to pull this one off. What do you think, Mary?'

A scraggy blonde-haired girl at the desk next to Cos wrung her hands and bounced her knees up and down. The number fifteen was embroidered on her pinny. She abandoned the section of rope she was pulling apart to grab her trusty wooden clipboard, which she twizzled absentmindedly between her hands.

'I dunno, Cos. She'll lock us away with no dinner when . . . I mean *if* she catches us.' As Mary spoke, her breath billowed out in puffs and her teeth chattered. The weather had been bitterly cold lately, and the Stains weren't for wasting roaring fireplaces on their charges.

'But I've devised a fail-proof plan!' Cos protested, her bottom lip protruding. Her friends were woefully pessimistic about the chances of all her – *rather fantastic* – ideas.

'I bet you haven't!' A loud voice huffed in consternation. Diya paused her task of rope-picking. She rolled herself away from her desk, the wheels on her wheelchair squeaking noisily.

Diya had brown skin and a swoosh of silky hair, an overstuffed tool belt slung across her waist and an oil slick smeared on her cheek. As a toddler Diya had been struck down with polio, a horrible disease that had left her legs paralysed. The number ten was visible on her crumpled dress. She raised a questioning eyebrow at Cos.

Cos sighed. She could almost picture the complex calculations running through Diya's gigantic brain that would inevitably judge Cos's ideas as lacking.

'If we take your past shenanigans into consideration,' Diya continued, spinning her favourite home-made spanner between her fingers, 'the projected success rate of this particular caper is nought point three per cent. Remember the time we crept into Miss Stain's bedroom in the dead of night because *you* thought she might be a bloodsucking demon in disguise?'

Cos crossed her arms. 'It was a reasonable theory!'

On the desk next to Diya Pearl stifled a rare giggle. She was carefully painting a purple emperor butterfly on to her wrist. It joined the other paintings of dragonflies, moths and bees that she'd decorated her ink-covered arms with. She'd also scribbled on her uniform, obscuring her assigned number: thirteen. Pearl, like Cos, was a medical mystery. Doctors called her behaviour *abnormal*, but Cos thought that short-changed Pearl's wonderfulness. Pearl liked spending time alone, found talking to new people tricky and hardly ever smiled, which made it even more special when Cos coaxed a grin out of her.

'Or –' Diya barely paused for breath – 'when you were convinced that running away to become pirates was a good idea. Miss Stain caught us before we made it out of the front door. We didn't even have a ship!'

'I still stand by that one,' Cos muttered under her breath.

'And I haven't got to the fortune-teller debacle yet!'

'Let's refocus on the plan at hand,' Cos said quickly. 'Pearl, how are your forgeries coming along?'

At the sound of her name Pearl hopped up from the desk she'd been sitting at, tucking her paintbrush behind her ear. 'Remarkably well, considering the last time I ate cake was three years, four months, two weeks, four days and approximately twelve hours ago.' She prised open her desk, revealing a whole host of cakes and pastries.

An 'Ooh' escaped Cos's mouth. Her tummy twisted in hungry knots as she eyed a cherry Bakewell. The Stains barely fed the girls enough gruel to get them through the day and the pastry looked scrumptious. The icing glistened in the dusty gloom of the schoolroom as Cos reached out a finger to poke the cake. It was rough to the touch and felt like rope. *It was rope.* Fake cakes were a key part of Cos's plan, and Pearl (as usual) had created them brilliantly.

'I think these might be your best fakes yet. Those fancy ladies won't be able to tell the difference until they take a bite.'

Pearl's mouth twitched into a slight smile that warmed the pit of Cos's stomach, like a sunny spring day after a hard winter.

Pearl was a master crafter. She could make the most amazing creations out of the huge coils of rope Mr Stain left piled on the schoolroom floor. The only other thing Pearl needed was paint and a brush. Cos was in charge of sneaking in Pearl's painting supplies, Diya's inventing bits and bobs, and any other contraband items her friends needed. She'd managed to strike up a friendship with the grocer's boy, and in return for tipping him off about when Miss Stain was out so he could deliver his goods without being shouted at, he brought her items from the outside world. She'd also become an expert at pinching things from the Stains and recycling old and unwanted rubbish the matron chucked out. With her paints Pearl had transformed the dull brown rope into a myriad of wonders.

Cos turned her attention to Mary. 'Have you plotted out the potential pitfalls?'

Mary twitched as she tiptoed towards the old apple crate where the children stored the nuts and bolts, paint supplies and Cos's collection of pilfered newspapers. Mary had what Miss Stain referred to as 'an annoying level of hysterical neurosis', but to Cos she was a protective friend who just worried a lot about getting everything right. Because of that Mary liked to plan for every possible (and sometimes nearly impossible) eventuality for everything that the girls did.

Mary grabbed an age-curled scrap of paper and unfurled it, placing it upon her Diya-made clipboard. Scrawled all over it were potential problems they might encounter on their flight to the kitchen.

'Our main obstacle will be Mr Stain – he's been patrolling the corridors even more than usual lately.' Mary trembled as she spoke.

Cos whistled as she pointed at the heading *PLAN IF TORNADO STRIKES DURING CAKE HEIST*. 'Do you think that's likely, Mar?'

Mary raised an eyebrow. 'You can never be too careful, Cos. We have to plan for *every* possibility.'

Cos clapped Mary on the back. 'And you have planned for every almost impossible possibility, Mar. With this plan we can't fail.'

Mary's grin became sure as she packed her clipboard and Pearl's cake forgeries into a large worn leather satchel that she slung across her shoulders.

Cos slunk towards Diya, who raised her eyebrows and folded her arms. Cos knew she'd have to pull out all the stops to persuade Diya that her plan was a good one. 'How's your latest invention coming along?'

Diya's face lit up like Mr Edison's electric light bulbs. She rolled forward, fetching a brand-new contraption from under her desk. With a flourish befitting a famous stage star, Diya presented her invention to the others. Cos could see that her friend had used chains (pinched from a failed velocipede venture the Stains had bought into), an old bellows (used to help those with chest issues breathe more freely) and a hand crank (chucked out by Miss Stain after her phonograph broke).

At first glance it looked like an ordinary, if very short, wooden ladder – small enough for any one of them to tuck under their arm. But as Cos peered closer, she noticed that the penultimate rung of the ladder was connected to a handle. Diya proudly placed the ladder upright on the floor and Pearl helped to steady it. Diya began winding the handle round and round. With every spin the ladder extended, shooting up towards the cobweb-covered rafters of the room. Even the girls who'd ignored Cos and continued picking apart rope paused to admire Diya's ladder.

Cos clapped her hands together. 'Brilliant. It's just what we need.'

Ambition flickered in Diya's brown eyes, a half-grin creeping across her face. 'I suppose it would be good to see the Phenomenal Protractible Ladder in action, to test if it really works in practice.' She hesitated suddenly, her eyes narrowing at Cos. 'But can you promise us Miss Stain won't catch us? I can't face having my ma's visit cancelled again.'

At the mention of the Stains' habit of scrapping family

visitations, three things happened:

Mary turned a shade of off-white that reminded Cos of the gruel they'd had for breakfast. The last letter Mary had received from her grandpa had mentioned that the workhouse had decided he was fit to work, and she'd spent a week fretting about his health.

Pearl hugged herself close, smearing the ink insects upon her arm into swirls of darkness that contrasted against her pale skin. Cos knew she was desperate to see whether her little sister had grown any taller since she'd seen her last.

Diya sniffed up her sadness. Her dad was away at sea, and she hadn't heard from him in months.

A sliver of sadness crept up Cos's back. Whispers travelled through the schoolroom and the other girls refused to meet her gaze. Cos, unlike her friends, had no family to speak of. She'd been at the home for as long as she could remember, and no one had ever visited her. She'd watched girls older than her age get out, sent away to work back-breaking jobs or live in adult homes the moment they became teenagers. Cos only had a year or two to unravel the truth of her past and find a proper home. Tucked away in the corner of her brain was the memory of a blurry smile, but Cos couldn't place it . . . *yet*. But every escapade out of the dormitory or the schoolroom gave her the chance to find some scrap of information that might lead her to her family.

Diya Nayak

Mary Turner

Pearl Wilson

Cosima . . . Unfortunate.

The others all belonged, even if they were separated from their families, but Cos had no one. On the rare occasions the authorities visited the home, no-surname Cos was always referred to as 'Cosima Unfortunate' – a nickname that felt like a stinging slap.

Cos shook her sadness off as she refocused on the plan at hand. As she did so, her hopelessness melted away.

'This one will work, I *promise* you. And we'll bring back cakes for everyone.' Smiles crossed the hunger-panged faces of all the girls. Some nodded gratefully at Cos, a few hunched shoulders relaxed, and murmurs of excited conversation echoed in the schoolroom.

The girls gathered closer to Cos.

'Here's the plan . . .'

CHAPTER TWO

Diya's fingers tapped impatiently on the armrest of her wheelchair as Cos frowned through the keyhole. Cos wiped the sweat beading on her forehead and returned to wiggling the old nail in the slot. Picking locks wasn't her strong point. Behind them, the other girls' excited chatter had turned to sighs.

'Cos!' Mary squeaked, her eyes darting from the clock tick-tocking on the schoolroom wall to the clipboard that she yanked from her satchel. 'We've only got two minutes left until Mr Stain makes his next round. If we don't hurry up, I'll have to start the "PLAN IF WE GET CAUGHT ESCAPING SCHOOLROOM".'

'I think it's time to give it up,' Diya said with a sigh. 'It's been ages and we've not even made it into the corridor.'

Determination took hold of Cos, and she tried again to coax the lock free. Suddenly a *click* sounded and the door creaked open. This passageway was at the heart of the building's ground floor, extending from the foyer all the way to the girls' schoolroom, before a right angle turned the corridor towards the Stains' private quarters. The corridor was packed with an array of weird objects: crystal balls, beauty creams that promised eternal youth and other useless items that sat unused and collecting dust in the bowels of the home. The Stains were constantly investing in schemes that they hoped would make them rich quick, and when they failed the siblings would dump whatever they'd bought in the corridor, leaving Diya a treasure trove of parts that she repurposed into inventions.

The Home for Unfortunate Girls felt even eerier in a snowstorm, teeming with darkness and the whistle of cruel winds that ripped through the paper-thin building. Cos's walking stick thudded on the floor, and she tried to dull the echoing sound.

She tiptoed away from the schoolroom, dodging a number of rotting floorboards, each step feeling more daring than the one before. Excitement thumped through her veins, spurred on by the thought of getting one over on the Stains and stealing some lip-smackingly delicious food. She couldn't remember the last time she'd eaten something that wasn't grey, cold and squelchy.

They'd reached the halfway point of the corridor when Mary tugged hard on Cos's sleeve. Her top lip wobbled like the gruel they'd had for breakfast. 'Mr Stain is due back in one minute.'

Tick-tock.

Diya's brow furrowed, as if she knew this was going to happen all along.

Tick-tock.

Pearl flinched in anticipation of Miss Stain's blow when their escape was discovered.

Tick-tock.

A word slipped from Cos's mouth that would have got her in heaps of trouble had an adult overheard. She forced out a slow breath as their time to hide slipped away. She was too far from the schoolroom to dash back; her bad knee made her walk slower than the others. She'd never make it.

'Think,' she whispered quickly, hoping that the others couldn't hear the undercurrent of panic in her voice. 'What can we do?'

'Psst.' Mary, a few steps behind Cos and clutching her clipboard with shaking hands, nodded to the left, indicating a broom cupboard. 'In my "PLAN IF WE GET CAUGHT IN THE CORRIDOR" I've written that we can hide in there.'

Cos nodded and, trying to ignore the stabbing pain in her ankles, stepped towards the door, prising it open for the others. Mary hurried inside. She pivoted around, searching for Pearl.

But Pearl, fast as the whipping wind, had run back the way they'd come – towards the shut schoolroom door.

Pearl shook her hair out of her eyes, grabbed her paintbrush and pulled out a small pot hidden within her overstuffed pinny, where she kept her most essential crafting supplies. She bit the lid from the pot, dunked her paintbrush into it and began smearing a gloopy mixture on to the edges of the door hatch.

Cos frowned. 'What are you doing, Pearl?' Cosima called across the hallway.

'Gluing the hatch together,' Pearl said matter-of-factly, as she finished and shoved her paintbrush back behind her ear. She pulled a long, sticky-looking substance from her pinny and plugged it into the keyhole, blocking the sliver of light peeking through. 'And jamming the keyhole. So Mr Stain can't tell that four of us are missing.'

Cos nodded with approval, just as the sound she dreaded most entered her ears. Footsteps echoed distantly, thudding closer and closer with every passing second.

Stomp-stomp-stomp-stomp.

Cos swore again. They needed to hide, and fast.

'Er, we've got another problem,' Diya said guiltily.

Cos swizzled on the spot to see Mary frantically trying (and failing) to squeeze Diya's wheelchair into the overstuffed broom cupboard. The chair thumped loudly as it caught on the door frame, its wheels squealing.

Cos frowned. They were making far too much noise. Even someone as unobservant as Mr Stain would notice the sound of a wheelchair crashing against the wall. 'Pearl,' she hissed, thinking fast, 'tell the others to sing.'

Pearl nodded and whispered through the door crack.

In a matter of seconds the girls left behind in the schoolroom began to warble loudly and off-key.

'This is the one possibility I didn't prepare for,' Mary rasped.

Cos furrowed her brow, trying to think up a solution, as Pearl dashed from the now sticky schoolroom door.

She hurried towards the broom cupboard, spotting that the wheels of Diya's chair were caught on the door edge. What could she do?

The plan struck her like lightning.

'Mary,' Cos whispered, 'clear as much space as possible in the cupboard and try to do it quietly.'

Mary nodded and began shoving the broken brooms, cleaning supplies and buckets to the far corners of the cupboard. The girls in the schoolroom singing their hearts out covered the ruckus.

Cos turned to Pearl next. 'Have you got anything *greasy* in your pinny pocket?' Pearl nodded and produced a small vial of something transparent and gloopy. 'Great. Rub it on Diya's wheels, where the metal meets the door.'

Pearl knelt and duly smeared the substance all over both wheels.

'Ahh,' Diya said breathlessly. 'I assume you're going to use Pearl's grease to try to unstick me. Smart, Cos!'

Pearl finished smudging the ointment on the wheels, and then she and Pearl held on to the handles of Diya's chair and drove it forward. Gritting her teeth, Cos pushed as hard as she could, hoping beyond hope that nothing dislocated. But, try as they might, Diya's wheelchair remained stubbornly stuck.

'Stop,' Diya said suddenly, a frown appearing on her face.

Cos knew that look. A half-formed idea was rapidly growing in her friend's huge brain. As Diya thought, Cos noticed that the footsteps were now deafening, hurtling towards them at the same speed as her panicked heartbeats. They needed to move fast.

'We'll need to exert more force on my chair for your idea to work,' Diya continued, clicking her tongue. 'I know – you need a run-up!'

Worry curled in Cos's stomach. Running wasn't something she ever did – it made the pain in her joints much worse *and* increased the risk of dislocations. She swallowed away her fear, stepping back with Pearl to the other side of the corridor.

Cos blew out a breath, screwed up her courage and nodded at Pearl. 'One, two, three – GO!'

Together they ran, hefting their shoulders into Diya's chair.

With a pop Diya's chair slid into the broom cupboard, colliding with the odds and ends Mary hadn't quite managed to shove to the back. Mary squealed as she dodged out of Diya's way. Mr Stain and his sweat-stained suit jacket flicked round the corner and the schoolroom girls' song reached its crescendo.

'Stop that caterwauling,' Mr Stain grunted. The girls in the schoolroom fell silent in an instant.

Pearl and Cos followed the others into the cupboard and shut the door softly behind them, swathing the girls in shadows. For a moment Cos couldn't see anything, until one of Diya's most useful inventions flickered into life. Diya had created the Luminous Lantern after one particularly horrid month when the Stains refused to buy matches for their candles in order to 'save on costs'. Using an upside-down glass jar, some wires and a stolen chunk of coal, Diya had managed to make a flickering, glowing light that was turned on with a switch.

Cos blinked as her eyes adjusted to seeing again.

The footsteps abruptly stopped.

Cos's breath of relief that they hadn't been discovered was covered up by a huff from Mr Stain.

'Bloomin' hatch.'

Cos grinned at Pearl, who looked – *rightly* – smug.

There was a jangle of metal as Mr Stain thrust his keys into the hole. A grumble told Cos that Pearl's second idea had also worked. Mr Stain was locked out of the schoolroom. He began thumping on the door, and Cos could hear the faint but terrified cries of the girls they'd left behind. Her jaw clenched with rage.

The Stains never failed to make every moment at the Home for Unfortunate Girls a living nightmare. Guilt shivered up Cos's spine – the cake heist had been her idea in the first place. But would a few mouthfuls of cake really make up for an angry Stain pummelling on a schoolroom door, scaring the other girls senseless? Cos bit her lip. She had to do something.

Cos turned and puzzled at the broken clothing lines, old cleaning rags and holey buckets that had been shoved to the back of the cupboard.

'What are you thinking?' Diya asked.

'What's Mr Stain scared of, more than anything in this world?' Cos said, a plan falling into place inside her head.

'Baths,' Pearl whispered, holding her nose.

'Insects,' said the others all at once.

Mr Stain screeched at the sight of creepy-crawlies.

Cos limped forward and picked up a cobweb-covered rag. 'Pearl, do you think you can turn this into a spider?'

Pearl grabbed the rag and began ripping it apart.

Next Cos grabbed a tangle of clothing line. 'We need a way to get Pearl's spider near Mr Stain without leaving the cupboard.'

'On it!' Diya said, placing her Luminous Lantern on the floor and unclipping a pair of tweezers from her tool belt. She grabbed the clothing line from Cos and got to work.

Cos turned to Mary. 'Mar, I'm counting on you to work out the throw.'

Mary trembled out a nod. 'We'll need to plan it exactly. It'll need the correct amount of forward thrust and height.'

'*Voilà!*' Pearl palmed Cos a spider so large she felt a shiver crawl up her back.

Pearl and Cos helped Diya untangle the clothing line, as Mary scribbled down a rough-looking diagram. Then they tied Pearl's spider to one end of the now unknotted line.

'You ready?' Cos asked, as the fake spider hopped up and down like a puppet on a string.

Mary wheezed out a nervous breath, then nodded.

Cos creaked the door open a sliver, peering through the crack. Mr Stain was now yanking the door handle, the soles of his shoes squeaking on the floor. Cos threaded the spider out into the corridor and handed the end of the line to Mary, squeezing behind her. Cos, Pearl and Diya leaned into the door, so all the girls could catch a glimpse of the action.

Mary's eyes darted from the piece of paper with her diagram plan on it to the spider, to the bulging back of Mr Stain's head. Then, with a deft flick of her wrist, the spider on the line flew skywards.

31

Cos held her breath as the rag spider soared through the air then fell a few feet behind Mr Stain. Disappointment coursed through her, but she tried hard not to let Mary see. 'That was only your first try, Mar, I'm sure you'll hit it next time,' she whispered.

Mary wound back the spider on the line and tried again. This time it landed even further away from Mr Stain, who had returned to pummelling his hammy fists against the door frame. She deflated, her breathing shaky.

Cos clasped hold of Mary's free hand. 'You can do it. We believe in you.'

Mary swallowed as she pulled the spider back towards them. She sent the spider soaring down the corridor for a third time, and this time it landed squarely on Mr Stain's shoulder. Mary wriggled the clothing line and the fake spider tickled Mr Stain's neck.

He froze, one arm mid-door-pummel, before turning towards the dancing spider and letting out a screech so high-pitched it hurt Cos's ears. Then, without looking back, he scarpered, running in the direction of his and his sister's private quarters.

Cos's chest felt less tight as she let the cupboard door creak wide, and the foursome made their way back into the corridor. Mary led the way towards the foyer. With every step – or wheel of her chair in Diya's case – the floor groaned like a ghoul fed up with haunting. Cos tried to keep up with the others, but it was tricky. Her knee throbbed and dread curled up in her stomach. Cos was sure a dislocation was coming. She paused for a moment, leaning on her walking stick.

Out of the corner of her eye Cos spotted Diya's frowning gaze and pushed her worried thoughts away. Diya could always tell when she was having a bad-joint day, but today Cos wanted to keep her pain a secret. She didn't want to worry her friends, not when they couldn't do anything.

Finally they reached the end of the corridor. The children peered into the foyer of the Home for Unfortunate Girls. Normally dust-covered furniture and paint-peeling walls greeted them, but because a gaggle of well-to-do ladies were due to visit, the Stains had forced one of the more able-bodied girls to spruce it up. The wilting vase of flowers and straightened picture frames didn't entirely mask the falling-apart-ness of the home. Unpaid letters stamped with shouting words like 'FINAL REMINDER' and 'BILLS' burst through the letter box. A wonky banner was strung across the foyer, with 'Welcome Your Ladyships' embroidered upon it. Cos resisted the temptation to roll her eyes. Inviting bored rich ladies for afternoon tea at a home for disabled girls was the Stains' surefire way to pocket much-needed money. The floor was so polished Cos could see a hazy reflection in it; tangled mud-coloured hair and a pale face stared back at her.

A rickety staircase stood in the centre of the foyer, leading up to the first floor of the building, where the girls slept in a spartan dormitory. Cos hated the stairs with a passion – walking up them multiplied her pain. But it was even worse for the girls in wheelchairs. They had to be carried up, before being plonked back in their chairs when they got to the first floor. On the far side of the foyer was a locked door: the kitchen. Next to the door, and placed too high in the wall for any child to reach, was a small serving hatch. It was used at mealtimes; plates of food were placed upon the narrow sill ready to be carried to the dining hall. It was, Cos had worked out, the only way to get into the kitchen without stealing Miss Stain's keys, which were permanently hung round her neck.

Beside the locked kitchen door was Miss Stain's office, the worst place in the whole home. It was where the matron dished out her most gruesome punishments, like plucking head hairs one by one or holding a lit match to the soles of feet. The office door was ajar. Cos suppressed a shiver as voices drifted towards them from within. One was horribly familiar: Miss Stain's screeching made Cos's head hum. The other was new; it was a booming baritone, and Cos immediately knew that it belonged to someone important – important people were never told to hush. Cos was told to be quiet at least five times a day.

'I've brought those books you were interested in, and the next instalment of your investment is overdue, my dear Stain. A slight inconvenience, but I am sure we can come to an arrangement to suit us both,' the man said.

Cos grinned. Miss Stain was suitably distracted. With a flick of her finger she gave the others the go-ahead, a mixture of terror and excitement churning in her stomach.

CHAPTER THREE

The plan was simple. Pearl was the strongest of them all, so she would carry the ladder into the hallway and help Diya unwind it to its full height. Mary was the smallest, so she would bring Pearl's fake cakes and squeeze through the serving hatch that led into the kitchen. With any luck the forged rope pastries would fool the adults until the evidence had been eaten.

Pearl, ladder tucked underarm, headed towards the serving hatch. The ink smudges on her arms looked like storm clouds now. She was followed by Diya. Cos kept one eye fixed on the office door, wordlessly hoping that it wouldn't suddenly fly open. Together Diya and Pearl carefully placed the ladder on to the floor, leaning it up against the wall. Its top rung barely skimmed Diya's lap. Cos allowed herself a calming breath as she turned back to mouth 'go' to Mary.

Mary vibrated with nerves as she slunk towards the hatch, Pearl's forged cakes hidden in her satchel.

Diya unwound the handle of her invention and the ladder rose. With each squeak of the handle Cos cringed, hoping that Miss Stain wouldn't hear. Finally the ladder was fully extended, coming to a stop at the windowsill of the serving hatch. It was the perfect height for the adults to fetch the girls' dinners but out of reach for Cos and her friends. Cos suspected the Stains had installed it to make sure none of them could get even a little bit more than the meagre portion of gruel doled out to them.

Cos ran over the next steps in her mind: Mary was going to scramble up the ladder, squeeze through the serving hatch, find the cake stand, steal the cakes and replace them with Pearl's forgeries. But Cos wasn't certain Mary was going to be able to do it. Her top lip wobbled and she sucked in a huge gulp of air.

Beside Mary, confusion clouded over Pearl's face.

'Are you all right?' she asked softly. Mary didn't answer.

Cos knew exactly what those signs usually foretold: a panic whirlwind. As fast as her aching legs would carry her, she crossed the foyer, leaving her lookout post outside Miss Stain's office door.

Cos clasped her friend's hand tightly; it was clammy to

the touch. 'Count to ten, Mar,' she whispered. 'Think of a calm place.'

Mary gripped on to Cos, eyes squeezed tightly shut and breath puffing in and out like a smoke-clogged factory chimney. Miss Stain and the strange man's conversation covered up the sound of Mary's hurried breaths, allowing the others to whisper words of encouragement. 'One, two, three,' Cos said, in her most soothing voice.

'Four,' hissed out Mary in between breaths. She opened her eyes, tears spilling down her cheeks. 'Five, six.'

'Seven,' said Diya, nodding at Mary. She wheeled herself closer to Cos and Mar and placed her palm on Mary's shoulder.

'Eight,' Pearl added, eyes resolutely on the floor.

'Nine . . .' Cos added.

Cos felt Mary's grip slacken, as her breaths slowed back to normal.

Mary wiped away the tears and smiled at her friends. 'Ten,' she said with a sigh. 'I'm sorry. I don't think I can do it, Cos.'

Cos grinned. 'It's all right.' She stuck out her chest like a story heroine. 'I'll do it!' She was the only other one that could: Diya's chair meant that the ladder was a no-go, and Pearl didn't like small spaces, so couldn't squeeze through the hatch. Cos ignored the niggle in her stomach. *Please nothing dislocate*, she thought.

Cos held out her walking stick. Mary smiled a watery smile

and took it from her, passing her the fakery-filled satchel.

Cos twisted her tangled fringe out of her eyes to show that she meant business, rolled her shoulders (luckily nothing dislocated) and stretched out her arms as if she were a boxer preparing for a bout. She balanced the satchel across her shoulders and hefted herself on to the first rung.

Each step upwards was met with a shooting pain up Cos's legs. Her bones felt as fragile as paper and liable to break at any point. She crept up each rung, hauling herself upwards, and finally reached the top of the ladder.

It should've been impossible, Cos thought with a grin, as she looked back down at the floor, which seemed very far away indeed. She shivered with excitement, ignoring her sweat-soaked skin, pounding heart and aching limbs. From when she was little doctors had said that her weak joints would render her crippled and unable to walk. And sometimes they did. But Cos was still determined to have adventures.

Cos gritted her teeth as she squeezed herself through the small serving hatch. Voices told her that Miss Stain and the man were still vigorously talking. She tumbled on to the kitchen counter, hoping that Miss Stain hadn't heard her far from elegant entrance into the room. She froze for a count, maybe two, but the voices continued.

Cos slid from the counter. The ornate cake stand was right in front of her on a wooden table in the centre of the kitchen.

She hurried towards it. It was stuffed full of deliciousness. Her stomach grumbled greedily and she just about resisted the urge to stuff one of the treats in her mouth right then and there.

Instead, she unpacked Pearl's creations on to the cake stand and grabbed as many of the real cakes as she could carry, piling them into the satchel.

With her satchel stuffed full, Cos rushed back to the hatch. She clambered up on to the side.

'Hurry up, Cos,' Diya whispered from outside. 'Mary thinks their conversation is going to end soon.'

Heart thumping, Cos took a deep breath and made to squeeze her way back through the window, several pastries heavier. But just before she did so, something caught her eye.

On the kitchen side, lying open, was Miss Stain's heavy age-cracked ledger. Cos's heart leaped. Miss Stain diligently recorded information about the girls (when they entered the home, who dropped them off, their disability) in her precious ledger, and normally it was kept under lock and key in her office. Cos spied a crumb-smeared plate and today's edition of the *Gazette* next to the ledger. Miss Stain must've been scoffing cakes and catching up with paperwork when the man had knocked on the door.

Cos's feet moved before her brain had even made a decision. She hopped back down from the counter and a pain like no other shot up her legs. She bit down on her lip to stop herself from crying out. Her eyes filled with water. Cos snorted up the tears and grabbed the ledger, flicking to the front.

Each page of the ledger was divided into a table with columns for information about each girl, with the very first column assigning each child a number. Some entries had been crossed out after girls had left or aged out of the home. Cos rifled through the pages, catching glimpses of number thirteen (Pearl), number ten (Diya) and number fifteen (Mary). But as she reached the very first page, Cos frowned. There was an entry for number two (Clementine, entered 1891, blind), but Cos's entry was almost unreadable, the ink smudged. Cos peered closer at the half-ruined page – the paper was crinkled and discoloured, as if something horrible had been spilt on it. She sniffed. The unmistakable smell of Miss Stain's favourite tipple wafted towards her.

The thrill that had rushed through Cos fell away. She stared at the blurry paper, willing away the tears that threatened to spill from her eyes. Cos sniffed them back – she wasn't going to waste her time on blubbering. Instead, she glared at the column on the far right, peering so close to the blotchy letters her eyelashes tickled the paper. She mouthed the words as she read: *Arrived in possession of a handkerchief.*

Cos's brain whirred into action. She glanced down at the entry for number two. The heading read *Any additional remarks,* and Miss Stain had written *ugly crier* underneath. Almost as sharply as it fell, Cos's heart rose again. A handkerchief. Cos had always believed she'd arrived at the home with nothing. Her thoughts rose like a hot-air balloon to the overstuffed apple crate where they kept their personal things like Pearl's painting supplies and Diya's spare nuts and bolts. Forgotten at the bottom of that crate, she was sure, was a moth-eaten and dust-covered scrap of fabric. Cos had always known it was there, but it had barely seen the light of day in years. Could that be the handkerchief that Miss Stain had written of? Cos ran her fingers over the faded ink – this was a clue, a breadcrumb on a treasure hunt.

A 'haw-haw-haw' echoed from Miss Stain's office. Cos jumped, hurriedly flicking back to the page she'd found the ledger open on. As she did so, the headline of the *Gazette* alongside it stole her attention: *THE STAR DIAMOND TIARA AT THE EMPIRE EXHIBITION*. Underneath was a black-and-white illustration of an opulent tiara, a dazzling jewel in its centre.

Almost without thinking, Cos pocketed the newspaper into her pinny pocket. She'd stolen every newspaper she could get her hands on since she'd learned her letters. Reading about the exciting events of the outside world made her dreary life at the home a little more bearable.

She hoisted herself on to the counter and squeezed back through the hatch, her feet feeling for the rungs of the ladder. She was so close to success!

Cos stepped on to the first rung as Miss Stain's voice rang in the air.

'I . . . I don't understand. You want to adopt *all* the girls? And what does this have to do with my debt?'

Cos froze as confusion pounded in her head. Adoption?

Girls from the home didn't get adopted! They were only under the Stains' care because the authorities decreed it, and many had families desperate to get them back. Cos rushed down the remainder of the ladder as the man continued to boom at Miss Stain.

Miss Stain sounded unsure, which made Cos's tummy twinge with nerves. Miss Stain was *never* unsure; it was always 'do this' and 'not that'.

Pearl wound the ladder down and the others began to tiptoe (or, in Diya's case, tip-wheel) to the corridor that led back to the schoolroom, but Cos hesitated. She had to find out who this strange man was and why he wanted to adopt them.

The others filed back into the corridor, elated that the cake heist had gone off without a hitch.

Cos stopped, making a snap decision. 'Get back to the schoolroom,' she whispered. 'I'll be there in a bit.'

'What are you doing?' hissed Diya.

Mary was thunderstruck. 'This is off plan.'

'Come *on*, Cos,' Pearl pleaded.

Cos shook her head as she stepped sideways and slipped behind a coat stand stuffed with Miss Stain's furs and stoles. Cos arranged the coats so that she was completely concealed, and able to peer into Miss Stain's office without being seen.

Miss Stain sat rod-straight at her desk, lips pursed and

eyebrows arched, staring at something Cos couldn't quite see on the man's outstretched wrist. Mounted on the wall behind the desk like trophies were her favourite instruments of punishment: a cane that had left many a red mark on Cos's thighs, razor-sharp scissors (used to shear the hair off unruly girls) and a stiff leather strap. Cos knew that locked away in the top drawer of the desk was Miss Stain's favourite tipple: Skullsplitter's Cure-All.

The man's voice was as slick as grease, and he spoke so fast that Cos couldn't quite catch his words. From her hiding place she could see that he was very tall and thin, had a fashionable handlebar moustache and beard, and a monocle tucked into the chest pocket of his ruby-coloured waistcoat. A shiver crept up Cos's back as she realised that something about him seemed familiar – maybe she'd read about him in a pilfered newspaper?

Miss Stain frowned down her crooked nose at the man. Cos noticed her lip wobble at the sight of whatever he had on his wrist. She was, Cos realised, a bit scared. Under the heavy furs Cos shifted to one side, but frustratingly she still couldn't see whatever it was.

The man pulled back his arm and let his shirt cuff fall over his wrist, his gold cufflinks glinting. He cleared his throat, and Cos could finally hear what he was saying. 'As you said, you've already invested all your hard-earned money in my exciting new project, so what's a few girls? When I prove it works, you'll be rich!'

Miss Stain's ivory cheeks coloured like a bruise. 'But surely, Lord Fitzroy, you are far too busy to even consider taking on twenty girls? I've read the papers; the exhibition opens this week. Why not wait a while?'

In her hiding place Cos's fingers brushed against the pages of her latest stolen newspaper. *Hadn't that headline mentioned something about an exhibition?*

Lord Fitzroy slammed his palms upon the desk, making Miss Stain jolt with shock. 'I am doing this now *precisely* because of the exhibition.' Spittle flew over the cringing Miss Stain, and Cos frowned. This all seemed very . . . *odd.* 'With the papers focused on the exhibition I can launch my project without the prying eyes and bleeding hearts of do-gooders who are determined to slow down scientific progress. I just need some children. Specifically defective children.'

In amongst the furs and stoles Cos's mouth felt as dry as old rope, and her stomach groaned, not with hunger this time, but a horrible mixture of fear and anger. She and her friends weren't defective; they were just different.

'But these children aren't up for sale!' Miss Stain spluttered. 'This isn't an orphanage; most do have families. We house girls with ailments that make it improper for them to be part of polite society.'

All of a sudden Lord Fitzroy strode away from Miss Stain, out of the office and towards the coat stand. Cos sucked in a deep breath, as though breathing in would make her less visible. She hoped beyond hope that he couldn't hear her heart thumping wildly against her ribcage. He neared and Cos finally caught a glimpse of his wrist. Etched on to it was an inky tattoo of a gnarled tree. Underneath it was a phrase in a strange language. Cos squinted at it, trying to make out the words. Cos mouthed them as she read, committing them to memory: *Non quantitas sed qualitas.*

Cos stifled a shiver as she leaned back into the safety of the coat stand. What could the tattoo and foreign words mean? And why was Miss Stain so afraid of it?

Lord Fitzroy plucked a coat from the coat stand and shouldered it on. 'I can see you are not as sympathetic to The Institute's aims as you should be.' His curling moustache twitched with disdain. 'I'll immediately begin steps to rescind your membership, and all the money you've invested will be lost. And obviously that means certain knowledge of mine will have to be made public.'

Cos furrowed her brows. *What was this 'Institute'? It sounded purposefully mysterious. And what did this lord and Miss Stain have to do with it?*

'No, your lordship, I am entirely in sympathy with The Institute.'

Cos tried to stay statue-still as Miss Stain pushed back

her squeaking desk chair and rushed after Lord Fitzroy, her pointed boots tap-tapping on the floor. 'But what will I say to the parents? What will I tell them when all their daughters go missing at once?'

Behind the furs, Cos stifled a gasp. But even as the surprise waned, an insidious pang of jealousy wormed its way into her stomach. *Miss Stain would have no one to tell if I disappeared. I'd just fade away, like a ghost.*

Irritation flickered across Lord Fitzroy's face, but he covered it up with a waxy smile. 'I'm sure you'll think up an imaginative ruse, Miss Stain. You seem to be a clever woman. After all, you found your way to my society.'

Miss Stain brightened, a wolfish grin across her face. 'Fine. If you let our investments stand and pay us, say, an extra fifty pounds, then we have a deal.' She turned on her heels and stomped back into her office. 'I can put off the families for a time, but I'll need a few days to get everything in order. We wouldn't want the authorities sniffing around.'

Lord Fitzroy's smile didn't quite reach his eyes. 'Of course, my dear Miss Stain.' He was back to being as sweet as sugar now that he'd got what he wanted. He followed her, pausing at the threshold of the office to gently close the door behind him.

Worries swam around Cos's head. She needed to get out of here *now* and think things through until it all made sense.

She went to step out from under the cover of the coat stand, and a twinge of pain surged through her knee as it went out of joint. For a moment Cos wobbled, then she hurtled floorward, bringing the coat stand along with her. Hats, coats and umbrellas scattered across the foyer floor as pain screamed through Cos's knee.

Cos scrunched up her face and hit her knee back into joint, whimpering from the agony. The stolen newspaper fell from her pinny; Cos hurriedly hid it under the waistband of her dress. Her friends, who hadn't returned to the schoolroom like Cos had asked, surged into the foyer, rushing to Cos's side.

Stomp-stomp-stomp-stomp.

Miss Stain stormed out from her office, her beady black eyes flicking from Cos and the crumb-smeared satchel to Pearl, Mary and Diya. Pearl's hands covered her ears, her eyes were squeezed shut, and she rocked to and fro. As Miss Stain neared her, Pearl cringed. Lord Fitzroy hurried after her, squinting at the girls through his monocle as if he were assessing broken artefacts at a museum.

Miss Stain bent forward, her teeth gritted in anger. 'Empty your bag,' she hissed.

Cos's heart sank. She slowly creaked herself into a sitting position, knee throbbing. She placed the stolen treats into Miss Stain's outstretched hands. The barest flicker of a smile passed Miss Stain's face as she let the cakes fall on to the floor and squashed them with the heel of her boot. Cos's stomach squeezed with a mixture of hunger and regret.

'Lord Fitzroy, I'd like to introduce you to some of the children you'll be adopting,' Miss Stain said brightly. She grabbed Cos, who was nearest to her, by the lapels of her uniform.

Cos screeched as she was yanked roughly upwards.

'This is number one. She's the resident troublemaker and is far too curious about her past. Her defective joints make her almost useless for chores.' Miss Stain let go of Cos, and Cos found herself sprawled on the floor for a second time.

Miss Stain grabbed the handles of Diya's wheelchair. She pushed her forward, showing her off to Lord Fitzroy. 'This horrid little urchin is number ten. She's of an exotic origin and has a most unusual name.'

Lord Fitzroy raised an eyebrow. 'Most peculiar – do we know her parentage?'

Miss Stain shrugged, and elbowed Diya to answer.

Diya uncurled ever so slightly, squared her shoulders and set her jaw. Cos was blown away by her bravery. 'My father is a lascar, sir. From India. My mother is from Stepney. And my name's *not* unusual in India.'

Lord Fitzroy seemed to think it beneath himself to reply to Diya. He harrumphed instead. 'What's a lascar?' he asked

Miss Stain, who shrugged in response.

Diya sucked in a breath. Cos saw her hands tighten into fists. 'A lascar is a sailor, a seaman, usually from Asia. My father arrived in Britain when his ship docked.'

Lord Fitzroy yawned, as though thoroughly bored by this explanation. 'Go on, Miss Stain.'

'She had infantile paralysis as a toddler, so is now confined to a chair. Good with her hands but tends to have ideas above her station.' She let go and Diya wheeled away to help Cos up from the floor.

Miss Stain rounded on a shaking Mary. She almost snarled at her. 'Number fifteen suffers dreadfully from neurosis. She is a damp squib of a human being, always shaking and fainting and prone to melodrama.

'And finally number thirteen.' She jabbed a pointed nail at Pearl, who stared resolutely at the floor as if she were ignoring everything that was going on. 'A very odd individual. Seldom talks, has appalling manners, is all-round useless.'

Even though she was racked with spasms on the floor, Cos noticed that Lord Fitzroy seemed particularly interested in Pearl. He moved closer to her and leaned down so his moustache almost bristled against her forehead. Cos wished she could shield her friend from his focus, bat away his stifling closeness. Pearl's lip wobbled as he frowned at her, her whole body recoiling from him.

'I see what you mean,' Fitzroy said slowly, clicking his fingers loudly by Pearl's ears. 'There's almost no reaction. How extraordinary.'

'Are these children suitable for your purposes?' Miss Stain asked.

Cos's stomach plummeted. Anger and worry buzzed inside her head. *This couldn't be happening.*

For a second Lord Fitzroy said nothing. Instead, his eyes coldly appraised the line of girls in front of him. He tapped his chin as he inspected the children closely, peering at their faces and tutting at the state of their clothes. He came to a stop in front of Pearl and nodded. 'They'll do. Are they a representative sample?' he asked eagerly, as if unfortunate girls were the latest fashionable thing to collect.

The buzzing inside Cos's head was deafening now. 'We're human beings,' she blurted out. 'Just like you.'

A venomous look from Miss Stain silenced her. Lord Fitzroy blinked at her, but his gaze was cold and blank, as if he were staring at a science experiment rather than a child.

'What others have you got?' he asked Miss Stain, ignoring Cos completely as he returned to talking over the girls' heads.

Cos thought she could see coins glint in Miss Stain's eyes. 'We've got a right mixture: deaf, blind, children who can't speak, the list goes on. Twenty girls in total, ranging from two to twelve years old, all defective in some way.'

Lord Fitzroy grunted in approval. 'I'll pick them up after you've completed the necessary paperwork. But I want them *all*.'

'Once we receive our payment in full, you'll be welcome to them.'

Lord Fitzroy let out a short, sharp bark that Cos realised was his laugh. 'You drive a hard bargain, Miss Stain.'

Triumph cracked across Miss Stain's face. 'Then we're in agreement?'

'Of course. But,' Fitzroy continued, grabbing Pearl's wrist with an iron grip, 'I'll take this one now, as a . . . *deposit*.'

An unearthly screech escaped Cos's throat. *No, no, no, this couldn't be happening.* Cos felt as if she were being ripped apart from the inside out.

Lord Fitzroy dragged Pearl across the foyer. She thrashed and cried as she was pulled away. Despite the pain, Cos surged towards her friend, followed by Diya and Mary. Cos caught the very edge of Pearl's fingertips and held on tight. Diya and Mary grabbed hold of Cos's waist and yanked back. Together they prised Pearl away from Lord Fitzroy, all of them landing in a tangled heap on the shiny foyer floor. Fitzroy let out an angry roar.

Miss Stain tiptoed to Lord Fitzroy's side, jittery like a rat being hunted. 'Your Lordship,' she simpered in a most un-Stain-like way. 'Perhaps it would be better if you pick *all* the girls up on Friday. That way I can get the paperwork in order. We don't want the authorities asking questions, not when your project is so close to fruition.'

Lord Fitzroy pursed his lips, his eyes bloodshot and bulging. Cos got the impression he'd never been told 'no' before, let alone 'wait a few days'. She heaved out nervous breaths on the floor, waiting for Fitzroy to protest, to demand that Pearl be handed over to him.

There was a clatter as Mr Stain burst into the foyer, keys still clenched in his hammy fists. Cos tasted the salt of tears on her tongue as she stopped herself from sighing her relief. *A distraction.*

'Miss Stain,' he thundered. 'Four girls are missing from— What's going on?' His confused gaze darted from the smushed cakes to the scowling Lord Fitzroy and the pile of girls on the floor.

Miss Stain snarled as she picked Pearl up by the scruff of her pinny. 'Lord Fitzroy,' she said pointedly, 'has presented us with a once-in-a-lifetime business opportunity. By Friday we'll be rich beyond our wildest dreams.'

Cos thought back to the unopened bills and the many failed get-rich-quick schemes. The Stains desperately needed money or else they'd end up in the workhouse. Being rich was the key to everything. People did anything for money, no matter how awful. A half-formed thought floated into her head – *could she and her friends use that greed to their advantage?*

'Ohhhh.' Mr Stain smiled, fists unclenching. 'That's good news.'

Lord Fitzroy smiled back, but to Cos it was more of a pained grimace. He patted his waistcoat down, and a black-and-white photo fluttered from his pocket. His lordship didn't notice it fall, but Cos did. She tucked it into her pinny, the stolen photo slotting in next to the stolen newspaper.

Fitzroy nodded at the Stain siblings as he slipped outside, his rage covered by a mask of pleasantness. 'I have to say, they're a fine collection of . . . *unfortunates.*'

CHAPTER FOUR

There was a fog in Cos's brain, even as she was elbow deep in soapy water. She leaned back on the wonky stool she was perched upon, her arms dripping water to the floor.

'Get on with it,' growled Mr Stain, skulking in the shadows of the doorway. 'You don't have all day.'

Cos plunged her hands back into the sink and tried to push away the haze in her brain. She grasped for ideas, thoughts – *anything* – but every single one seemed insubstantial, like clouds of breath on a chilly morning. Brain fog engulfed Cos after every dislocation. All she wanted to do was fall into a restless sleep and wake up when the pain was less gnawing.

But instead, as soon as Lord Fitzroy left, Miss Stain had frogmarched Cos and her friends to the belly of the scullery and demanded they scrub the good china till it shone. She'd instructed Mr Stain to supervise the girls' every move before bustling off into town, in search of more pastries for the ladies. With Miss Stain gone the tension in the Home for Unfortunate Girls subsided a little. It seemed as though the building itself had let out a sigh of relief.

In the scullery Pearl hovered nervously behind Cos as Mary and Diya dried the china. Tin saucepans and bowls hung on metal hooks on the white-tiled walls around them as the tiny room filled with steam.

Craaaaack.

Cos twizzled on her stool, sending a splatter of water shooting across the room. Mr Stain had marched in, snatched a tea towel, and thwacked it round Pearl's head. A trembling Pearl flinched from him. Cos buzzed with anger, balling her hands into fists. She hated the Stains. She hated their cruelty and greed and petty meanness. Most of all, she hated the fact that she had no power to stop them.

'I said, get on with it,' he spat through gritted teeth.

Reluctantly Pearl tiptoed towards the sink and, cringing, put her hands in the water. Cos made for a painful step upwards, ready to fly at Mr Stain in a tornado of anger, but Diya grabbed hold of the back of her pinny.

'It's not worth it,' Diya mouthed. 'And it won't help Pearl.'

Cos pummelled the anger down inside herself.

Mr Stain snorted and backed away, settling back into his

perch in the doorway. 'Better. Now maybe you'll be—'

'Mr Stain?' An obtrusive voice cut through his words from outside the scullery. Miss Stain was back. 'Get out here this instant!'

Mr Stain grunted. He jabbed his stubby finger at Cos and her friends. 'No funny business whilst I'm gone.'

He slammed the door closed and stomped off, leaving the girls alone for the first time since their cake heist had been uncovered.

'What went wrong?' Mary asked, after Mr Stain's footsteps had faded into nothingness.

Diya dropped her tea towel and crossed her arms. 'What always happens. Cosima went off plan, Mary.'

Shame coursed through Cos. 'I'm sorry . . . I just wanted to know who that man was.'

'Well, now that horrible man nearly stole Pearl away and is coming back for us and—' Diya sucked in a breath as she turned away from the others, shoulders shaking. She sniffed and faced Cos again. 'And we don't even know why.'

Amidst all the sadness and guilt and anger churning in Cos's stomach that question had lingered. *What does Lord Fitzroy want with twenty disabled girls?*

Cos set her jaw with determination. 'We'll stop him and the Stains, I promise.'

'How?' Diya demanded. This time she was less upset and

more furious. 'We have no idea who this Lord Fitzroy even is, and soon he'll be back to get the rest of us. We're going to disappear and never see our families again.'

A sob escaped Mary. 'I have to see my grandpa soon, Cos. He's so ill. I'm so afraid. I'm so afraid that . . . that . . . he'll be even worse since he's been in the workhouse. They've given him a job picking rope, Cos. He's far too sick to work.'

Cos tried to quell the jealousy that had sprung unbidden in her chest, which was clawing up her throat. *At least you have a family.*

Diya shivered. 'Rope picking happens at every workhouse. I suspect that's where the Stains got the idea.'

An uneasy silence settled over the scullery. For once Cos's mind went blank. She felt as dim as the gloomy gas lamps that lined the street outside. She plunged her shaking hands into her pinny and heard paper crinkling. *The stolen newspaper!*

Cos dried her hand on a tea towel and whipped the newspaper out from her pocket. 'Aha,' she said. 'Lord Fitzroy mentioned something called "the Empire Exhibition" when he was talking to Miss Stain, and I knew I'd seen that somewhere before. It's an article in today's edition of the *Gazette!*'

'What does it say?' Pearl said in little more than a whisper as she wiped her hands down her pinny. Pearl hated the touch of hot water and the dry feel of towels, and Cos knew she was very stressed now Mr Stain had demanded she wash up.

The others gathered round her as Cos flicked through the paper to the page she needed, skimming an article about a roving woman reporter that she'd normally find rather interesting. She cleared her throat:

'Throngs of people are expected in London when the Empire Exhibition finally casts its doors open and the learned, the wealthy and the noble descend on this mighty symbol of achievement in Kensington. Thereafter the public shall be free to explore the wonders and curiosities of Her Majesty's Empire. Not since the Great Exhibition of 1851 has such pomp and splendour visited the capital.

'This grand display of empire is the brainchild of Lord Francis Fitzroy, the distinguished explorer, who has returned triumphantly to England after an absence of a decade. Lord Fitzroy has spent his career travelling all over the world, collecting and curating rare specimens of art, fossils, creatures, inventions and, most spectacularly, jewels. These precious stones, from all corners of the empire, will be displayed at his Exhibition. Lord Fitzroy liberated these jewels from the colonies so they could be cared for properly in the Motherland.'

Diya scowled. '"Liberated" is just a fancy word for stolen. I don't understand the British Empire – why do people celebrate conquering other countries who are perfectly capable of governing themselves?'

Mary let out a shaky breath. 'You're right, Diya.' She

nudged Cos, sniffing up her remaining tears. 'Is there more?'

Cos continued. *'However, the main attraction of this grand event will be the golden tiara, within which sits the Star Diamond. This priceless coronet was forged in celebration of Lord Fitzroy's discovery of the Star in India, and is believed to be the most valuable tiara in the world.'*

'Maybe he wants to do something horrible to us. Like force us to mine for gold in tunnels deep underground or put us to work in a dangerous factory.' Mary's voice raced at the speed of a locomotive; her eyes were as wide as gas lamps. Her mind always dashed to the worst-possible outcome.

Cos frowned at the tiny inked words. 'It says here that Lord Fitzroy is a "distinguished explorer".' For some reason that made her feel even more uneasy. *What does an explorer want with twenty disabled children?*

Cos's thoughts were tangled into unpickable knots. She folded the newspaper and tucked it underarm.

'Maybe –' Pearl shrugged innocently – 'he does just want to adopt us, so we can see the world outside the home. Besides, it can't be worse than living with the Stains.'

Cos's heart simultaneously leaped and sank at Pearl's words. Pearl saw the world through a rose-tinted lens, and it made Cos love her friend and fear for her at the same time. Cos knew that there were people in the outside world just as cruel and callous as Mr and Miss Stain, and she suspected Lord Fitzroy was one of them.

Pearl wasn't a fan of touch, so Cos wrapped her arms tightly round herself. 'This hug is for you, Pearly.' Pearl's mouth twitched into a small smile in response. 'But I don't think that Lord Fitzroy is a good man or has good intentions at all. In fact, he gave me the creeps.'

Mary and Diya nodded in agreement.

'Plus,' Cos said with a shiver, 'the Stains seemed to know him. You should have seen the tattoo he showed Miss Stain. It was on his wrist and she seemed almost . . . *scared* of it. And it had these strange words underneath it.'

'Hmm.' Diya pushed her glasses up her nose. 'Scared? That's odd. What did it say?'

Cos shrugged. 'They weren't in English, but I think I can remember them.' She scrunched up her face, trying to picture the exact phrase. *'Non,* erm. *Non quantitas?'* Cos clicked her tongue. 'Aha! I think it was *Non quantitas sed qualitas.'*

Diya blinked. 'That sounds like Latin! Inventors use that language all the time. I may be able to translate it. But why would Miss Stain be scared of a tattoo? And why would a lord even have a tattoo in the first place? What did it look like?'

'It was a tree.'

Without a word Pearl dug around in her pinny pocket, withdrawing a teeny paint pot. She unhooked her trusty paintbrush from her ear and dipped it in the paint, before searching for a spare bit of skin to draw upon. She finally found a bit (in between her shoulder and her elbow) and began to sketch.

She drew a lush tree filled with greenery and branches that stretched wide.

Cos frowned. 'That's beautiful, Pearl. But Fitzroy's tree was more . . . dead. Its branches were withered and droopy, like it hadn't seen water or sunshine for years.'

Pearl nodded, smudged her tree into nothingness, and found another bare spot of skin in the crook of her elbow. This time she sketched a tree of nightmares: black and as skinny as a skeleton it loomed dark on Pearl's skin; its branches seemed to stretch towards Cos like claws.

'That's it!' she exclaimed. 'That's perfect, Pearl.'

'Buuuut, what does it mean?' Mary quivered as she spoke.

Cos tapped her chin. 'That is the question. It obviously means *something* to Lord Fitzroy and the Stains. We've got to figure out what. That will be the key to stopping Lord Fitzroy from adopting us.'

Cos instinctively turned to Mary. She was always the best

when coming up with step-by-step plans.

Mary smiled nervously. 'Well, first things first, we need to stop Lord Fitzroy from adopting us. And to do that we have to figure out *why* he's adopting us. There might be a clue at the exhibition he mentioned.' Mary paused for dramatic effect, her eyes shining with excitement. 'And to figure that out we'll need to visit.'

A reverent hush filled the scullery, tempered by a snort from Diya. The Stains only let the girls leave the home when they were whisked away for painful and scary hospital appointments. Cos hadn't stepped outside in years.

The silence that had fallen was broken by a rapid *stomp-stomp-stomp* from outside. Without a word Cos hid the newspaper in her pinny, pivoted on her stool and plunged her hands back into the soapy water. Pearl reluctantly dipped a single finger into the basin, Diya rolled back over to the drying rack, her wheels squeaking, and Mary hid her terrified face behind a tea towel.

With a slam the door crashed open. 'Their ladyships are due any moment,' grumbled Mr Stain. 'You lot are to wait upon them.' He stomped off as fast as he arrived.

The girls groaned. Waiting on rich ladies was horrible, and, particularly for Diya and Cos, very difficult to manage. Using a wheelchair or a walking stick to get around meant balancing trays full of tea, and that was tricky. It would be even tougher for Cos just after a dislocation.

'Go to the exhibition, figure out what Lord Fitzroy wants, find a way to stop him adopting us,' Mary whispered under her breath.

Cos's throat felt rope-dry. Visiting *the* attraction to see in London was more than impossible – it was unthinkable.

Diya sighed, confirming Cos's unspoken fears. 'I think stopping Fitzroy will be a lot harder than you think, Cos. Remember, we're kids. And, more than that, we're *unfortunates*.'

Cos set her jaw. However difficult, she refused to give up. 'Which means that adults always underestimate us. I know we didn't quite pull off the cake heist, but think of all the other jobs we've done!'

'My favourite was the Great Drawers Disappearance of '98.' Pearl giggled.

'Miss Stain was knickerless for a whole month in the middle of winter. Served her right for cancelling family visits for the billionth time. *And* Pearly made some beautiful dolls for the younger girls out of the pilfered material.' Cos grinned at her friends.

'I think the time we replaced her gin with rainwater was the best one.' A smile crept across Mary's face. 'She may have been in a foul mood for weeks, but it was worth it.'

Diya huffed in an attempt to try to hide her grin. 'That one was good, but I think the day Pearl glued Mr Stain shut in the laundry room was even better. Miss Stain had to send for a handyman to get him out, remember?'

Cos snorted at the memory of Mr Stain pummelling his fists on the door. 'Exactly! That *proves* we can pull off shenanigans.'

'This is *more* than shenanigans, Cos,' Diya said with a shiver. 'Lord Fitzroy is dangerous, and rich, and powerful. We're a group of disabled children with nothing.'

Cos nodded. And there was nothing they could do – if they followed the letter of the law – to change that. She plucked the newspaper from her pinny again and stared at the drawing of the tiara, an idea sparking in her mind. 'If only we were half as rich as him. Then he wouldn't dare take us.'

Diya opened her mouth to ask another question, but, before she could, a doorbell rang. A chorus of high-pitched squeals and coos sounded from the foyer. The ladies had arrived.

CHAPTER FIVE

'Again, I apologise *profusely* for the lack of cake, Your Ladyships,' Miss Stain said for (at Cos's count) the twentieth time since they'd arrived. She glared at Cos as she spoke. Her search for cake replacements had gone poorly; the bakery was all out.

They were gathered in the dining hall, where two of the circular tables were now adorned with drooping bouquets of flowers. The same prune-faced ladies that had attended every one of Miss Stain's afternoon teas since Cos could remember were clustered together at a table, chit-chatting and haw-haw-hawing at each other. In all the afternoon teas Cos and her friends had been paraded at, not one of the ladies had uttered a word to her. Instead, they gawked at the girls as if they were zoo animals. Cos knew that they only visited so they could appear to be public-spirited.

Cos was marched into the dining hall, Miss Stain's pinched nails gripping her shoulder. 'Behave or else . . .' she demanded through gritted teeth. 'And don't breathe a word to the other girls about Lord Fitzroy.'

The girls they'd left behind in the schoolroom had filed in without meeting Cos's eye. She felt her cheeks warm with shame; she'd promised them cake and failed. Worse than that, her actions had led to every one of them being in danger. She busied herself with preparing the steaming-hot tea and coffee and tried to push away the gnawing guilt.

Mr Stain stood guard in the shadows of the doorway, arms crossed. Miss Stain hovered like a wasp in search of a sugary drink, children flinching as she neared them. She cleared her throat and the muttering faded into silence.

Miss Stain's smile was glassy and false. 'My girls are very excited to act as your serving girls today and will be—'

Miss Stain's speech was cut off by the sound of glass smashing outside the dining hall. She scowled, jabbing a pointed finger at her brother, who hurried out of the room. He returned a few moments later, his fist wrapped tightly round the upper arm of a younger lady, who, although being shunted into the dining hall like a common criminal, had a swagger befitting royalty. Cos was immediately impressed by the rebelliousness of it all.

'Found her rummaging around in your office,' growled Mr

Stain, shaking his prisoner roughly. 'She broke your bottle of Skullsplitter's.'

Cos cringed. Spilling even a drop of the Stains' alcohol was, in Miss Stain's opinion, akin to murder. The matron twitched with anger, a vein pulsing in her neck as she stared down at the newcomer. This frigid welcome didn't seem to bother the woman, though. Cos noticed that the lady's fingers were stained dark, and as Mr Stain jolted her roughly about, cogs fell from her pocket, pinging loudly on the floor. In one of her hands she clutched an open bag, the battered spine of a book poking out.

'Apologies,' said the woman, although she didn't seem sorry at all. She wrenched herself free from Mr Stain's grip. 'I'm here for the Ladies' Tea, but having entered your magnificent abode, I found myself lost.'

Miss Stain sucked on her teeth, thinking hard. Cos's gut told her that the strange woman was lying. She didn't seem like the type to get lost. Miss Stain clearly thought so too, as she coldly appraised the woman's fashionable attire, spoiled only by the cogs, stained fingers and cracked bag.

Diya elbowed Cos in the ribs. 'Look at that book,' she hissed. The spine read: *The Lady's Guide to the Study of Engineering.* 'She's a lady engineer,' she hissed, eyes shining with excitement. 'A *real* lady engineer!' Diya gripped Cos's hand. Lady engineers were right next to lady inventors in Diya's mind.

'I don't recall sending an invite to someone new,' a purse-lipped Miss Stain muttered.

'Lord Fitzroy suggested I attend,' the woman replied breezily.

Miss Stain jolted, her expression inscrutable. Cos was equally befuddled. *This strange lady knows Lord Fitzroy?* Miss Stain swallowed her scowl and replaced it with a thin-lipped smile, gesturing for the woman to sit.

She plonked herself on to a chair at an empty table in the most unladylike fashion, slamming down her satchel. The other ladies tutted.

Cos peered closely at a piece of paper squeezed next to the book in the lady's satchel. She could just make out the words 'Lord Francis Fitzroy, WORLD-FAMOUS EXPLORER, proudly presents: THE EMPIRE EXHIBITION' written across it.

'And who, may I ask, are you?' Miss Stain questioned. 'I only admit ladies of calibre to this establishment. Does your family appear in *Burke's Peerage*?' Cos noticed that Miss Stain was being far less polite to the gathered ladies than usual. Cos knew why; she didn't need them or their money any more, not with Lord Fitzroy's offer on the table.

'I'm Agatha Noone, lady engineer and, no, you won't find the Noones in *Burke's Peerage*. I'm displaying my latest contraption, a cylinder engine, at the Empire Exhibition.'

Cos could tell that nervous excitement was shooting

through her friends. This was it – their ticket to discovering why Lord Fitzroy wanted them. Diya gave her hand a squeeze. But for some reason Cos felt uneasy.

She stared at Miss Noone, trying to take in everything about this strange new person. Apart from her stained fingers (which Cos thought were probably caused by long hours working with grime and oil), she looked like an entirely respectable person. Her hair was coiffed in the latest fashion that Miss Stain had tried and failed to emulate, her dress was smart but simple, and her intelligent and level gaze made Cos feel a little . . . *exposed*. It was as if this Miss Noone could stare straight into the depths of her soul.

'Have you heard of the Empire Exhibition, Miss Stain?' asked Miss Noone, as she unclasped the small leather satchel slung across her shoulders, withdrawing a small notebook and fountain pen.

Miss Stain pursed her lips. 'Of course, Miss Noone. It's the talk of London, as you well know, being an exhibitor.'

'Quite,' replied Miss Noone, scribbling in the notebook she'd pulled from her bag. 'And do you know Lord Fitzroy *personally*?'

Cos raised her eyebrow and caught a glance at Miss Stain's stunned expression. This Miss Noone asked a lot of probing questions for an engineer. Something shifted within Cos. Miss Noone was very curious.

'Of course not,' Miss Stain replied sharply. Her whole

body tightened up with the lie. Cos shared a worried look with Diya. 'He's an important, busy man. He wouldn't have anything to do with a home for unfortunates.' She clapped her hands together. 'Well, enough of all this chatter. Girls, tea.'

A clatter of china and the hiss of hot water could be heard as the girls started preparing the hot drinks. The other kids clustered round Cos and her friends, peppering them with questions.

'*We heard a commotion,*' signed one.

'What happened?' asked another.

'Did you manage to pilfer the cakes?' demanded a very hungry girl, her tummy rumbling loudly.

Cos tried to crack a reassuring smile. 'Everything is fine. But no cakes, I'm afraid.'

'Less chit-chatting, more tea-making,' Mr Stain hissed angrily at them, out of earshot from their esteemed guests. The girls bolted away from Cos and her friends, bustling round the tea trolleys.

Mary, Diya, Pearl and Cos huddled together.

'This is our way into the exhibition if we can get her to like us,' whispered Mary, as she spooned sugar cubes into a bowl.

'And she's a modern woman.' Diya swooned in a completely un-Diya-like way.

Cos frowned, pouring tea into a cup. 'Hmm.'

'Come on, Cos.' Pearl nudged Cos. 'How else are we going

to get there? We have no other way. This is our one-in-a-million chance to stop Lord Fitzroy.'

But there was a tug in Cos's stomach that told her it was too good to be true. She sighed as she picked up a tray with a teacup, saucer and a steaming teapot in one hand. She limped forward, leaning on her walking stick. The tray wobbled precariously.

'Do you need any help?' Mary's voice shook with worry.

Cos shook her head, gritted her teeth and made her way towards the table where Miss Noone sat, writing frantically in her notebook. Cos was only two steps away when her knee twinged in agony. The tray slipped from her grip and smashed to the floor.

Shards of china scattered across the dining hall, tea splashing everywhere. Miss Stain erupted, *stomp-stomp-stomping* towards Cos.

'YOU IDIOT!' she snarled, spittle flying into Cos's face. 'Pick it all up this instant.'

Miss Noone pushed back her chair and stood, before scrambling on the floor to pick up china shards. 'No, no, no, it's all right, Miss Stain. Let me help.'

Miss Stain drew back her mouth into a wolfish grimace.

The ladies on the other table tittered, as Miss Stain swallowed her anger and turned away from Cos's mess.

Cos shifted her weight on to her walking stick and tried to help Miss Noone fish the remaining cup splinters off the floor. Diya wheeled herself across the hall and gathered up the tray as Mary and Pearl grabbed some scraps of fabric and began wiping up the tea spillage.

'I'm so sorry, Miss Noone.' Cos tried to blink away the tears that threatened to spill from her eyes.

Miss Noone winked at her. 'A little mess never hurt anyone. And call me Aggie. I detest formalities.'

Cos grinned back, despite herself. *It's nice*, she thought, *for an adult to treat me like a person, rather than a problem.*

'Ahem!' snapped Miss Stain, rounding back on Cos and Aggie. 'Get to work.'

But Cos ignored her. She pushed away her doubts and instead put on her winningest smile. The others were right. Aggie might just be their route into the exhibition.

Cos just had to persuade her. 'Aggie,' she said, 'can you tell us more about the Empire Exhibition? It sounds *very* interesting.'

CHAPTER SIX

M iss Stain stomped towards Cos, grabbing her by the crook of her elbow and shaking her roughly. Cos cringed, hoping that her joints would stay in place. 'I apologise profusely, Miss Noone, for this girl's insolence. Rest assured, number one will be severely punished.'

Aggie stood up, thudding her palms on the table. 'No, Miss Stain. I applaud your charge's curiosity! Curiosity is an essential attribute for all young ladies.'

Miss Stain let go of Cos, her jaw twitching with anger. Cos's mouth fell open. She couldn't remember the last time an adult had stood up for her.

Aggie peered through her spectacles at Cos. 'What did you say your name was?'

'Number one,' Miss Stain said quickly.

Aggie frowned slightly. 'But . . . that's not her actual name?'

Miss Stain let out an exasperated sigh. 'Well, no, but for reasons of . . .' Her words trailed off.

Cos stepped forward. 'Cosima. Cos for short.'

'A beautiful name. Did you know it's derived from the word "cosmos", which means universal? That means everything – the earth, the sea, the sky and the stars.'

'Oh,' Cos said, heat pricking at her cheeks, 'I didn't know that.'

Aggie smiled. 'I'm sorry, Cos, I've forgotten what your question was.'

'*SheaskedifyoucouldtellusmoreabouttheExhibition,*' Mary said all in one breath, stepping forward to be level with Cos. 'Will there be any animals there?'

Mary's question seemed to freeze Aggie's expression into one of unease. 'Er, I don't believe so.' Aggie glanced down at the leaflet in her bag. 'But there will be animal specimens on display.'

Mary knitted her eyebrows. '*Specimens?*'

'A specimen, Mary,' Diya interjected, 'is an object used for scientific study.'

'You are absolutely correct!' Aggie beamed at Diya. 'Do I detect a budding scientific mind?'

Somewhere behind her, Cos heard Miss Stain splutter.

Diya blushed with pride. 'I'm an inventor, Miss Noone.'

'How impressive! And what about you?' Aggie fixed her

gaze on Pearl, who pulled at the cuffs of her dress and stared resolutely at the floor.

'Pearly is a brilliant maker. She can turn almost anything into art.' Diya smiled reassuringly at Pearl.

'It's wonderful that you are all so talented.' Aggie tucked an errant curl behind her ear and sighed. 'You remind me a little of myself when I was younger – I loved to learn. So how did you all hear about the exhibition?'

The others clambered to chat to Aggie, as Cos felt herself step backwards and melt into the cover of the crowd. Even the girls who had missed the cake heist had shuffled towards Aggie, eager for a bit of kind adult contact. The other ladies tutted and scowled, whilst the Stains silently seethed.

'What's on your mind?' Diya slipped her hand into Cos's, their conversation covered by the girls' excited chatter. 'Why aren't you spinning Aggie wild tales about our desperate need to visit this Exhibition?'

Cos thought for a moment before answering, frowning slightly. 'I'm not sure. Miss Noone, Aggie, is rather curious, isn't she?'

Diya scoffed. 'Of course she's curious, Cos! She's a lady engineer. She's probably faced obstacle after obstacle in order to pursue her career. You'd *have* to be curious to do that. Besides, she's our one chance of finding out more about Fitzroy.'

'Exactly,' Cos replied, eyeing Aggie as the engineer

fired question after question at the others. 'It's almost too convenient, isn't it? And she seems very interested in us and Lord Fitzroy's connection to the home.'

Diya snorted, dropping Cos's hand. 'Come on, Cos, we're relying on you.'

The weight of expectation thumped in Cos's chest. If she didn't figure a way out of this Lord Fitzroy debacle, then not only would she have put her friends in danger and inadvertently ripped them away from their families, but also (and this didn't bear thinking about) she might lose the chance to find out more about where she came from. *For ever.*

The awful possibility steeled her and she stepped forward. She knew she needed to plant the idea of taking the children to the exhibition into Aggie's mind and make her think it was all her idea. Cos cleared her throat loudly and the other girls' chatter faded away.

'We all love learning, and the Stains are careful to ensure we get our lessons. But we rarely leave our home.' She sighed dramatically. 'What we wouldn't give to go on a day trip.' Cos's words hung heavily in the air.

An odd expression crossed Aggie's face, but she didn't reply to Cos. She ran her thumb over the words on her leaflet: *Gaze at wonders from around the world.* 'Yes, I suppose you'd love to get out and about more,' she said.

'Due to our financial situation and the girls' various ailments,

Miss Noone, we are unable to take them out of the home.' Miss Stain placed a warning hand on the small of Cos's back.

Aggie frowned. 'Ever?'

Miss Stain pursed her lips. 'Ever,' she hissed through gritted teeth. 'And I must add that it is so inappropriate for these children to socialise with . . . . with . . .' She spluttered as she searched for the right words. '*Normal* people. They should not be seen and not be heard.'

The prune-faced ladies on the other table nodded their agreement to Miss Stain's words in between slurps of tea. A shiver crept up Cos's spine. It was almost as if Miss Stain wanted to pretend her charges and their disabilities didn't exist.

Aggie ignored them all. Her gaze was fixed upon the girls, and Cos could almost see the cogs spinning in her brain; the lady engineer was forming a plan. 'I don't think that's inappropriate at all.' She turned to Miss Stain, who had a look of horror dawning on her face, and the other ladies, who scowled. 'Twenty girls let loose in an enormous building with interesting items all around. It will be raucous. Preposterous!'

Aggie screeched her chair back and stood. 'In fact, I think it's rather a good idea. I'm at the exhibition first thing tomorrow to make sure none of the screws have come loose on my engine. I'll pick up the girls on my way there and show them around for the day. No cost to you, of course.'

Miss Stain opened and closed her mouth, but no sounds

came out. The other ladies muttered behind gloved hands.

'I won't take no for an answer, Miss Stain.' Determination was caught in Aggie's eyes. 'Besides, I'm sure you could do with a day off.'

A strangled squeal erupted from Miss Stain's throat. Her shoulders slumped. 'Fine.'

Cos smirked under a curtain of hair so the Stains couldn't see. *Yes!*

'Brilliant.' Aggie placed her notebook and engineering tome back in her bag before standing up. 'Here,' she said, thrusting the leaflet about the exhibition into Cos's hand. Dark smudges of oil stained the corner of the paper. 'You can read up on this ahead of tomorrow.'

Cos bought the leaflet close to her face, expecting to smell the burning scent of oil – familiar because of all Diya's inventions. But instead she sniffed something sooty and metallic. Cos wasn't sure what it was, but it definitely wasn't oil. Cos suspected Aggie might not be exactly what she appeared to be either.

Curious.

The Stains' punishment was horrible.

Cos dragged her tired feet up the rickety staircase, leaning heavily on her walking stick. Her knee throbbed with every step upwards; her whole body ached. After the ladies had left,

Miss Stain had made her scrub the entire ground floor of the home with nothing but a sponge and bucket filled with frigid water. Cos's knuckles were blistered and cracked, her legs felt like lead, and shivers coursed through her body. Outside the windows of the Home for Unfortunate Girls, snow had finally stopped falling. Instead, a bitter frost took root on the cobblestoned London streets.

Cos moved as quietly as she could, past crooked doors, a chorus of snores echoing through the shadowed corridors. Eventually she reached the last room at the far end of the home. Cos pushed open the creaking door, and a whispered cheer went up. The familiar sight of cobwebbed rafters, threadbare plank beds and her friends' wide-eyed faces warmed her heart. The other girls, exhausted by the afternoon tea, were tucked up in bed, fast asleep – only Mary, Pearl and Diya had waited up for her. Cos felt a pang of regret in her stomach, remembering her broken promise to bring them back some cake.

'Cos!' Mary exclaimed, as she enveloped her in a hug. Cos flinched, too sore to be touched. Mary gasped. 'I'm sorry – are you all right?'

But before Cos could answer, Diya rushed forward, eyes wide with excitement. 'I translated the Latin bit of Lord Fitzroy's tattoo,' she spluttered, brandishing her precious collection of inventing pamphlets that Pearl had retrieved from searching through the neighbours' bins when the Stains forced her to take the rubbish out.

'*Non quantitas sed qualitas* means it's not the quantity, but the quality.'

'Hmm,' Cos said, a little taken aback. She'd hoped that the tattoo quote might shed some light on Lord Fitzroy and his plans for them. After all, it had been that which had rattled Miss Stain so much.

'Sounds like gibberish to me.' Pearl shrugged.

'Maybe,' Mary said breathlessly, 'he means to do away with us all together! He kept calling us "degenerates". He obviously doesn't think we're quality.'

Pearl scoffed. 'I think you're reading too much into it, Mar. It might just be his family motto.'

'Whatever it means, we need to find out.' Cos limped towards a rope pulley and yanked it, and a blackboard hovered down from the rafters above.

They'd rescued the old blackboard from the schoolroom, and Diya had hidden it from the Stains in the rafters of the dormitory. It was perfect for planning out Stain-annoying shenanigans. Cos grabbed an old rag and cleared the board of drawings of cake designs, before Pearl chucked her a piece of chalk. In her spidery handwriting Cos wrote *FOUR days till Lord Fitzroy picks us up!* Then she scribbled a heading: *Lord Fitzroy's Plan*. Under that she added bullet points:

- *The Institute — non quantitas sed qualitas, which means it's not the quantity, but the quality.*

Pearl furrowed her brow. 'What's that got to do with a dead tree?'

Diya's grin faltered. 'I suppose it's a mystery.'

Cos grimaced. Her brain was too fuzzy to solve anything right now. She handed the chalk to Pearl, who sketched the creepy skeleton tree on to the blackboard.

'Are you sure you're all right?' Mary asked again.

Cos shrugged as she lowered herself on to her bed. 'I'll be fine in the morning,' she lied. 'I just need a good night's sleep. I heard Aggie leave, though. She told the Stains she would pick us up first thing tomorrow.'

Pearl's arms tightly wrapped round her chest. 'So, it's really happening? We're going to the exhibition? We can find out why Lord Fitzroy wants us?'

Diya nodded. 'And knowing *why* he wants us will help us figure out how to stop the Stains giving us to him.'

Cos saw relief shoot through the girls. Mary squeezed Cos's hand, and they shared a smile. Cos glanced round at the other sleeping girls, rummaged in her pinny pocket and withdrew the stained and rumpled leaflet Aggie had given her earlier.

Something else fluttered to the ground.

'What's this?' Pearl knelt and picked up the small black-and-white photo.

'I'd forgotten about that!' Cos took the photo from Pearl and peered closely at it. Two haunted-looking children stared back at her: a teenage girl holding hands with a smaller boy in the centre of a grand living room. The boy's hair was unruly and he wore a scowl, and the girl's cheeks were pinched and she had what looked like a star clipped into her hair. Behind the children, Cos could see a wall dotted with picture frames and a well-stocked fireplace. The bottom of the photo was jagged and rough, as if it had been ripped. She realised with a start that the bottom half of the image had been torn away. Cos brushed her fingers against it, wondering what was missing. 'Lord Fitzroy dropped this when he was leaving.'

The others gathered round Cos's shoulders, eagerly staring at it. Other than the occasional grainy images in stolen newspapers, it was the first photo they'd ever seen.

'They look sad,' said Pearl.

Diya shrugged. 'It's probably just a photo of Fitzroy's kids.'

Cos shook her head. 'It looks older than that.' She pointed at the well-worn and dog-eared corners at the top of the image.

'You're right,' Diya said, and Cos noted the tone of surprise in her friend's voice. She yanked the photo from Cos, peering closely at it. 'It's not a daguerreotype, or even a collodion positive – they're too early for this.'

'A daguerreo-*what*?' Pearl asked.

'It's a type of photograph,' Diya said. 'This is a tintype.' She handed the photo back to Cos, a proud look upon her face.

'What does that mean?' Mary frowned.

Diya sighed, as if it were obvious. 'Cos is right – this photograph is old. Probably from twenty or so years ago. That's when this method of photography – tintypes – was most popular. I read about it in a copy of *The Inventor's Journal* Pearl found for me.'

'Well, even so,' Mary reasoned, 'this photo won't have anything to do with his plan for us. Plenty of people carry around photos of their loved ones. If I had a photo of my grandpa, I'd treasure it for ever.'

'I'd get one with me and my sister,' Pearl muttered quietly.

'Mine would be my dad standing at the bow of his ship.' Diya smiled at the possibility.

Jealousy soared in Cos's chest again, threatening to spill out and spew angry, unfair words at her friends. She'd never had anyone to take a photo of. Instead, she whispered, 'but why is it ripped?'

'And this is what we'll see tomorrow at the exhibition?'

Mary swiped the leaflet from Cos's lap. She seemed to have tired of the conversation about Cos's found photo. She wrinkled her nose at it. 'What's this on it?' she asked, pointing to Aggie's smudged fingerprints.

'It's obviously oil,' Diya said, preening a little. 'Engineers, like inventors, always have oil on their hands.

Diya's words dragged Cos's attention away from the photo. 'It's not oil,' she said quickly. 'It doesn't smell like it.'

Diya looked flabbergasted.

'Can I have a look?' Pearl asked softly.

Mary handed the leaflet over to her. Pearl looked so closely at the stain that she went almost cross-eyed. Then, to Cos's surprise, she licked it.

'It's ink,' Pearl concluded.

'Ink?' repeated Mary.

'Why would an engineer have ink on her hands?' Diya asked.

Questions swirled in Cos's head as she handed the leaflet and the strange photo to Pearl, who duly stuck them both to the blackboard with some of her glue before winding it back up to the rafters.

Cos laid back in her bed, wincing as she swung her legs up.

'I don't know, Diya,' she replied. 'But I think we're going to have to find out.'

Diya extinguished the glow of the Luminous Lantern and Cos pulled the threadbare blanket over her. She waited till she was sure her friends had drifted off to sleep before she slid the stolen newspaper from her pinny, hiding it under her pillow. Then she bum-shuffled towards the foot of her bed and began to rummage through the old apple crate. She peeled through years of girls' possessions – broken ear trumpets, prototypes of Diya's inventions, Pearl's crafting supplies and, of course, *rope*. Cos dug all the way to the very bottom, disturbing a nest of spiders that scurried over her hands, until her fingers stumbled across the handkerchief. She knew she'd seen it there.

At first glance it wasn't much to look at. The years at the bottom of the crate had made it fade to a greyish shade, and there was what looked like a knot of different-coloured string in a clump on it. Cos frowned – handkerchiefs were supposed to be for wiping noses, weren't they? She resisted the urge to yank the knot away – this was her only link to her past, but a bubble of anger rose in her. Why hadn't she realised the hankie was important sooner? Why had her parents left such an inscrutable clue? The string caught in her fingers, and she blew out a frustrated breath. As she turned it over in her hands, her frustration shifted to shock, and then confusion. On the back of the handkerchief was an intricately decorated embroidery.

It covered almost the entire other side of the handkerchief, and Cos realised with a start that it was the reason for the clump of thread. She frowned as she tried to make sense of the picture. A series of black lines spread across the fabric and looked a little like a spiderweb, and dotted between them were squares of greenery. And then at certain points there were little symbols stitched into the handkerchief: at the top right was a wonky heart, coloured red. To the left of the heart were a series of thick grey bars, a sunrise shadowing the outline of a spiky-looking plant behind them. Just below that was an image very familiar to Cos – a knot of rope. To the right of that a star – yellow and almost, Cos thought, shining, was stitched on top of one of the spiderweb black lines. A few lines away from that was a drawing of an open book. And finally, at the bottom of the handkerchief, was an X, stitched shakily into the fabric.

Cos stifled a gasp – *a treasure map.*

The Luminous Lantern flickered back into life. Diya sleepily shoved her upside-down glasses on to her nose, yawning into the flickering light. In the beds next to her Mary and Pearl stirred and yawned into wakefulness.

'I know that gasp anywhere, Cosima Unfortunate,' Diya whispered, but there was kindness hidden behind her scowl. 'What are you up to?'

Cos hugged her found handkerchief to her chest. For some reason she'd wanted the clues to her past to be hers and hers alone, just like the others had their own families to themselves. But, as she blinked into the curious faces of her best friends, she knew she owed them the truth – now and always.

'When I was pinching the cakes,' admitted Cos, 'I came across Miss Stain's ledger.'

Her friends' faces were 'O's of surprise. They knew just how carefully Miss Stain guarded her ledger. The other girls slept on, oblivious to the conversation.

'And it said that I had arrived at the home in possession of a handkerchief,' Cos continued. 'Miss Stain always said my parents had abandoned me with nothing. But she lied. When I read the entry, I remembered a bit of fabric that I'd tossed in the apple crate, years ago. I came up here and found it. And look.' She turned the handkerchief round, showing them the embroidered landscape.

'It's beautiful,' Pearl said, her eyes shining. 'A real piece of art.'

'It is,' Cos said, but inside her chest she felt as though her heart was fraying piece by piece. 'But what does it mean? I'm sure it's a message from my parents – or whoever dropped me here. A message meant for me. Or a map maybe? But I can't work it out.'

The others puzzled at the fabric.

'Can I touch it?' Mary asked. Cos fought the urge to flinch – after all, it was only a hankie – but now she knew the answers it might hold, it was infinitely more precious.

With a shaking hand Cos nodded. Mary stood and tiptoed towards her bed. She took the handkerchief reverently and began peering closely at it – holding it near the Luminous Lantern for light. After a few minutes of puzzled silence, Mary nodded. 'Cos,' she said carefully, 'it is definitely a map.'

Cos peered over Mary's shoulder. Suddenly she saw that the spiderweb lines were roads and streets and the squares of greenery parks. *Could the map be of Kensington? Of the streets and buildings that surrounded the Home for Unfortunate Girls?*

'So these symbols,' Cos said – pointing at the heart, the book and star, 'maybe they're places nearby that are important to me, and to my parents. And the X – could that be where my parents are?' Cos's heart swelled with hope.

Diya gestured to Mary to pass the hankie to her. Cos nodded her agreement, and Diya set her discerning gaze upon it, peering at the map like it was one of her complicated inventing problems. 'Ancient engineers used symbols sometimes on their inventions. It was a way to share ideas with a fellow engineer without having to speak the same language. We just need to work out what these ones mean.'

Cos nodded vigorously from her bed. 'This is brilliant! The first real clue to my parents' whereabouts.'

Mary fiddled nervously with her long blonde locks. 'This map is just an embroidery, so the streets might not be accurate. And even if they are, if you've had it since you were a baby, then it was sewn twelve years ago, so buildings and streets might have been demolished or built in that time. And this could be a map of anywhere in London – England, even! I just don't want you to get your hopes up *too* much.'

Cos swallowed. That might be a problem. Her hopes had already soared. This was the first clue she'd ever found to her past, and she couldn't help but be excited. Maybe she'd been forcibly removed by the Stains? Maybe her parents had searched every home in London but the one she was in? Maybe they were patiently waiting night after night for her return?

Pearl scrambled to her feet and settled in between Mary and Diya on Diya's bed. Unlike the others, she decided to look at the handkerchief from beneath. 'I think this was done in a hurry – the embroiderer didn't have enough time to keep their stitches neat and tidy. And they were new to sewing – look at the wonky heart. And have you seen this?' She held out the corner of the hankie so Cos could see.

On it were faded gold initials that read 'W. F.' Cos had been so transfixed by the embroidery that she hadn't noticed. *Another confusing clue.*

'This hankie,' Pearl said, as she gently rubbed her thumb against the material, 'was once expensive. It feels like silk, you see. And these initials were put there by someone professional – not the same person who did the embroidery.'

'So,' said Cos, trying to put the puzzle pieces in order in her head, 'this hankie probably once belonged to someone rich, someone with the initials W. F. But later on someone else embroidered this map on to it. And to find where X is we need to work out what the other symbols mean.'

Everyone nodded.

Possibilities swam through Cos's head as she stared so hard at the hankie that her eyesight went a little blurry. 'So perhaps,' she said, sounding unsure, 'this handkerchief was made for W. F., a well-off gentleman – my father. He gifted it to his sweetheart, a poor but beautiful seamstress – my mother – who, when she realised the authorities would take away her disabled baby – left me a clue to her location.'

'Maybe,' Pearl whispered, but Cos noticed that her friend didn't sound convinced.

'I think a professional seamstress might be a little neater with her stitches.' Diya ran her fingers through the knot of thread.

'Diya's right,' Mary added. 'There are so many other possibilities. You don't know for sure that your parents are the ones that left the hankie for you – it could've just as easily been a nurse or a churchwarden. Even if your mother *was* the one who embroidered the map, the W. F. initials might be a red herring. She could've just come across the hankie by chance. And we have to consider that the map might not lead anywhere – it might just be a pretty picture.' She counted the problems off on her fingers.

'No,' Cos said decisively. She felt in her gut that the hankie had to mean something. 'I can't explain it, but I know it will lead me to my parents.'

'Cos,' said Diya, and she could see her friend was choosing her words very carefully. 'I know this is exciting, and I know you want answers, but you've got all the time in the world to find your family. We need to focus on what's important right now – and that's stopping Lord Fitzroy.'

Cos tried to cover the hurt on her face with an airy smile. 'Of course!' But bitterness snaked up her insides. It was easy for Diya to say that – when she had a mum that visited and wrote and loved her. Cos had nothing. 'It's late, and we've got a big day tomorrow. Let's get some sleep.'

For the second time that night Diya extinguished the Luminous Lamp, and Mary and Pearl picked their way back to their beds, with Mary handing the hankie over to Cos.

Cos laid back in bed, pain pulsing through her body and questions running through her head. She drifted off to sleep, holding the hankie tight. She was too tired to start unravelling its mysteries now, but as soon as she could she would figure out where her parents were and why they'd left her with it.

CHAPTER SEVEN

Morning brought the kind of frosty sunlight that only comes the day after a snowstorm. Ice glistened on the inside of the dormitory windows, children shivered under thin blankets, and for what seemed like the billionth day in a row bedside glasses of water were frozen solid. Cos lay in her tiny cot bed, handkerchief held tight in her hands. As shards of hazy sunlight sneaked through the window, she rolled herself to a seated position, stretched, and clicked everything back into place.

'Morning,' said Mary with a yawn, wiping her eyes and blinking in the light. A murmur of sleepiness crept through the rest of the dormitory as the other girls began to wake.

'Today's the day!' Cos whispered, as she placed a tentative foot on the creaking floor. She scrunched her face together and hoped that everything would hold together. She stood, then let out a deep breath. *Nothing dislocated. Phew.*

Anticipation thumped through Cos's heart as the dormitory door slammed open. Miss Stain swept inside to begin mechanically helping girls get ready for the day, assisting their dressing and moving them from beds into wheelchairs. She handed Cos her walking stick with a scowl. Cos tied her newly found handkerchief round her neck like a scarf, the embroidered map hidden against her neck and behind her tangle of hair.

A short while later Cos clattered down the rickety staircase to the ground floor, followed by the girls who were able to walk. Mary had carefully packed her clipboard of plans for what-ifs into the satchel that swung from her shoulder. Diya and all the girls in chairs were heaved out of them one by one by Mr Stain, carried down the staircase and then plonked back in their carriages. It was a scary and humiliating experience.

As they waited at the bottom of the stairs, Cos caught snatches of breathless conversation:

'Do you think there will be fossils at the exhibition?' one girl signed. *'I've always wanted to see a real dinosaur skeleton in person, not just in a book!'*

'Can you imagine what we'll have for lunch? The food must be splendid! Do you think Miss Noone will treat us to a hot cocoa?' asked another, rubbing her hungry belly.

'I'm going to have a look at those speckled hens,' said Dolly – who was the youngest resident of the home.

'*Specimens*, Dolly,' Diya corrected gently.

But Cos couldn't pull her thoughts away from her discovery of the handkerchief. Instead of talking with the others, in her head she ran through a list of potential W names for her long-lost father.

William.

Walter.

Woodrow.

Warren.

None of them sounded quite right, though. Cos was sure that something in her gut would tell her when she'd hit on his true name.

The excited chatter continued throughout breakfast (it was, as usual, gloopy grey gruel) and as they shouldered on their coats, hats and mittens in the foyer. It only dissipated when the familiar *stomp-stomp-stomp* of Miss Stain's high-heeled boots echoed down the staircase. The girls silently arranged themselves in a long line. Cos found herself shoulder to shoulder between Mary and Pearl as Miss Stain descended from the last step. Pearl fiddled nervously with the cuffs of her dress, pulling them down to cover the new ink drawings on her arms and refused to meet Miss Stain's gaze.

Miss Stain coughed and arched an eyebrow pointedly at

Pearl, and Pearl sucked in a breath and forced herself to stop fiddling. Each and every girl tried to look at the Stains without flinching. Cos's strategy was to focus on a speck of mould on the distant wall and push everything else away.

'Now –' Miss Stain paced back and forth as she spoke, as if she were a commander of an army – 'as per usual, today I expect you all to behave with the utmost consideration of how your conduct will reflect upon me. You will, at all times, speak only when spoken to, remain in sight of Miss Noone, and, of course, never communicate in any way with outsiders. Remember what I have taught you about the outside world; it is cruel and callous to people like you. If I hear one word about rule-breaking, I will make your lives unbearable.'

The doorbell rang and fear squirmed in Cos's stomach. Everything hinged on today. As horrible as the Home for Unfortunate Girls was, it was all Cos knew.

Mr Stain opened the door and cold air slammed into Cos's chest, blowing away her doubtful thoughts.

Aggie stepped elegantly into the hallway. Her eyes darted around, endlessly searching the nooks and crannies of the foyer. Cos's gaze swivelled to the visitor's hands – they were still ink-stained. 'Morning, girls,' she said cheerfully.

Cos chanced a glance at the Stains; they were apoplectic with rage that Aggie hadn't even offered them a hello: Mr Stain flexed his hands in and out of fists, and Miss Stain looked like a kettle on the brink of boiling.

Aggie winked at the girls. 'Shall we set off then? It's only a short walk, one street over.'

Outside was so much . . . *more* than Cos had imagined. She'd read about London in the newspaper scraps she'd managed to pilfer from the Stains and heard stories from the grocer's boy in snatches when Miss Stain wasn't breathing down her neck, but being in the open air sent tingles racing through her bones. It was almost *too* overwhelming for Pearl. No sooner had she stepped across the boundary, than Pearl had frozen stiff, unable to move.

She'd uttered just two words. 'Too much.'

'Too much' attacks were similar to Mary's panic whirlwinds, except they rooted Pearl to the spot. Triggered by 'too much' newness, it took Pearl a little longer than others to get used to changes. And leaving the home for the first time in years was a huge change.

'What's going on?' Aggie asked, faced crinkled with concern. 'Anything I can do to help?'

Mary shook her head. 'We just need to give her some space. Girls?'

Like they'd done many times before, the girls of the home linked arms and surrounded Pearl in a loose circle, shielding her from the street. Mary kept her keen-eyed gaze on the circle, advising when the spaces between them grew too wide, and occasionally whispering words of encouragement to Pearl. Wind whistled through Cos's hair as she waited, teeth chattering.

After a few minutes, Pearl gulped a big breath and blinked in the cold air. 'I'm all right, I think,' she said, a watery smile briefly crossing her face. 'We're ready to go, Aggie.'

The street was crammed with strangers, and Cos peered at as many of their faces as possible, hoping to see something familiar, the same hazel-coloured eyes or a cheek dimple that mirrored hers, but . . . nothing. The chance was tiny, she knew, but she still hoped.

Snow dusted the crooked roofs of the skinny houses lining the cobblestoned street where the Home for Unfortunate Girls stood. Horse-drawn cabs and omnibuses trundled past. Smog hung heavy in the air, and when Cos breathed in too deeply she spluttered at the bitter taste of coal. She drew close her threadbare coat, the wind chilling her to the bone. The shouts of newspaper hawkers and hot-eel vendors echoed in Cos's ears as their group marched along slippy pavements past gawking eyes.

Cos couldn't blame them. She supposed it was a little strange to see twenty identically dressed children, some walking with crutches, some travelling in wheelchairs, moving down the street. Aggie buzzed around them, a whirlwind of activity. She soothed the cries of a girl overwhelmed by the sights and sounds of the outside, she cleared snow from wheelchair wheels, and helped the group navigate the bustle and noise of the London streets.

The cold pinched the girls' noses red and bit at their fingers and cheeks. The girls in wheelchairs had it worst of all. Their wheels slid across the ice, making it difficult for them to steer.

Diya navigated her way through a particularly slippery patch, steering herself close to Cos, Mary and Pearl. 'So,' she whispered, 'what's the plan?'

Cos dragged her thoughts away from long-lost parents and secret maps, and back to the danger posed by Lord Fitzroy. She checked around to make sure none of the other girls were listening in. But she needn't have worried; they were far too busy taking in the world, whooping and marvelling with the sheer joy of being outside.

'If Aggie is anything like the Stains, she'll keep a close eye on us. We'll need to cause a diversion if we want to get away and search,' Cos muttered, her breath blowing out in clouds.

'A diversion?' whispered Mary, wringing her hands nervously.

Cos nodded, scrambling for an idea. 'Maybe if we hang back from the others, we might be able to sneak away?'

Pearl made a face and Diya sighed. A squeak crept out of Mary's trembling lips.

Cos knew it wasn't one of her strongest ideas. She was

so used to planning shenanigans within the confines of the home, where she knew each and every room like the back of her hand. The thought of doing something in a place so new and strange slammed into her like a vicious gust of wind. But Cos swallowed away the fear. She could do this. She *had* to do it – for her friends.

The girls rounded the corner at the end of the street, and Cos skidded to a halt to avoid smacking into the back end of a huge crowd. The shabbiness of the previous road melted away; instead of tiny dilapidated cottages, grand red-brick buildings rose into the blue sky above. Cos stood on her tiptoes and tried to peer over the heads of people to see what all the fuss was about.

The great glass building ahead of them sparkled in the early-morning light, hinting at the wonders contained within. Whispers raced up and down the crowd ahead, of what secrets lay undiscovered, of the curiosities that were about to be displayed for all the world to see, of strange new inventions with cogs and whirrs. Cos felt shivers run up her spine.

'People are so excited they've been crowding Exhibition Road for weeks. It isn't even open yet,' said Aggie, as she dodged past a couple of workmen hefting a large canvas on their shoulders. 'But Lord Fitzroy is very insistent that he wants to keep the exhibition top secret till the public are allowed in. He's even banned the press.'

The girls weaved past the gathered people clothed in their very best. Small boys perched in nearby trees just to get a peek inside. Cos was swept along with the rest of the group. Aggie marched purposefully towards a building surrounded by horse-drawn carriages and people toing and froing. Trees lined the street, preventing the crowds from seeing within the exhibition's great glass walls. The girls followed, mouths agape.

Cos noticed that the Treasure Palace seemed to be divided into three sections: a huge central foyer and two curved wings shaped like spirals. Through the glass walls of the building, Cos could also see it was filled with greenery – lush elm trees even poked out of the very top of the roof. Huge metal beams formed the skeleton of the building and a band of silver ran round the base of the Empire Exhibition.

'The trees were here before the exhibition, and instead of chopping them down they incorporated them into the building,' Aggie explained.

Between the trees stood a bronze statue of Britannia that stretched towards the ceiling. Cos knew it was a statue of Britannia because Miss Stain talked about it all the time as the perfect symbol of British might, much to Diya's displeasure. Britannia was an armoured woman standing tall with a fearsome trident in her grasp. The bronze version of the woman was four times the height of a normal adult, her trident stretching to the great glass roof above.

There wasn't a door at the entrance to the exhibition, just a huge intricately decorated gate. It was two-tiered, supported by eight gold pillars and stretched wide across the threshold. A copper dome sat atop the second tier, and, as they neared, Cos saw that each of the pillars was carved with floral decorations. An inscription on the front of the gate read *Where there is virtue, there is victory.*

Cos heard Diya let out a gasp. Her friend wheeled towards the nearest pillar, running her hands over the carved decorations. 'Is this from India?'

'Yes, Diya!' Aggie replied. 'This is the Jaipur Gate, handcrafted by skilled craftsmen and shipped here to be the entrance to Lord Fitzroy's Exhibition.'

Cos gaped whilst Aggie showed a smartly dressed man an official-looking piece of paper, and with a nod he unlocked and opened the gates and Cos and the rest of the girls slipped into the bustling building. Behind them came a chorus of disgruntled moaning from the crowd.

'This Treasure Palace was actually modelled on the famous Crystal Palace from the Great Exhibition of 1851,' Aggie said, as she swept further into the building. 'And, just like its predecessor, the entire building is completely temporary. It was constructed this past month and when the exhibition finishes next year, it will be pulled down.'

Wonder took over Cos's brain as she stared up at the

impossibly big structure, its light reflecting off the snowflakes falling outside. She twirled slowly round, leaning on her walking stick for support, and drifted away from the others.

At opposite sides of the entrance Cos glimpsed the two wings of the Empire Exhibition. To her right, under a huge banner reading *Marvels of Culture*, she could see the first of many galleries – *The Gallery of Inventions*. Diya squealed as a complex contraption with spinning cogs was wheeled past them.

'The exhibition is split into two halves,' Aggie said. 'There's the Marvels of Culture, which displays wonders of innovation and creativity in the Gallery of Inventions, the Light Stadium and the Jewels Gallery.' Then she pointed to Cos's left, to the wing titled *Empire Pavilions*. 'And the Empire Pavilions shows items from the colonies of the British Empire.'

Diya let out an annoyed sigh. Cos saw Mary give her a supportive squeeze.

'At the very end of the pavilions is the Demonstration Hall,' Aggie continued, 'a theatre-like room where Lord Fitzroy will show the very latest scientific and technological innovations.'

All around them precious items from far-off countries were being carefully carried in and transported to the many pavilions that Cos caught a distance glimpse of. Large canvas tents fluttered in the cavernous space, each one fronted with a stall filled to the brim with objects and artworks transported from distant countries. Cos gasped as her eyes drank in the wonders of India — purple-velvet thrones and carpets of a thousand colours. Canada had sent elaborately painted sleighs and snowshoes; Australia had sent possum skins; the Gold Coast an elephant's tusk. Gloved men swept back and forth, busy unpacking crates, polishing frames and hoisting artefacts in readiness for the grand opening. The sound of hammering echoed through the hall as the final touches were being made, and in the distance clanging whirrs told Cos that brand-new inventions were being tested.

Guilt racked through Cos, as she remembered why they were here. Not to look at pretty or interesting things, but to try to understand what Lord Fitzroy wanted with them. Cos gripped her walking stick tightly, steadying herself.

She turned back to her friends and frowned at what she saw.

Aggie was crouched down on the ground, her voluminous skirts poufing out all around her. She was whispering to the girls, and every single one of them appeared to be listening carefully. Cos limped closer, hoping to catch what Aggie was saying. Instead, as she neared, Aggie stood up, smoothed out her skirt, and raised her hands.

'Welcome —' Aggie's voice shook with excitement, her words echoing round the cathedral-like space — 'to the Empire Exhibition!'

But before Cos could even begin to take it all in, Mary let out an unearthly scream.

CHAPTER EIGHT

Cos immediately knew the reason for Mary's terror – her friend had spotted someone terrifying before everyone else.

Footsteps thundered into the hall. Moustache first, Lord Fitzroy hurtled towards them, bushy eyebrows knitted in anger, and a silver key swinging from a chain on his belt. Cos felt the blood drain from her body to be replaced by an icy dread. She stepped towards Mary, giving her friend's hand a squeeze as her scream fizzled out.

'*Now, girls,*' Aggie hissed out of the side of her mouth.

In an instant the girls scattered. They headed in every conceivable direction. One girl in a wheelchair spun back towards the entrance, bumping into a man hefting a carefully wrapped package. Knocked off balance, the man dropped what he was holding and Cos heard the sound of breaking china. Dolly and some of the speedier home residents sprinted towards the statue and began to clamber up it. Other girls made their way beyond the Britannia statue, towards the Marvels of Culture and the Empire Pavilions.

Only Cos, Mary, Pearl and Diya remained, standing beside Aggie as Lord Fitzroy stomped towards them. They linked arms with each other, a wall of unfortunate girls. Cos could feel Pearl's hands flap this way and that.

Fitzroy had emerged from a small door at the far side of the foyer. Cos squinted at it – could the reason why he wanted them be somewhere in there, in a Fitzroy-only annexe of the Empire Exhibition? As Fitzroy and his furiousness stormed ever closer, she felt rooted to the floor.

'What's happening?' she whispered.

Pearl shrugged, her fingers flicking. 'Aggie told us to cause chaos – that we could do whatever we wanted – make as much mess as possible, touch anything and everything, even break stuff.'

'She said cause chaos?' Diya was frowning slightly. 'I would've thought that an engineer like her would want to protect her new cylinder engine at all costs.'

In the distance Dolly whooped as she straddled Britannia's left arm.

'Who are you?' Fitzroy demanded. 'And what on earth is

this gaggle of girls doing in my exhibition?' He frowned as Dolly waved one-handedly at Aggie from her perch on the statue. 'Are they –' Fitzroy's face paled like off milk – '*defective?*' He turned back to Aggie. 'Who. Are. You?'

'Miss Agatha Noone, Your Lordship,' Aggie said, dipping into a shallow curtsy and retrieving her notebook from her bag. She flicked it open, her pen poised above the paper. 'I'm an engineer and exhibitor. My machine, the cylinder engine, is in the Gallery of Inventions.'

'Fitzroy frowned, drumming his fingers. Hmm. I'm sure I would've remembered—'

Aggie cut him off. 'Do you know these girls, sir?'

Lord Fitzroy twitched at the question, his gaze running coldly over the girls and coming to a halt at Cos. He looked at her for a moment too long. He scoffed. 'Of course not. I don't associate myself with such degenerates. Besides, these children will get nothing out of the Exhibits. They don't have the capacity to learn . . .'

Lord Fitzroy began to talk nonsense, and, just like with the Stains, Cos didn't listen. She was confused. Why had Aggie told the girls to cause chaos? It made no sense! But, on the other hand, Aggie's idea had given them an opportunity to search the building for reasons why Lord Fitzroy wanted to adopt them.

Cos gave her friends a nudge. 'Let's split up and search,' she whispered. 'Pearl and Mary, you two start with the Marvels of

Culture. Me and Diya will search the Empire Pavilions.'

Pearl and Mary nodded and darted off.

Cos and Diya headed for the pavilions. This wing of the Empire Exhibition was a spiral-shaped corridor; it curled round and round and was dotted with smaller stalls dedicated to each of the countries that formed the British Empire. The first one they came across was for the Gold Coast.

Draped in brightly coloured fabric, the Gold Coast stall was a riot of sights and smells. Cos couldn't help but admire the beautiful paintings on display that depicted women balancing huge baskets of ripe fruit on their heads. Small delicately carved wooden statues were on the stall and a huge vat sat beside them. A couple of the girls from the home stood nearby, slurping from mugs.

'It's a drink called brukina,' said one, grinning at Cos and Diya as she licked her lips. 'It's delicious.'

Diya chivvied Cos along, and they passed many more pavilions – Australia, British Malaysia and Fiji to name a few. They peered behind curtains and searched the shadowed crevices of the building, but there was no inkling of why Lord Fitzroy wanted them.

Diya scowled and glowered at each pavilion as they passed, and Cos could understand why. Each of the stalls were beautiful – showcasing artwork, food and drink, and clothes from the respective countries – but they were displayed as if they were curiosities to be peered at by the public, possessions of the empire.

Diya seethed as they finally came to the Indian pavilion, her hands pressed tightly into fists. She wheeled closer, distracted from their hunt for clues. 'This isn't India,' she hissed, as she nodded at jewel-toned shawls that hung from the side of the sparsely decorated stall. 'This is just a watered-down British friendly version of India.'

Cos spluttered. She couldn't find the right words – maybe there weren't any – to explain to her friend just how sorry she was. The girls of the home all had it hard, but Diya was looked down upon doubly – because she was doubly different. It wasn't right, and it wasn't fair, but unfortunately it was the reality.

Diya tore her eyes away from the stall and pushed off, wheeling away as fast as she could. Cos struggled to keep up with her, and as she rounded the final spiral the pain pulsed through her knee. She bit back a scream, then gently swung her leg back and forth to check it was still in joint. When she decided that it was, she stepped forward, only to spot Diya frowning suspiciously at a set of double doors. She tugged on the handle. 'It's locked.'

The plaque above the door read *Demonstration Hall*.

Cos tried peering through the keyhole, but all she could see were a lot of chairs, all facing a raised stage with velvet curtains that met in the middle.

Finally Diya sighed. 'It just looks like some sort of theatre. Let's go and see if Pearl and Mary have found anything.'

They met the other two under the greenery of one of the indoor elm trees in the central atrium of the palace. Pearl and Mary didn't need to say a word, their glum faces told Cos they hadn't found anything to explain what Lord Fitzroy might want with them either. The group fell into an uneasy silence. Cos noticed that Mary's lips were tightly pursed, as if she were thinking over an idea.

'I bet he's written down whatever he's planning and is keeping it in a staff-only area,' Mary finally burst out. 'Somewhere private, where the public can't get to.'

'And where exactly is the "staff-only" area?' Diya's inquisitive eyebrow was back.

'Well,' Cos said, as she limped away from the elm tree. Her friends followed. 'Fitzroy came through *that* door.' She pointed at the unimposing door to the right of the Britannia statue. 'So I bet his office is back there.'

The group weaved past hurrying workmen, making their way across the central plaza to the door. Cos stretched out her fingers, knuckles cracking painfully, before grasping the door handle. She gritted her teeth as she leaned into the door, but it was stuck fast. Sighing, Cos dug around in her pinny pocket to retrieve her home-made lockpick – a rusty nail.

Diya nudged her, holding out a curved wire. 'Try this instead. I started working on it after the cake heist. I call it the Pilferer Powertool.'

Cos took Diya's latest invention and shoved it into the keyhole. With a twist and a click the door swung open. Diya shot Cos a triumphant look.

Without a backward glance they slipped inside, and they found themselves in a shadow-filled corridor that seemed to stretch endlessly in both directions.

Diya harrumphed. 'I knew I should've brought my Luminous Lantern.'

Cos stepped into the darkness and something crunched loudly under her heel, sending warning prickles into the sole of her shoe. She froze. 'What was *that*?'

Pearl squeezed past Cos, crouching down to pick up a razor-sharp fragment. 'Broken glass,' she said. 'Hold on to Mary's shoulder, I can get the pieces out.'

Cos's eyes adjusted to the darkness, and she could just about see the shattered glass, scattered across the corridor.

Ignoring the shooting pain, she leaned on to Mary and gingerly lifted her foot, as Pearl began carefully pulling shards of glass out of the bottom of her shoe.

'Why would someone leave a drinking glass in the middle of a corridor?' Cos thought out loud.

Behind her, Diya gasped. 'Pearl, can you pass me that sliver?' Diya pointed at a shard that looked identical to the hundreds of other splinters scattered across the floor.

Pearl plucked up the fragment and handed it to Diya, who squinted at it closely.

Diya clicked her tongue, and Cos knew she was mulling an idea over. This isn't a normal glass – see how the lip curls?' she said, after a final examination of the glass. 'I think it's a test tube.'

Cos frowned. 'A what?'

Diya folded her arms. 'A test tube is a thin glass tube used in science experiments.'

Cos's frown remained.

Diya huffed. 'Pearl?'

In a matter of moments Pearl whipped out a paintbrush and a gloopy paint pot. In a freckle-dotted space of skin, she sketched a finger-shaped glass.

'Ohh.' Realisation dawned over Cos – she *had* seen test tubes before, in the pages of the dog-eared science books in the schoolroom.

'But it's very strange. Why would something used in experiments be lying abandoned in a corridor?' Pearl furrowed her brows as she pocketed her brush and paint and stood up.

Cos shrugged, glad that both her feet were now firmly planted on the floor. 'Could it belong to an exhibitor? Aggie mentioned that lots of inventions were being shown at the exhibition. Maybe it's from one of those?'

Pearl 'hmmed', and Cos knew her friend wasn't convinced.

'Well,' Diya continued, 'a broken test tube won't help us work out why Fitzroy wants us. Me and Pearl will go this way, you and Mary go the other. Be careful.' With that Diya spun herself away. Pearl waved goodbye and also disappeared.

Cos turned and stepped judderingly into the darkness of the corridor. Mary reached out and held her hand, steadying Cos's courage. The corridor seemed even more ominous now there were only two of them, the shadows stretching eerily and every sound edged with danger. They picked their way slowly down the hallway, trying every door they came across – all were locked. Uneasiness settled in Cos's stomach as the possibility of finding anything about Fitzroy's plans faded away.

Mary shook with nerves, her breath puffing in and out. 'I think I'm going to have to go back,' she squeaked.

'Do you need me to come?' Cos asked quickly.

Mary shook her head, disappearing back the way they'd come. Cos tried to push away her fears as she stumbled further down the darkened corridor. She hoped that, at the opposite end, Diya and Pearl were having more luck. Just as she was about to give up and turn back, Cos's eyes picked out something moving ahead of her. There was the creak of a door and a small figure slipped into the corridor.

Cos narrowed her eyes. The figure was small, a child's size, but in the shadows of the corridor Cos couldn't make out much more.

'Hello?' Cos called.

The figure darted away and something glinting clanged to the floor. Cos frowned, heart thumping. She moved as fast as her sore joints would allow her, stooping to pick up whatever had dropped on to the floor.

She stared at the item in her palm. It was a golden pocket watch. Cos ran her fingers over its shining surface and opened the clasps. Inside, a handsome clock face stared back at her. Opposite the clock, a phrase was engraved in swirling handwriting: *To Franny, love Mina.* Underneath that, braided into a plait and behind a glass pane, was a lock of copper hair and a small star clip that shone even in the gloom of the corridor.

Want gripped Cos's heart. She'd never had anything so shiny or special before. The girl who had owned the clip had to have led a charmed life. Cos ran her fingers over the clip, and it fell away from the hair, clinking to the floor. Cos retrieved it. She tried fixing it back on to the plait, but Miss Stain had taught her nothing about hair – as Cos's own tangled mane confirmed – and the star clip simply fell away. Cos suddenly felt as though she had intruded upon (and broken) something very private. The pocket watch was obviously a treasured keepsake, perhaps of a sweetheart or best friend.

She closed it sharpish and tucked it into her pocket, telling herself that she'd fix it properly later. Cos set her jaw, rolled the clicks out of her shoulders, and, gripping tightly on to her walking stick, followed in the direction that the figure had disappeared.

She picked her way through the long corridor before coming across a door that was ajar. She slipped through it and found herself on the exhibition floor again, at the mouth of the Marvels of Culture wing. She spotted a flutter of movement as the figure ran round the bend that curled into the inner section of the spiral wing.

Cos knew she should only be focused on following, but she couldn't quell the excitement that rose in her chest as she neared the Gallery of Inventions and all its whirring cogs and *brr*-ing machinery. *Diya would love this!* She passed it slowly and moved onwards to the Light Stadium. The huge gallery dazzled like stars – every inch was covered in flickering light bulbs, demonstrating the immense power of electricity. Past the see-through walls of the building, Cos could see the huge trees that lined the street and the bustle of crowds behind them. Onwards she went, curling past paintings and sculptures, until she came to the strange gallery at the very centre of the spiral.

The banner above it read *The Jewel Gallery*. Heavy velvet curtains were drawn across the space, blocking its contents from sight, but Cos saw the curtains twitch with movement.

Curiosity rushed through Cos. Ignoring a knee crunch, she stepped towards the Jewel Gallery and yanked the curtains apart. As she slipped inside, she smacked into someone and fell flat on her back. The watch she'd picked up tumbled from her pocket, skating across the polished floor.

She froze, as she always did when she had a fall. She mentally checked her body to make sure everything was in joint. When she decided she was all right, she rocketed up to sitting. 'What do you think you're doing?' she whispered.

The boy stuck out his hand to help her up, and Cos got her first good look at him. He was around her age, dressed in holey trousers and a tatty coat. He leaned forward and his coat billowed, revealing sparkling watches, bracelets and other fine items attached to fabric hooks.

'A thief.'

CHAPTER NINE

'I'm not a thief,' protested the boy, pulling his wool coat closed. He had brown skin, curly hair and piercing eyes. 'I'm a magician.'

In the heavy gloom of the Jewel Gallery, the maybe-magician took out a matchbox and struck a match, handing it to Cos. Her attention was momentarily snatched by the flickering flame.

The boy plucked an impossible flower from behind Cos's ear, which he handed to her. Cos blinked as she took it, trying hard to hide the marvel she felt. 'Well, what's with all the jewellery then?'

The boy's face fell, as he withdrew a deck of worn playing cards from his coat and began to shuffle them as he spoke. 'I've fallen on hard times, that's all. But I'm an ethical thief,

I only take from those with too much.'

Cos frowned. *Ethical thieving?* But before she could question him, the heavy velvet curtains of the Jewel Gallery flapped open and a skulking man stepped inside.

The boy ducked down behind a glass cabinet, and Cos found herself copying him, blowing out her match and dropping it and the flower on the floor. She bent and a crack ripped from her kneecap, echoing round the space. Cos grabbed her knee, relief spreading through her when she found her joint was still in place.

'Hmm,' said a gruff voice. Claws scratched against the floor, something whined.

'A guard,' hissed the boy. 'And his dog.'

A chill took hold in Cos's gut. She carried out some fast Mary-esque possibilities in her brain and decided on an escape plan. 'We can hide ourselves till he's gone,' she whispered barely audibly.

The boy tutted and rolled his eyes, taking in her wonky stance and makeshift walking stick. The hackles on Cos's back rose with indignation. She sucked in a furious breath. She was tired of everyone underestimating her or disregarding her entirely because of her disability. *I'll show you.*

She grabbed the boy's hand. Still crouched, she pulled him towards the very back of the Jewel Gallery. Careful to keep her walking stick lifted so it didn't make a sound, Cos led the way through the labyrinth of display cases.

On the opposite side of the gallery the measured steps of the security man mirrored Cos's tiptoeing. His canine companion sniffed as it followed its master. Even though Cos's eyes watered with pain, and her brain buzzed with the effort of walking without her trusty stick, she kept going.

Finally they reached the very back of the gallery. In the gloom Cos found the meeting of the curtains. She lifted the material up, and together she and the boy squeezed themselves in and listened – she could hear the rapid *thud-thud-thud* of her heart as the man and his dog inspected the gallery.

The sound of footsteps crept closer, and Cos put her finger to her mouth as the security guard came perilously near to their hiding place. For a moment all she could hear was his footsteps and her heart thumping wildly, and then they faded away.

Cos peeked out of the curtains just as the guard leaned down to pick something up.

The guard straightened and Cos saw that he was holding the glinting pocket watch tightly. With a grin the man turned on his heels and stomped out of the gallery. All of a sudden the star clip weighed heavy in her pinny pocket.

'He's gone,' Cos said softly.

Together they slipped out of their hiding place. Cos nodded towards the empty space where the pocket watch had fallen, raising her eyebrows. 'Ethical thieving?'

The boy shrugged. 'That toff isn't gonna miss a trinket –
look at all this.' He gestured towards the huge iron-barred cage
in front of them. Within the cage sat a glass cabinet and below
it was a safe. 'I grabbed it when he stormed out to shout at
that lady, picked the lock on the entrance to the staff area, and
would've got out of here with it if you hadn't disturbed me.'

Cos ignored his complaints, pressing her face up against
the bars. The view seemed familiar somehow. With a start she
thought of the embroidered hankie round her neck. Without
thinking she took it off and unfurled it to look at the map.

'Wow,' said the boy, as he peered over her shoulder. His
eyes widened as he took it all in.

'I knew it!' Cos exclaimed.

Next to her the boy frowned.

'This map was probably embroidered on to the hankie and
left for me by my parents,' Cos explained. 'It's the only way I'll
find them. And this –' Cos pointed to the tiny stitched bars
with the sunrise behind it – 'I think, might be a symbol for a
prison. If I can work out *which* prison it stands for, that might
help me figure out *where* X is in real life.'

The boy scowled as he snatched the handkerchief from
her, and she bit her tongue to stop herself from shouting 'Be
careful!' at him.

He peered so closely at the handkerchief that his grubby
nose almost touched it. 'I think you're right,' he said finally,

chucking the hankie in Cos's direction as if it were rubbish. 'They're prison bars.'

'How do you know?'

The boy glared at her but pink blotches coloured his cheeks. '*That*,' he said darkly, pointing at the embroidered bars, 'is a very specific view. One you don't forget. Her Majesty's Prison Wormwood Scrubs. It's not too far from here – Shepherd's Bush way.' He shook off a shiver.

Icy realisation crashed over Cos. The symbol *did* represent a prison. One, it seemed, the ethical thief had been in. An 'Oh' escaped her mouth.

The boy tutted. 'They lock people up for anything,' he muttered indignantly. 'It's hard not to be a criminal when you're so poor you can't afford to eat.'

Embarrassment curled up in the pit of Cos's stomach. She of all people knew just how unfair the world was to those who the people in charge thought less of. She met the boy's glare. 'I'm sorry. You're right. I've been locked up since I can remember because I'm different. I just don't understand how the bars relate to my parents . . .'

'That plant is a wormwood. Every morning, as the sun rose, you'd see the spiky leaves shadowed against the sky.' The boy's words were little more than a whisper. 'The view of the wormwood and the sunrise, you would only know . . .'

'If you were an inmate!' Cos breathed. She faltered. *Does that mean one of my parents was a crook?* She shook the thought away. They were probably wrongly imprisoned, just like her at the home or the ethical thief. Or perhaps they were outlaws, locked away for their love. She retied the hankie round her neck, careful to hide the map. 'Thank you.'

She turned away, refocusing on the glass cabinet in front of her. Sitting resplendently on a ruby-coloured cushion within it was a glittering tiara. In the very centre of the crown was a diamond that sparkled and glowed in the soft light. Surrounding the tiara, on ruby cushions of their own, were several other jewels: one was the colour of blood, another shifted from green to pink to purple, yet another was a green the same colour as the strange boy's eyes, and the final one was the brightest blue. A seed of an idea bloomed in her thoughts, but Cos pushed it away. It was silly, *impossible* even. They'd never be able to pull something like that off.

'They're priceless. That's what rich people call things that are *really* expensive,' said the boy, as if reading her mind. 'But you'd have to be crazy to try to nick them – they're unstealable.'

Her gaze drifted back to the sparkling jewels encased in glass behind the iron bars. 'Why are they unstealable?' she asked, nodding towards the cage.

'Ah,' the boy said, tapping his nose, 'see that?' He pointed to the keyhole on one side of the iron cage. 'It's an unpickable lock. You *have* to use the master key. And if that toff has got even half a brain, he'll keep it somewhere safe.'

Cos raised an eyebrow. She moved closer to the jewels, catching her companion's reflection in the glass.

'Even if you get past the iron bars, then you have the problem of the glass cabinet.'

Cos frowned. 'Huh?'

The boy's words tumbled out of him so fast Cos could

126

barely make them out. 'It's an open secret amongst the London underworld – designed especially for this Exhibition. The latest in anti-theft technology. If the glass is smashed, the jewels fall into the safe below. And obviously that's uncrackable.'

Cos considered the difficulties. Maybe an ordinary person would be put off by an unpickable lock, untouchable glass and an uncrackable safe, but Cos didn't think it was *impossible*. As she thought, the boy opened and closed his mouth, as if he were considering something.

Cos swallowed a snigger and turned to face him. 'Spit it out.'

He huffed loudly, as if what he was about to say was very hard indeed. 'Sorry about tutting at you before. And rolling my eyes. It was wrong to judge you like that before I'd even said a word to you. I know what that's like. Feeling like an outsider.'

Something warm crept into Cos's chest, just as a sudden surge of confidence swept over her. She and her friends were capable of anything – they were smart, inventive and never gave up – and, most of all, they were constantly underestimated by almost everyone around them.

The boy grinned at her and stuck his hand out. 'I'm Miles, by the way.'

'Cos,' she replied, shaking his hand. *Miles*, she thought, *suits him*. She stared at the shine of the golden tiara, as she turned the idea over in her mind. 'Miles, what if I told you that I know a way we can make both our lives a lot better?'

Miles's disbelieving expression was so like Diya's, Cos bit back a giggle. 'How—'

Lord Fitzroy barged into the gallery, his black eyes glinting with rage. Instinctively Miles slipped behind the heavy curtains. Cos crouched behind the jewel cabinet, hoping she wouldn't be discovered. Her eyes began to water, as the strain of sneaking around and standing began to weigh heavily.

'Where did you find it, Mr Bashum?' bellowed Lord Fitzroy, his eyes wild. He clutched the pocket watch in one fist, and in the other he gripped the silver key hanging from his belt. So the pocket watch was Fitzroy's. A squeeze of guilt gripped her heart as she ran her fingers over the star clip – she was as much a thief as Miles, even if it had been accidental.

The security guard from before shrugged, his hand wrapped tightly round the leash of the dog, who was snarling at the fuss Fitzroy was making.

'But you don't understand,' spluttered Fitzroy, as he peered under cabinets and heaved up the bottom of the curtains. He brandished the pocket watch at Mr Bashum. 'I have this on my person at all times; it never leaves me. There was something precious in it, something that's now gone. There must be a thief in the building.'

Cos swallowed as she glanced in the direction of the lump in the curtain. The pain of crouching was too much now. She stood upright, and the floor creaked traitorously. Fitzroy's eyes snapped to her. Mr Bashum's dog strained against its leash, barking and growling loudly at Cos. Fear slammed into her, and for one tiny millisecond Cos wanted to go home.

Lord Fitzroy's gaze rested coldly on her walking stick and his lips puckered to a sneer. 'You!' he spat, as if she were his deadly enemy. Amidst the terror, Cos wondered why he hated her so much. She'd only met him twice, barely said a few words to him, and yet his spiteful gaze always seemed to single her out. Cos knew what was coming next. Lord Fitzroy was going to steal her away right this instant. And nobody was going to stop him.

Bashum moved swiftly towards her; Cos felt herself shrink as he approached and placed a meaty hand on her shoulder.

'It won't be her,' Fitzroy hissed, his gaze shifting back to his pocket watch. He ran a finger over it gently, and Cos wondered if she'd imagined his attention. 'She's one of the unfortunates. Probably hasn't even got the wherewithal to steal.'

His words felt like a gut punch, and Cos could feel her cheeks heat with colour. Mutinous thoughts crept into her head.

'Cosima!' Aggie slipped into the Jewel Gallery. Relief pulsed through Cos at the sight of a friendly face. 'There you are.'

Girls appeared from behind Aggie's voluminous skirt, stepping into the Jewel Gallery with their mouths wide open and eyes full of wonder.

Aggie held up the corner of the curtain so that the girls in wheelchairs could get in. The last girls to shuffle into the gallery were Mary, Pearl and Diya. Cos raised her eyebrow in a silent question. All three shook their heads, and Cos sighed.

Fitzroy turned his rage on Aggie. 'Get control of your charges, Miss, Miss . . .'

'Noone,' Aggie added helpfully.

'Prepare your invention, then leave,' he spat, 'and take these degenerates with you.' With that Fitzroy turned on his coat-tails and stormed off, followed swiftly by Mr Bashum.

'What a pair of charming gentlemen,' Aggie said with a shrug when he'd gone, and Cos swallowed away a smile.

An excited 'Ooh' stole Cos's attention.

'What's this?' Dolly's face was pressed up against the iron cage.

'Ah, I can tell you all about the jewels,' Aggie said. 'As an exhibitor I've read up on Lord Fitzroy's . . . *achievements*. This one is the world-famous Rainbow Opal. It was found by Lord Fitzroy in Australia. As you can see, its name comes from the many colours it reflects. Isn't it beautiful?' She pointed towards a glittering green gem. Pearl silently sketched its every curve on to her arm. 'And this is the Thunder Emerald. Named because Lord Fitzroy came across it during a thunderstorm in Mashonaland.'

'Miss Noone?' whined Dolly. She was enamoured with a

sea-coloured jewel next to the Thunder Emerald. 'What's this one called?'

'Ah!' Aggie exclaimed. 'That, Dolly, is my personal favourite. It's called the Ocean Sapphire.'

'Because it looks like the sea?'

'Exactly, Dolly. It reminded Lord Fitzroy of stormy waves when he discovered this sparkler in the Cape of Good Hope. But by the time he'd transported it to England, the blue was calmer, like the clear blue of the sea on a hot summer's day. It changes every so often.'

'I like this one best.' Diya's fists were clenched round the bars of the iron cage. 'The one in the tiara. It's called the Star Diamond. It was taken from India. That's where my father's from.'

'Diya is right. That is the Star Diamond from India,' Aggie said. 'Lord Fitzroy had it placed as the centrepiece of the tiara.' Cos and Pearl shuffled closer to Aggie, and Pearl began sketching the tiara on her forearm. The gathered girls oohed as they stared at the glistening crown.

'And finally the Midnight Ruby.' Aggie pointed to the deep red jewel nearest to the tiara. 'Found in Egypt.'

The sixteen girls were transfixed for a moment, but soon their focus was pulled by the other Exhibition wonders.

'Race you lot to the dinosaur bones,' Dolly said, a mischievous glint in her eye. She led the stampede from the

Jewel Gallery as girls ran, limped and wheeled after her. Only Cos, Diya, Pearl, Mary and Aggie remained.

A dusty silence descended.

'So does your engine run on internal combustion?' Diya asked Aggie. 'Can we get to see it?'

Aggie's expression was fixed. She coughed and began to rummage in her bag. Cos realised with a start that she was scrambling for an answer.

'Sometimes,' she said finally, in a strangled voice. 'Excuse me for a moment, girls.'

Diya frowned at the empty space where Aggie had stood. 'You can't have an engine that only works on internal combustion *sometimes*. That's scientifically impossible!'

Cos nodded. 'I agree. I don't entirely trust her.'

'Whilst that may be, Cos,' Mary said softly, 'Aggie isn't who we should be focusing on now. Nothing here has given us any clue about why Lord Fitzroy wants us, or how to stop him.'

'Don't worry, I've got an idea!' Cos said.

Diya groaned and Mary looked nauseous.

'Cos, are you *sure* your idea is good?' Pearl asked. 'Most of the time they're pretty hare-brained.'

Cos tried to brush off her friends' criticisms. She turned back to the curtain, but the Miles-shaped lump had gone. Cos sighed, digging her spare hand in her pocket. Her fingers came across something. She pulled it out. It was one of the playing cards Miles had been shuffling earlier. She turned it over, in shaky almost illegible handwriting on the back was one word:

MIDNIGHT.

CHAPTER TEN

M iss Stain welcomed the girls with a smile almost as frigid as the air in the foyer. A scowling Mr Stain stood by her shoulder, not bothering to help the kids pull off their coats and scarves.

As soon as Aggie was gone, Miss Stain's overstretched smile contorted into fury. She turned towards the girls and hissed, 'All of you into your dormitory! You will catch up on all the work you missed today whilst you were out. I want the same amount of rope picked that you would usually do. There will be no sleep until you have done so.'

Girls who had spent the day peering up in wonder at display cabinets and racing round the exhibition galleries drooped, eyes now firmly planted on the floor. Cos swallowed away a groan as she tramped up the rickety stairs with the others.

Walking aids thudded and wheelchairs squeaked as they made their way to a night of work.

Mr Stain unlocked the dormitory door and the girls filed in and slumped on to their threadbare beds. With a grimace he lobbed in a huge pile of unpicked rope, lit a few measly candles so the girls could just about see, and then stomped out, slamming and locking the door.

Diya nudged Cos and together they shuffled towards four beds, huddling together round a solitary candle that was perched on Pearl's bedside table. Like the other girls, the foursome settled down to their evening of work.

A few hours of yawns and sore fingers later, all the other girls had fallen asleep, heads lolling against their pillows. Cos blew out a sad breath as she checked that they were all sleeping, each of them clutching their picked-apart rope as if it were a dolly. The last time Mr Stain had peered through the hatch in the door he'd hiccupped loudly and almost fallen over. Cos was pretty sure he'd nicked a few drinks from his sister's tipple collection and would now be snoring loudly in his bed. Only the four unfortunates remained awake.

Cos tugged on the rope pulley, pulling down the blackboard. She rubbed out FOUR and replaced it with THREE *days till Lord Fitzroy picks us up!* Then, in the top left-hand corner, she wrote in small letters: *The Map Hankie.* Underneath that she

135

scribbled *Iron bars – HM Prison Wormwood Scrubs.*

Diya pulled a face. 'How did you figure that out?'

'I'll explain in a bit,' Cos promised. 'Wormwood Scrubs is in Shepherd's Bush. Mary, can we work out where the X is now?'

Mary tried and failed to cover up her cringe. 'Well, it's a good start, but we need to find the location of more of the symbols if I'm going to be able to pinpoint it.'

Cos's chest squeezed with disappointment. So she had four more symbols to figure out, and no idea what any of them meant. She turned away from her friends as she added the new information from Lord Fitzroy's pocket watch, writing *To Franny, love Mina* under the *Lord Fitzroy* heading.

'What's that from, Cos?' Pearl asked, eyebrows knitted.

'A pocket watch belonging to Lord Fitzroy,' she explained. 'I saw it at the exhibition. Inside it was a lock of red hair, the phrase and *this.*'

Cos pulled out the star clip from her pocket. It glinted in the flickering candlelight. The others oohed with awe. It really was very beautiful.

'You took that?' Mary huffed, a note of judgement in her voice.

'Only accidentally,' Cos explained. 'It fell out of the pocket watch, and before I could return it, Fitzroy had the pocket watch back.'

'Maybe it belonged to the Mina mentioned in the phrase?'

Diya suggested.

But as she stared at the dazzlingly stoned star, Cos couldn't help but feel that the tiny, beautiful-but-useless hair accessory was meant to be hers. After all, hadn't Aggie said that her name meant cosmos or universal? And stars were a crucial part of the cosmos. For a split-second Cos thought about pinning back her tangled fringe with the clip. It was just *so* pretty. But the second either of the Stains saw the stolen star clip, it would be snatched away and sold. Cos reverently hid the clip under her pillow.

'I wonder who Mina is?' said Pearl, just as Mary asked, 'And could Franny be a nickname for Lord *Francis* Fitzroy?'

Cos shrugged, the questions shaking her from her thoughts. 'I'm not sure.'

An uneasy silence settled over the dormitory for a moment or two.

'So,' Diya asked, 'what's your idea?'

Then, whispering softly over a chorus of snores and by the light of Diya's Luminous Lantern, Cos began to tell them her plan.

'We're going to steal Fitzroy's golden tiara from the Empire Exhibition. It's worth a lot of money, so if we sell it, that money could save us.'

The idea had been bubbling in her brain for hours now, but she still couldn't quite pick the right words as the others gasped. 'It'll be just like the cake heist!' she spluttered.

Diya frowned. 'The one that went horribly wrong and led to, A., us getting zero cakes and, B., Miss Stain forcing us to scrub all the china in the scullery?'

'No, not that bit.' Cos tripped over her words. 'This time it'll all come off.' She smiled reassuringly at the worried faces of her friends as she gingerly stood up and limped to her bed, where she retrieved the newspaper she'd stolen from the Stains the day before. 'If we're rich, that will shield us from Lord Fitzroy.'

Diya scowled. 'What? How?'

Cos blew out a breath to steady her courage, flicking to the article about the Empire Exhibition. 'Money is how Lord Fitzroy is so powerful. Money is why the Stains are giving us to Fitzroy. Whatever Lord Fitzroy wants with us, the only way we can stop it is if we have money. We use the money we make to buy off the Stains, stop Lord Fitzroy and employ a new, kinder matron.'

Mary looked as though she'd been slapped. 'We can't steal! Besides, stealing is wrong.' Mary's voice was hushed, as if she were afraid that Fitzroy could hear her all the way from the exhibition.

Cos sighed. 'But, Mar, think about it: even though we don't know why Lord Fitzroy wants twenty disabled girls, it doesn't take Diya levels of genius to figure out that it's probably for

138

something bad. If we steal the tiara, we can get enough money to stop the Stains and Lord Fitzroy! Really, it can't be *that* wrong if we manage to save twenty kids.'

Mary pursed her lips. 'Two wrongs don't make a right, Cos.' Her voice was barely more than a whisper.

'Lord Fitzroy has stolen almost every single thing in the exhibition, Mary,' Diya said softly, staring closely at the newspaper. 'From the jewels to the artwork, all the items have been taken away from countries Lord Fitzroy visited. Countries Britain has forced to be a part of the empire. Stealing the tiara is far less awful than all the things Fitzroy's nicked.'

Silence followed as the others digested Diya's words.

'And something's not quite right with Aggie as well.'

'But she's so nice!' Mary whined.

'She is,' Diya agreed, 'but it was very odd that she told all of us to run round the exhibition, an exhibition where she's displaying her work. It doesn't seem like something a responsible engineer would do.'

Cos tapped her chin. 'Exactly. And I think everything's connected – the tattoo on Lord Fitzroy's wrist, the lady engineer *and* the Empire Exhibition.

'And the broken test tube,' Pearl added. 'I think that's connected too.'

Cos brushed off Pearl's suggestion. 'The point is, stealing

the tiara is the only way we're going to get out of this mess.'

'Hmm,' said Mary, 'I'm not sure that quite follows.'

Cos turned to the blackboard, writing on it: *Aggie* and *the Empire Exhibition*. She drew an arrow between those words and the previous things she'd written about Fitzroy and his tattoo. She even wrote, in slightly smaller letters, *The Mystery of the Broken Test Tube* – much to Pearl's delight.

Pearl drew in a big breath, looking at her arms. They were inked with items she'd spotted at the exhibition, including the tiara. 'If we're stealing the tiara, I have an idea. I could make a replica tiara out of leftover rope and paint it gold. That way, no one will even know it's missing.'

'You're a genius, Pearl!' Cos exclaimed. 'Nobody will even be looking for a tiara; we'll be able to sell it to any old jeweller.'

'But . . . maybe . . . perhaps . . .' Diya seemed to be in a world of her own. 'The tiara is made of gold. If I can melt it down, we could turn it into bullion. I'm pretty sure Miss Stain dumped a mould in the corridor when their turning-metal-into-gold scheme failed.'

'Bull-a-what?' Cos said.

Diya let out a short sharp laugh. 'That's how money is kept in banks. They store it in gold bars called bullion. Even if Pearl's fakes fool Fitzroy, no jeweller is going to buy a golden tiara from a group of disabled kids. The only way stealing the treasure would even *half* be worth it is to turn it into money.'

'Perfect!' Cos said, the plan slotting together inside her head.

'Don't get ahead of yourself,' Diya warned. 'For that I'd have to construct some sort of smelter – which would be very difficult. And that's not all – I'd have to make more Luminous Lanterns if we're going to infiltrate the exhibition.'

'But if we can pull it off,' said Cos, excitement fizzing through her, 'then we'll be able to get rid of the Stains and stop whatever Fitzroy's planning for us.'

What she kept back from her friends was her secret hope that the money would also help *her* find her family. She turned back to the blackboard, chalking another heading on it: THE STAR DIAMOND HEIST.

She cleared her throat and wrote a to-do list as she spoke. 'So, Pearl, you're going to make a replica tiara, and Diya is going to build more mechanical instruments we might need. Mary –' she turned to her friend, who was fiddling frantically with her clipboard – 'I want you to find us a way into the building.'

'You want me to plan a way to sneak into a see-through building?' squeaked Mary. 'That's impossible, Cos! Even for me.'

Cos placed a hand on Mary's shoulder. 'It's not impossible, only highly improbable – and you always tell me about the importance of planning for every eventuality. I know you can do it, Mar.'

Diya sighed, clicking her tongue. 'I'm not sold on this heist idea. I think we should focus our efforts on finding out *why* Lord Fitzroy wants us and how we can get out of it. Maybe we can get a message to our families?'

Cos squirmed uncomfortably, touching the handkerchief that was still tied round her neck. She had no family to get a message to – *yet*. If she lost Diya, Mary and Pearl, she would be all on her own. 'No!'

A few of the sleeping girls stirred but didn't wake.

'Even if you're able to tell your families, they'll inform the authorities, and you know how useless the authorities are when it comes to the Stains.'

Cos thought back to the last time the authorities 'inspected' the home. Instead of talking to the girls and finding out what living there was really like, the inspectors drank a whole bottle of Miss Stain's Skullsplitter's Cure-All and stumbled out sick to their stomach. 'If we pull this off, we'll be rich, and nobody messes with rich people.' She stared round at her friends, hoping for their support.

Diya sighed. 'But, Cos, do you really think four disabled kids can do a job this big?'

Cos nodded decisively. 'Yes.'

Pearl fiddled with her coil of rope, her eyes not meeting Cos's.

Cos's heartbeat thundered in her eyes, as she struggled to find the words to address her friends' worries. She could normally persuade them that her plans were doable — that she had thought them through, that it would make their lives better and that the worst thing that would happen would be a punishment from Miss Stain. But this time she couldn't. If they failed, Lord Fitzroy would steal them away and Cos had a sneaking suspicion his plans for them would be even worse than living with the Stains.

Words died on Cos's lips. Her silver tongue had deserted her. The other girls' gentle snores and the thumping of her heart were the only things she could hear. Despair rose in her like bile, but before Cos mustered up the courage to admit defeat there was a *tap* at the window that splintered the quiet.

CHAPTER ELEVEN

Mary hopped up from her bed, frowning. Diya wrapped her fist round her favourite wrench on her tool belt, her face taut with fear. Pearl crooked an eyebrow. The clock affixed to the dormitory wall began to chime, striking for midnight. The sleeping girls snored on, used to the clock's hourly peals.

BING-BONG.

Cos pushed her chair back and picked her way as quietly as possible towards the window. The night was so cold a web of frost had already formed on the inside of the glass. She set aside her walking stick and pushed up the pane. Her breath blew out in clouds as she leaned over the windowsill.

BING-BONG.

A shadowy figure waved up at Cos from the pavement

below. *Miles.* Cos grinned. Confidence surged back into her. She turned to her friends; confusion was etched across their faces.

BING-BONG.

'Pearl, can you find me the longest, sturdiest and least unpicked bit of rope?'

Pearl nodded, and without question began searching the room.

Diya's eyebrows were so high they almost disappeared into her hairline. 'Cos, what's going on?'

Mary dashed across the wooden floor, rope in hand. She stuck her head out of the window, blonde hair haloing her face. She turned back to the others, her face a picture of shock. 'There's a *boy* outside!' she whispered.

Diya shot Cos a suspicious look. 'What have you done?'

Cos shrugged noncommittally. 'I'll explain everything, promise, as soon as we get him inside. Diya, do you have that winch-crane-hoist thingamabob?'

BING-BONG.

At the mention of one of her favourite inventions Diya went a little starry-eyed. She reversed her wheelchair towards her invention station, the empty cupboard she'd transformed into a storage area at the back of the dormitory.

BING-BONG.

'Mary, can you try to clear a channel without waking the others?'

Mary began pushing the beds of the sleeping girls to the side of the dormitory. A few stirred but all remained sleeping. Mary was careful not to let the beds squeak as she moved them.

BING-BONG.

Diya busied herself with heaving the winch out of her station. She wheeled herself to the wall opposite the open window and placed it on the floor.

BING-BONG.

Pearl wrapped a bulky coil of rope round her shoulders like a snake.

Diya rubbed an invisible mark off her invention. 'The Wondrous Winch is ready, Cos. But I still don't get why we need—'

'Does it work?' Cos said quickly.

'Well, er, yes,' Diya spluttered. 'I haven't tested it properly, but I think so.'

BING-BONG.

'Great! Pearly, can you wrap the rope round the barrel and tie a knot tight? Mary, great clearing. Can you drape the other end of Pearl's rope out of the window? And, Diya, get ready to pull.'

BING-BONG.

Cos and Mary carefully lowered the rope out of the window. 'Grab hold of the end – we'll pull you up!' she whispered, the cold air stinging her teeth.

Miles looked as though he might protest, but then he grabbed the end of the rope and started to hoist himself up the wall. The rope went taut.

BING-BONG.

Cos grabbed the section nearest her and pulled back, the rope burning her palms. The effort hit her like a gut punch. Miles's weight was so much more than she had imagined. 'Pull, girls, pull!' she hissed. The others joined in, yanking the rope upwards.

BING-BONG.

At the back of the room Diya began spinning the crank, shortening the rope and pulling Miles ever closer to the open window.

Diya cringed and puffed out, 'This'd better be worth it, Cos.'

BING-BONG.

As the final clock strike rang out, fingertips appeared on the windowsill and a ragged boy rolled into the room. Cos, Pearl and Mary smacked to the floor as the rope went slack. For a couple of moments all the girls froze. Cos listened intently for footsteps, but none sounded, and the girls who had stirred in their sleep snuggled back down.

Miles picked himself up, brushing off his threadbare clothes and shaking snowflakes from his hair. He looked

unsure of himself, then he affixed a bright smile to his face, twirled and smoke exploded from his feet. 'Ta-da!'

Cos cringed, but the other girls were obviously so exhausted that none of them woke.

Pearl covered her ears with her hands. She hated unexpected sounds.

'How'd you do that?' Mary asked, as the last of the smoke dissipated.

Miles tapped his nose. 'A magician's secret,' he said.

His gaze darted around the dormitory, taking in the sleeping girls and Diya's Wondrous Winch. The other girls stared open-mouthed at him. Boys were an anomaly at the Home for Unfortunate Girls; the girls weren't allowed to mix with them. None of them had so much as seen one since they'd been admitted to the home.

'Hi.' Miles lowered his voice to a whisper. 'I'm Miles.' He turned to Cos. 'So what's your plan then?'

The other girls shot Cos a look of shock.

Cos dusted her uniform off, and Pearl and Mary helped her off the floor. 'Hear me out, everyone. Miles is a magician. And a thief. He picks locks and does tricks. He's the one who worked out that the bars on my hankie referred to Wormwood Scrubs prison. He's the missing puzzle piece for the heist!'

'Huh?' Miles and the girls said at exactly the same time.

But before Cos could explain, footsteps thundered along the corridor outside the dormitory. The girls went rigid with fear.

'Quick – the cupboard,' Mary whispered. She and Pearl chivvied Miles towards Diya's invention station. 'Please don't make a sound.'

Diya turned off her Luminous Lantern and she and Cos moved as fast as possible towards their beds. Diya pushed herself out of her chair, as Cos carefully lowered herself to her threadbare mattress, pulling the blanket up to her neck and pretending to be asleep.

Mary shut the door softly on Miles's surprised face, then she and Pearl hurried to their beds, just as the dormitory door crashed open and the skulking figure of Mr Stain leered towards them, his shadow stretching eerily into the dormitory.

Cos peered through her eyelashes as Mr Stain scowled at the sleeping girls, his face illuminated by a flickering candle. She tried to still her shaking limbs.

'You lot'd better be asleep,' he hissed into the darkness. Cos thought she could catch the dizzying smell of liquor on his breath, even from a distance.

When nobody answered, Mr Stain hissed in anger and kicked his boot into the dormitory door. Yelling in pain and clutching his foot, the noise finally woke the other girls. They yawned and rubbed sleepy dust from their eyes.

'I *knew* you were awake,' Mr Stain said triumphantly, spittle flying from his mouth. 'No breakfast in the morning and you'll pick double the amount of rope tomorrow.'

The girls groaned as Mr Stain creaked the door shut and drunkenly lumbered away. Cos stayed still until she was sure the other girls had fallen back asleep, before she tiptoed across the floorboards and turned the Luminous Lantern back on.

Miles opened the cupboard door a crack and peered out. 'Is he gone?' he whispered. Cos nodded, and Miles slipped through the doorway. 'He's horrible,' he said with a shiver, as Diya, Pearl and Mary sat up in their beds. 'Now, can you please explain what's going on?'

'Yes, Cos, *explain*,' Diya said, folding her arms.

Four sets of eyes fixed on Cos. She steadied herself, then explained the plan.

Miles listened carefully, hand on chin, as silence stretched over the dorm. 'I don't think it's impossible,' he said. 'And we have a head start – Cos and I already know where the key to the jewel cage is.'

Cos frowned. 'Do we?'

Miles rolled his eyes, as if it were obvious. 'On Fitzroy's belt!'

An 'Oh' slipped from Cos's lips. She grinned, cheeks warm, before a snag wound its way into her head. 'So he keeps the key on him? At all times?' This might be more difficult that she had envisioned.

'Well, if you *can* steal the key from Lord Fitzroy –' Diya pushed her glasses back up her nose –'and we find a way to break into the building, I suppose Cos's plan isn't completely impossible. But I think we shouldn't just steal the tiara. I think we need to steal Fitzroy's other jewels as well.'

Cos frowned, completely confused. Only a few minutes ago, Diya seemed as though she was the least convinced about this plan. 'What? Why?'

Diya was so excited she was shaking. She nodded at Pearl, who rolled up her sleeves. Alongside the tiara on her left forearm the other jewels were inked across her arms. 'Because they're already stolen! They aren't Britain's. We should steal them back and send them to the people they were stolen from.' Diya's expression was resolute. She'd obviously thought this through.

Cos opened her mouth to protest. After all, stealing other jewels would make the heist that much more complicated and increase their work threefold. Poor Pearl would have to make replicas of all the jewels as well as the tiara. But the determination in her friend's eye silenced Cos.

'I have a few ideas about tools that will help,' Diya said, regaining a bit of her usual composure. 'Perhaps I can make portable Luminous Lanterns, one for each of us, that we could attach to our foreheads.'

Cos nodded. Enthusiasm surged through her again. This *was* actually happening.

'I have an idea about us getting into the building,' Mary squeaked. 'I've been working on a plan to get us to the library so we can find out about Lord Fitzroy's past. Well, the library *should* also have building plans. Maybe looking at those will help us break into the exhibition?'

'Smart!' Miles said softly.

'But what about the key?' Mary asked. 'How are you going to steal it from Lord Fitzroy without him noticing immediately?'

A wry smile appeared on Miles's face. 'That's why you need an expert at sleight of hand. We won't actually steal the key itself, just borrow it for a few minutes so I can make a wax replica.'

Cos let out a breath as the plan came together in her head. 'All right, so Mary's job is to find the blueprint and plan us a way in, Pearl will make replicas of the items we're going to steal so the theft isn't discovered, Diya's going to invent some tools to help us with the heist and build a smelter, and, Miles, you're going to make a mould of the key so we can break into the iron cage.' The others nodded. 'And I'll be on hand to help you, smooth over any difficulties and make sure nothing goes wrong.'

Miles failed to suppress a shiver as a gust of wind blew through the open window, bringing with it a scattering of snowflakes.

Cos took off her blanket and wrapped it round his shoulders as Mary and Pearl hurried to the windowsill and heaved it shut. 'Miles, you can stay with us. The Home for Unfortunate

Girls may be awful, but it's better than the streets.' She turned to Diya. 'Can he hide in your invention station?'

'Sure.' Diya's penetrating gaze fixed upon Cos. 'You're missing one crucial point of the heist, though.'

Cos frowned. 'And what's that?'

A smile flickered over Diya's face. 'Well, firstly, you have to convince the Stains and the other girls that absolutely nothing is up – when we're hiding a boy in the dormitory, sneaking out without permission and building a smelter good enough to melt solid gold.'

Cos swallowed. She hadn't quite thought of the enormity of it all. 'And,' she said, her voice scratchy and hollow as she glanced at the clock that was now well past midnight, 'we've only got two more days before Lord Fitzroy collects us.'

'Exactly,' Diya said gravely, as she wound up the blackboard.

CHAPTER TWELVE

Cos tried very hard not to yawn into the faces of all the girls the following morning. She was only partially successful.

The sky was as gloomy and smog-filled as Cos's mood. She'd spent a sleepless night tossing and turning. For their plan to work the girls needed all the help they could muster. They had to keep the Stains distracted – and for that the girls that weren't part of the heist plot had a very important role to play.

'Everyone, please concentrate. We need you to distract the Stains today.'

'But why?' asked one, brow furrowed.

'We can't explain now, but it's so important that they don't check on the dormitory. We need you to keep them downstairs until Mr Stain comes up with our lunchtime gruel.'

'I know what we can do!' shouted Dolly. Beside Cos, Mary

winced. The girls had purposefully got up earlier than usual so they could have their meeting without the Stains prying. Cos hoped that they hadn't heard Dolly's excited squeal. 'Why don't we let a rat loose in Miss Stain's office? You know how she hates rodents!'

'Or,' signed one of the other girls, *'we could hide Mr Stain's shoes when he has his afternoon nap? He'd be furious.'*

'What about if we steal some of that fancy syrup Miss Stain likes to drizzle on her breakfast and pour it all over the floors?' suggested another. 'They'd both be slipping and sliding all over the place.'

Cos grinned, goose pimples prickling up her forearm. These were the kind of shenanigans she loved, and they were just the sort of activities that would, A., make the Stains stinking mad and, B., keep both adults busy so that they didn't notice Mary and Cos were missing.

Cos nodded her encouragement, and the girls thought up ever more ambitious prank ideas, until the familiar *clack-clack-clack* of the Stains' footfalls filled the air. All the girls, in a flurry of panicked movement, rushed for their beds. Cos had only just pulled the threadbare cover over her head when the door slammed open.

'Up now!' Miss Stain screeched. 'You're to pick four pounds of rope today or there will be no dinner.' Her brother, skulking beside her, began counting the girls under his breath.

The girls stretched and yawned as Miss Stain roughly handed some their walking aids and helped others dress. Cos nodded at Diya, Mary and Pearl, and as they'd planned, they began uncontrollably coughing.

Miss Stain straightened, her eyebrow arched.

Cos spluttered into the crook of her elbow. 'Sorry, miss,' she said, as sincerely as she could muster. 'I think we've caught a chill.'

Mr Stain scowled at Cos, before ushering the non-coughing girls towards the dormitory door.

Cos stared at Miss Stain. She could almost hear the whirr of the cogs turning in the matron's head. Lord Fitzroy was expecting twenty disabled girls; if the Stains didn't deliver, he might pay them less money.

Miss Stain licked her lips as she thought. 'Hmm. Well, if that is the case, I don't want you lot infecting the others. You four will stay in here until you've recovered.'

A smile crept out of the side of Cos's mouth. She immediately regretted it.

Miss Stain spotted her happiness and a snarl appeared on her face. 'Don't you think this'll mean you get a day lolling about in bed,' she said sharply. She clicked her fingers, and her brother disappeared, returning a few minutes later with a coil of rope that he lobbed on to the floor. 'This'd better be picked by lunchtime.'

The smile fell from Cos's face. Miss Stain shot her a look of vicious triumph as she took hold of the door handle and shut the door. As Miss Stain's footsteps faded away, Miles opened the cupboard door and stepped into the dormitory.

'Well, that went well.' Diya's shoulders slumped as she stared at the coil of rope on the floor.

Cos rubbed the bridge of her nose, but pain was stuck fast in her body. 'We'll worry about the rope later. Let's focus on preparations. What have we all got to do today?'

Pearl grabbed a hunk of rope. 'I'll create the tiara and the jewels.'

'And I'll start inventing,' Diya said, twirling her spanner between her fingers.

'And me, Miles and Mary will go to the library, research Lord Fitzroy's past and find the blueprint for the Empire Exhibition.'

'Here are your disguises,' Pearl said, as she handed Cos a bundle of clothes made from old curtain scraps.

'Thanks, Pearly.' Cos turned to Miles and Mary. 'Are we all ready to do this?'

Miles nodded confidently, but Mary looked to be on the verge of tears as she clutched her satchel close. The trio pulled on Pearl's disguises, transforming them into respectable schoolchildren on a research trip.

'Remember,' warned Diya, as she fetched a brand-new

rope ladder from the cupboard, 'you all have to be back by lunchtime. Mr Stain is *very* fastidious with his roll call, and he'll count to make sure all of us are here. If you aren't back, the Stains will know we're planning something and there is no way we'll be able to pull off the heist.'

'I know,' replied Cos, as Miles lifted the window open, letting in the chill from outside. 'I promise we'll be back in time.' She glanced at the clock on the wall. It had just gone seven twenty. The Stains gave each of the girls a few spoonfuls of gruel at twelve sharp. That gave them just over four and a half hours to get back.

Diya and Pearl heaved the extendable ladder over to the window. Diya unwound the handle and the ladder edged downwards. Soon it snaked all the way to the ground. Miles went first, sliding down. Mary and Cos followed. Cos waved goodbye to her friends and followed Mary and Miles on to the London streets.

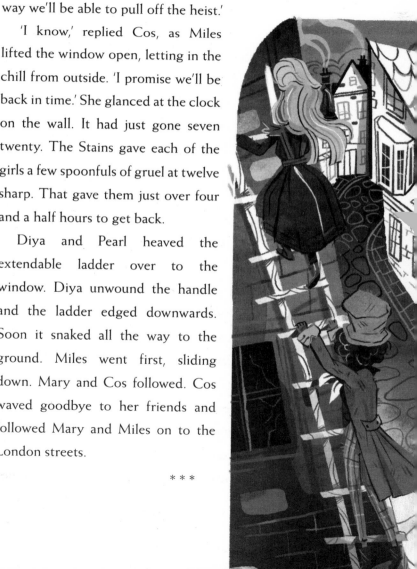

* * *

It took them far too long to get to the library. The wind whipped Cos's hair into even more of a tangle as they picked their way past shivering figures sitting huddled in doorways, and flat-capped men heaving their barrows of goods over the cobblestones. This time the sooty smell didn't bother Cos so much, but there was smog everywhere – it clung to each building, staining them rain-cloud grey. There was a constant rumble of noise in the city, a combination of chatter and shouts, the *brr* of the nearby factory chimneys and the thrum of traffic that thronged about the streets.

Mary had planned their route carefully, having worked out that the library was only a fifteen-minute walk from the home, but Cos's pain meant that the journey faltered forward in stops and starts, and Mary's panic threatened to bubble over as the streets they were on became busier. The accusatory stares from strangers made Cos's skin itch, and she struggled to steady her courage. Miss Stain couldn't be right; not everyone would hate her for who she was.

Cos saw Mary gulp down a steadying breath at a particularly busy intersection, crammed with omnibuses and horse-drawn carriages. She offered her friend a reassuring smile and leaned closer to her. 'Remember,' Cos whispered, 'libraries are famously quiet.'

That seemed to calm Mary down a little, and soon a red-brick facade reared up at the very end of the street they'd turned on to. Arched windows dominated the building, Union Jack flags blew in the blustery weather, and a gilded sign announcing *The Kensington Library* was above the smartly painted door.

Businessmen in top hats and tails tutted as Cos paused for what felt like the billionth time, screwing her eyes tightly shut in an effort to push away the agony.

'Can I do anything to help?' Miles's voice was hazy, as though he were very far away, but Cos knew he stood right next to her, helping her stay upright.

She shook her head as Mary heaved open the library door and they slipped inside.

The foyer of the library was a bustle of activity. Learned-looking men with twirled moustaches rushed this way and that, carrying stacks of books. Ladies dressed in frills and silk laughed lightly as they swept past Cos, whacking into her shoulder as if she were invisible.

Everything looked so grand. A grandfather clock tick-tocked away in the corner. Cos winced as she noticed it was now half past eight. Time was slipping away from them. Arched doors led to various rooms: *The Ladies' Reading Room, Guilds & Society Records* and *The Library & Archives*. Cos shuffled forward, uncomfortable in her disguise as Mary led them towards the library and archives.

Miles pushed open the door and Cos found herself in a

shadowy room lined with shelves of books, their leather covers cracked with age. For some reason Cos felt as if she should whisper, lest she disturb the words. The sheer number of books overwhelmed her – she could see tomes covering everything from geography to Shakespeare and philosophical tracts. *Where on earth do we start?*

'Don't worry,' Mary said breathlessly. She shuffled her planning papers. Her nerves seemed to have calmed since they'd entered the hallowed book-lined room. 'I've got everything under control.' She licked her fingers and picked out two pieces of paper headed with the phrases *Lord Fitzroy's Past* and *The Exhibition Blueprints*.

Mary handed a piece of paper to Miles. 'Can you look for a book called *Burke's Peerage*? It's a list of the gentry that live in the country. Lord Fitzroy's family should be in there, and we might find out more about his past.'

Miles's brow was furrowed as he mouthed *'Burke's Peerage'* over and over. 'Any idea what it looks like?'

'Sorry, no,' Mary replied with a wince. 'I've never actually seen it in person; I only heard about it from the Stains when they told us –' Mary faltered – 'that the people in *Burke's Peerage* were the best of the best and we were . . . *broken rejects.*'

'It's all right, I'll start at the Bs. It's bound to be somewhere in there,' Miles said, clutching the paper and stalking away. A few seconds later he hurried back. 'You're not broken, by the way. That's complete tosh.' He nodded at Cos and Mary before disappearing back in between the shelves.

Mary puffed out a calming breath. 'Right, and whilst Miles is doing that we'll hunt for the blueprints.' Mary grabbed hold of Cos's hands and pulled her in the opposite direction to where Miles had gone.

They traipsed through the bookshelves, skirting past scholars nose-deep in tomes and ladies giggling over the latest romance. Cos struggled to keep pace with a jittery Mary and was relieved when they finally stepped out of the shadows of the bookshelves.

Ahead of them the room opened into a small alcove. A few imposing desks and chairs were in the very centre of the space. Ancient-looking objects sat on wooden bureaux that lined the walls. A wizened man, bent double with age, rifled through the bureau drawers, before slowly making his way back into the bookshelves.

Cos frowned. 'Is this the . . .?'

'Archive,' Mary said breathlessly, letting Cos's hand fall. She studied her plan carefully. 'And, according to my research, archives ought to be organised.' She stepped away from Cos, peering at the labels attached to the bureaux. She stopped at one that read *Building Floor Plans – Borough of Kensington*.

Cos hovered behind her. She bent over and heaved the bureau drawer open. Almost immediately she and Mary were engulfed in the dusty smell of the past. The drawers were full to the brim with age-curled yellowed documents.

Ever so gingerly Mary pulled the corner of the first paper upwards. A drawing of a grand building was etched across the page. At its corner was a small coronet.

'I think it's Kensington Palace!' Mary exclaimed, reverently refiling the plan. 'Where the queen was born.'

Cos flicked through some of the papers, blowing an exasperated breath out of her cheeks. 'There are so many.'

Mary set her jaw with determination. 'Well, we're only going to find it if we start looking,' she said decisively, pulling out an armful of papers and walking over to the desk. Cos pulled out a chunky stack of papers and the smell of dust drifted into her nostrils. She followed Mary over to the desk, plonking herself down in the chair.

CHAPTER THIRTEEN

Time seemed to fall away from them as Cos's eyes went blurry from the effort of peering at the old building plans. She saw the insides of many grand buildings that she'd heard of before – the National History Museum, Kensington Town Hall – but not the exhibition. Cos huffed, cracking her fingers, just as Miles emerged from the bookshelves carrying a huge red book with gilded gold letters on its spine.

'Found it!' he said triumphantly. Energy surged through Cos, as she and Mary cleared the desk. Miles placed the book down, licked his finger and flicked through the pages until he came to the right one. Their shoulders jostled together as they all peered at the entry, which was headed by an emblem of a tree in bloom:

FITZROY

Lord Francis Fitzroy of Kensington in the City of London. Educ, Eton College and King's College, Cambridge (BA 1888, MA 1890). Pres. of The Institute, MP for Chelsea, Parl. Sec. to the Empire Minister, Vice-Chanc. Hospital for Crippled Children. B. 23rd September 1867, second child and first son of Lord and Lady Fitzroy (Willamina Fitzroy, d. 1888). No issue. For more information on the illustrious pedigree of the Fitzroy clan, please refer to A Chronological Genealogy of the Fitzroys *by H. A. Fitzroy.*

Cos stifled a gasp as she frowned at the page. The tree emblem sent a shiver through her. It was almost the exact opposite of the tattoo on Lord Fitzroy's wrist, which was a skeleton of a tree, whereas this one was in bloom.

Beside her, Mary tutted. 'It doesn't really tell us much.' She sighed. 'He's gone to fancy schools, hobnobbed with government ministers, and it seems he works a lot with people like us and the empire. As if Diya couldn't despise him any more.'

The words 'people like us' reverberated in Cos's brain. It seemed to be a recurring motif in Lord Fitzroy's life – but why? Someone as rich and privileged as Fitzroy would probably never come across people poor enough to be placed in workhouses, or disabled children. It seemed odd somehow. Cos thought back to that old ripped photograph that had fallen from the lord's breast pocket. Maybe that held a clue.

She peered closer at the page – there was what looked like a grubby little mark under 'no issue', as if someone had run their fingers under it. Cos frowned – it seemed as though somebody else was interested in Lord Fitzroy's past. If only she knew what 'no issue' meant. She'd have to ask Diya when they got back home.

And there were those words again:

The Institute

When Lord Fitzroy had come to the home to speak to Miss Stain, he'd mentioned The Institute – could whatever The Institute was have something to do with his plans for her and her friends?

Cos felt a little deflated. She'd hoped the library would give her answers, but it only seemed to add to her many questions. 'What about this book mentioned? The Chrono-thingamabob?'

'Give me a second.' Miles disappeared back into the stacks and returned with a much smaller book. It was leather-bound and gilded, and Cos reached for it hungrily.

It opened with a cloud of dust that tickled the back of her throat. A piece of paper fell from the book and on to the library floor. Cos ignored it, flicking through the book as fast as she could. But other than beautifully illustrated family trees and confusing pages of old-fashioned writing, the book about the Fitzroy family didn't tell her much. In fact, it didn't even include the current Lord Fitzroy.

A frustrated groan escaped Cos's mouth as she shut the smaller book and pushed it away. She returned to *Burke's Peerage*, hoping that she'd missed something.

'Cos, could this be something important?' Mary squeaked.

She was holding up the slip of paper that had fallen from the Fitzroy book. On it was a beautiful watercolour sketch of a young man sitting cross-legged on a desk. Behind the man were bookshelves, each one filled with tomes.

'That looks familiar,' Miles said, tapping his chin thoughtfully.

'The man?' Cos asked, as she stared at the sketch. He had wild hair, a pale face and a furrowed brow. He looked like he was in the middle of a plan. Surrounding him were teetering stacks of books and unfurled scrolls. But his clothes stuck out – they were tattered and ill-fitting, like the man was out of place.

'Don't be silly – the background! Take a step back.'

Cos duly did, followed by Mary and Miles. Miles pointed and Cos gasped. They were in the same place! From the ink-stained and dented desk to the colours of the leather-bound tomes, the sketch was done exactly where Cos stood. A shiver crept up her back.

'There's a title as well,' Mary said, as soon as the surprise of the discovery had worn off. 'And a signature.' She cleared her throat. '*E researching at the library, by M. F.*'

'M. F. *has* to be a Fitzroy.' Cos returned to the small genealogical book, only to be disappointed when the only Fitzroy with a first name beginning with M had died over 150 years before. She blew out a snort of frustration. Mary handed her the sketch, and Cos tucked it into her pinny pocket – another perplexing clue! Cos tried to quell her disappointment as she slammed both books shut, sending up a cloud of dust.

Mary squealed with excitement. 'Wait a moment! Cos, show me your hankie again.'

Cos untied it and handed it over to Mary.

'I'm right!' she said, pointing at the symbol of the book. 'I think this stands for a library – maybe even this one!'

Cos shuffled closer to Mary, peering at her shaking finger.

'See, the book is embroidered to the bottom left of this rectangle of green. Perhaps that green bit stands for Kensington Gardens? I'd have to look into it more to confirm it, but I'm pretty sure the book stands for *a* library at least.'

'Brilliant.' Cos gave Mary a quick squeeze, her disappointment replaced by soaring excitement.

She grinned, for ever grateful that Mary planned everything down to the minute detail. 'So that's two symbols almost figured out,' she said. 'We're getting closer to finding where X marks.'

But even as she hoped, questions ran through Cos's head. What did a library have to do with her parents? She ran her hands over the spines of a nearby book stack. Maybe books were a crucial part of their story?

'All very exciting,' Miles muttered, 'but can we concentrate? How are you getting on with finding the Empire Exhibition plans?'

Mary sighed as she returned to the bureau drawer, rifling through the many building plans that remained. 'Cos and I have spent ages searching, but we can't find the Empire Exhibition anywhere.'

'Hmm.' Miles's fingers wriggled above the drawer, his lips pursed as if puzzling out a problem. He pinched out one of the papers, and, to Cos's surprise, the words 'the Empire Exhibition' were written across it. 'Bingo,' said Miles with an easy smile.

Mary eagerly took the building plan, as Cos turned to Miles. 'How did you do that?'

'It's part of my thieves' tool kit,' Miles explained. 'Looking carefully at everything. You said that the Empire Exhibition was new, right? So I figured that the plan wouldn't be all tattered like most of these. I picked the one that looked the freshest.' He turned to Mary, who was scribbling frantically on the paper attached to her clipboard. 'What are you doing?'

'Sketching a rough plan,' Mary answered, 'so when we get back to the home, Pearl can draw us a much better one.'

Miles shrugged. 'Why don't we just take it?'

'We can't steal it. Building plans are important – that's why it's in an archive. Someone else might have use for it. Besides, we don't need to steal it,' Mary said breathlessly, as she slotted the Empire Exhibition plan back into the bureau drawer.

'Brilliant!' Miles said. 'Then we can get going.' He plucked an unfamiliar pocket watch out of his jacket.

Mary shot him a scandalised glance.

'Force of habit. Once a pickpocket, always a pickpocket. But I'll give it back, promise. It's eleven o'clock. That gives us plenty of time to get back before lunch.'

They carefully packed the stack of other plans back in the bureau drawer, and Miles returned *Burke's Peerage* and *A Chronological Genealogy of the Fitzroys* to the stacks. But Cos couldn't shake a worried niggle from her stomach that they were missing something – a crucial part of the puzzle.

Cos mulled her worries over as she limped after her friends back through the bookshelves and towards the door. Miles held it open for her and she stepped through. She was so caught up in her thoughts that she nearly didn't clock the familiar-looking woman that swept past them into the Guild and Societies Records room.

Elegantly coiffed hair.

Spectacles.

Ink-stained fingers.

Aggie.

Cos halted, her eyes wide and fingertips tingling. *Of course.* Aggie had burst into their lives by searching Miss Stain's office and asking probing questions about Lord Fitzroy. Could the smudge on *Burke's Peerage* have come from her ink-stained fingers?

From here Cos could see the grandfather clock tick-tocking time away. She knew that the smart and sensible thing to do would be to stick to the plan and take what they knew straight back to the home before Mr Stain did his lunchtime checks. But something deep in her gut told her to follow Aggie.

Mary tracked Cos's gaze. 'No, Cos, we can't go off plan again. Remember what happened with the cake heist!'

'But there's something *strange* about her,' insisted Cos, the pull in her stomach growing ever stronger. 'I want to find out what it is.'

'We've only got twenty-five minutes to get back to the home,' Miles warned. 'Otherwise everything is off.'

Cos swallowed and nodded. 'I know – it's silly and impulsive – but I've got to try. You two get back. Stuff my bed with rope and pretend I'm deathly ill. Mr Stain might not check.'

'No,' Mary said decisively. 'If we're doing this, we're

doing it together. Besides, I can tell your knees are bad, so I'm not going to leave you alone.'

Cos smiled gratefully at her friend. She nodded and glanced at Miles. He sighed, took one final glance at the stolen pocket watch, and stepped towards the door Aggie had disappeared through, pushing it open. The three of them slipped inside.

The Guild and Societies Records room was a lot different from the Library and Archive. Instead of lines of bookshelves, it was split into cubicles separated by wooden dividers.

Cos couldn't see Aggie when she first stepped into the room. She peeked round the nearest wooden divider; a bearded man was puzzling over a leather-bound book on a desk, surrounded by papers. Behind him was a storage locker. The next few cubicles were also occupied by men, too engrossed in their work to even notice that they were being spied on. Frustration grew in Cos. She was *sure* Aggie had come in here.

Cos put her finger to her mouth and gestured for the other two to follow her. In the next cubicle another man frowned at a book, the one after that was empty, but then . . .

Cos stifled her gasp. A diminutive, smartly dressed lady was examining a small file at a desk, a stern-looking librarian at her side. Cos, Mary and Miles hid in the empty cubicle, standing flat against the wooden divider. For a few moments all Cos could hear was the shuffling of paper. Questions ran through her head. What was Aggie searching for?

Miles nudged Cos, nodding at the flickering lights of the candles that lined the walls of the room. 'That reminds me, I've got to grab some wax for the key mould,' he muttered, as he stepped away.

'There's only one record, and the information it contains is scanty,' Aggie complained. 'The Institute – an improving guild. Fitzroy's obviously the president, and there's an address, but that's it.'

Beside Cos, Mary vibrated with fear. But Cos was far too intrigued to be scared. *An improving guild? What on earth does that mean? And what would such a guild want with disabled children?* If only Aggie had read the address of The Institute's headquarters out loud . . .

'Please calm down, Miss Noone,' whispered the librarian. 'This is a scholarly establishment. You are being . . . *hysterical.*'

Aggie huffed. 'Hysteria isn't real. It's just what men call women when they want them to go away. And I'm not going away, Mr whatever-your-name-is. This file on The Institute is woefully inadequate. It hardly says anything about what this society's purpose is. Can you explain why their records are so sparse?'

The librarian spluttered. 'Can I ask how this is any of your business, Miss Noone? Your library registration card notes your occupation as a lady engineer. What is a lady engineer doing nosing about in the Guild and Societies Records room?'

'Are you concerned about my credentials, sir?' Aggie's voice sounded pinched and hurt, as if she were gravely upset.

'There have been reports recently in the press of certain shady characters who spend their working lives causing strife and trouble for others,' whispered the librarian. 'In the past three months I believe you have come to this library with three different identities: Lady Diana Guys, a gentlewoman interested in the effects of pesticides, Mrs Ignotum, an expert in the treatment of matchmakers, and now you are this Miss Noone, lady engineer. Who are you really?'

'It doesn't matter who I am,' snapped Aggie, and Cos heard her stamp the floor impatiently. 'It matters who Fitzroy is. He's got secrets, mark my words. And what The Institute is doing might be the biggest secret of all.'

There was silence for a moment before the librarian sighed. 'Fine. I can't promise anything, *Miss Noone*, but there may be some more information on this guild in our collections space. Follow me.'

Cos and Mary pinned themselves flat against the divider as two sets of footsteps hurried away. Aggie and the librarian disappeared through a set of creaking double doors on the opposite side of the room.

Mary tugged on Cos's sleeve. 'Can we go yet?'

'Nearly. Keep a lookout for me, Mar.'

Heart pounding, Cos dashed from their hiding place and into the cubicle Aggie and the librarian had recently deserted.

On the other side of the divider Mary groaned. 'Please hurry, Cos. I don't think I can hold back the panic whirlwind much longer.'

From the snippet of conversation they'd overheard Cos had expected to find a piece of paper on a desk. Instead, she was greeted with a bulging folder with *Kensington Guilds* across the front cover.

A curse escaped Cos's mouth. She hurried towards the folder and heaved it open, spilling a pile of aged paper on to the floor. As she scrambled to pick it up, her knee cracked. Cos allowed herself a moment to feel the pain before she sniffed up her tears, shoved the fallen paper back in its pocket, and began to flick through the folder as fast as possible.

Cos could hear the familiar puffs of breath that signalled the beginning of Mary's panic whirlwind. The thought of her friend panicking all on her own in an unfamiliar place made Cos's heart hurt, but she *had* to find The Institute's address. Unfortunately there seemed to be no rhyme or reason to the *Kensington Guilds* folder. The Weavers were first, followed by the Cobblers (Cos came across half a sole stuck in between their records), then came the Hatmakers. The muscles in her arms burned as she turned the pages, finger pressed against the cracked paper, mouthing the words she read. There was a thumping in her chest as she heard Mary's panicked breaths descend into quiet sobs, and she kept her ears out for the return of Aggie and the librarian.

An ink-stained fingerprint told her she'd reached the page Aggie had been studying. The lady engineer was right – The Institute's records were sparse – but the address was there: 1 Callender Road, South Kensington, London. Cos whispered a triumphant 'Yes!' as she slammed the folder closed.

It was at that moment that everything fell apart.

There was a slam as the double doors of the Guilds and Society Records room opened. A desperate but muffled squeal told Cos that Aggie and the librarian were heading her way. Footsteps thundered closer. Cos scanned the cubicle, but there was nowhere to hide. She had to bite back a yelp with every step she took. Sweat beaded on her forehead. She was going to be caught. This was the cake heist all over again.

'Oh my!'

The shout shattered Cos's alarm. She risked a peek round the cubicle divider. The librarian was sprawled on the floor, his glasses askew. Aggie leaned forward to help him back up. The other patrons, previously engrossed in their research, had gathered round to see what the fuss was about. Cos's eagle eyes spotted a coil of rope on the floor.

As she tottered back to Mary, Cos overheard a whispered conversation.

'I wouldn't have thought hysteria would be enough to land you in a home.'

'Well, it's still a defect. And when they took my grandpa into the workhouse, there was no one left to look after me. I was too nervous for school, and too young for work.'

Cos rounded the cubicle barrier to see Miles and Mary hugging. She bit back a surprised 'Huh', as Mary caught Cos's eye and smiled a watery grin at her. Her friend's face was tear-streaked and ruby red, but with Miles's help Mary had vanquished her panic whirlwind.

'Did you trip the librarian up?' Cos whispered.

Mary nodded snottily, shuffling away from Miles and linking arms with Cos. 'He's not hurt, is he? It was the only plan I had left. Did you find what you were looking for?'

'He's fine,' Cos promised. 'And, yes, I did.'

Miles checked the coast was clear before they headed towards the door. 'Got the wax,' he said lightly, 'for the key mould. *And* I returned the pocket watch to its rightful owner.'

The relief from sneaking out of the Guild and Societies Records room wore off, and Cos was aware of the gentle tick-tocks of the grandfather clock. She stopped, the world around her woozy. To steady herself she bent over and let out a breath, wiping sweat from her forehead.

'What's the matter?' asked Miles.

Cos nodded at the clock. 'We've got ten minutes to get back to the home before Mr Stain checks the dormitory and finds two of us missing. It took us far longer than that to get here, and my knee is –' Cos paused, hating what she was about to admit – 'so much worse now.'

'There's no way we'll make it back in time,' Mary said glumly. 'Sorry, I should've kept a closer eye on the clock.'

'It's not your fault, Mar, it's mine,' Cos admitted, her heart beating in time with the clock as the three slipped out of the library building and into the bitter chill of London winter. 'I went off plan . . . *again.*'

Miles sighed sympathetically before his gaze settled on the bike rack beside Cos. A smile creased on his face.

'What is it?'

Miles grinned. 'Ever ridden on the handlebars of a bike? You can put your legs up safely above the spokes, so your knee won't get injured any more, and Mary and I can squeeze on the seat and do all the pedalling.'

Despite the pain she was in, Cos cracked a smile.

CHAPTER FOURTEEN

'ARGHHHHHHH!'

Cos screamed into the London chill as they sped through the streets, her hair whipping in the wind.

Miles had masterfully and quickly borrowed a bicycle from the stand (Cos felt a twang of guilt at the theft, but reasoned that this *was* an emergency), and soon enough they were whizzing back to the home. Miles was doing the pedalling; Cos perched in the basket, her feet on the handlebars and her hands clutching her walking stick. Mary perched on the edge of the seat behind Miles, eyes squeezed tightly shut and satchel grasped against her chest. Every now and again she would yell out directions for Miles to follow.

Pain coursed through every limb of Cos's body; her knee throbbed terribly. The bike weaved between a throng of traffic, leaving the library far behind and whooshing past the house fronts of Kensington. They zoomed through the greenery of London, Cos holding on for dear life, ignoring the wobbly feeling in her stomach. They clattered down cobbled streets and into a more familiar part of the city. It reminded Cos of the view she saw from the dormitory window – all crooked roofs and crowded streets, and dingy falling-apart buildings. They screeched to a halt outside the Home for Unfortunate Girls. The three abandoned the bicycle in the street, and Miles shouted up to the dormitory window whilst the other two, breathless and sweating, waited not so patiently for Diya to lower her extendable ladder out of the window.

Cos's heart thumped in her throat. She had no idea what time it was, or if Mr Stain had already discovered that they were missing. Mary scrambled up first, her limbs quivering with nerves. Miles took Cos's walking stick and went next, disappearing through the window in almost no time at all. Cos swallowed as she hoisted herself on to the first rung of the ladder. She bit her lip as she forced her heavy legs upwards. Slowly but surely Cos almost made it to the window ledge of the dormitory. Pearl's face appeared above her.

'Hurry, I can hear Mr Stain coming,' she squeaked.

Cos gritted her teeth – one rung to go. She was so close. She took a final step upwards and a twinge of pain surged through her knee as it went out of joint. For a moment Cos wobbled at the top of the ladder, her arms windmilling in an attempt to right herself.

Panic took hold of Cos. She felt herself beginning to fall backwards – towards the cold hard ground. Then, with a jolt, she was catapulted forward, through the open dormitory window. She hit the floor hard, but her knee crunched back into joint.

Diya unhooked something from the front of Cos's shirt, as she and Pearl helped Cos into bed, pulling the covers up to Cos's neck. Mary was already huddled in her bed, and Cos guessed Miles had hidden himself in Diya's invention station.

Mr Stain's beady eye peered through the peephole and began counting the girls. When he was satisfied, he unlocked and opened the heavy door and shunted four measly bowls of gruel into the room. 'Lunch,' he growled, before slamming the door and stomping away.

The weight on Cos's chest lifted somewhat. 'How did you get me in? I thought I was a goner.'

Diya lifted up a new contraption – a hook attached to a length of rope and a metal tube. 'I'm going to call this the Great Grabber. I fired it at your chest and yanked you in. It's not quite as accurate as I'd like it to be yet, but we're going to use it to lift the glass of the cabinet where the jewels are – so the glass doesn't break and trigger an alarm.' She placed the Great Grabber carefully on to the floor as Cos gingerly pushed off her bedcovers and Miles slipped out of the invention station.

'Those contraptions are incredible!' Miles said, jabbing his thumb back at the tangle of prototype inventions that filled Diya's storage area. Cos was amazed he had managed to squeeze himself in amongst the Phenomenal Protractible Ladder and the old and broken versions of Luminous Lanterns. 'How'd you get the supplies to make all this?'

Cos could have sworn Diya blushed.

'Most materials are just ordinary household items repurposed,' Diya explained, as she pushed herself off her bed and into her chair. 'Empty Skullsplitter's bottles, old brooms, broken ear trumpets. And of course all the tat the Stains buy to make money – usually they just leave things lying around, and I borrow them.' Diya shrugged as she wheeled towards her invention station, making sure that the doors were firmly closed. 'We hide everything in here, away from the Stains' prying eyes.'

'And the girls,' Pearl piped up. 'We don't want them getting into trouble.'

Mary nodded. 'If only we know, then only we can get punished.'

'But enough about that,' Diya interrupted, creasing her eyebrows. 'What took you so long?'

'Cos went off plan again.' Mary shook as she spoke, teeth chattering.

Diya shot Cos a disapproving look.

Pearl groaned. She was perched on her cot bed, nose buried in an unfamiliar book.

Cos frowned. 'What have you got there, Pearly?'

Pearl shrugged. 'It's one of those books Lord Fitzroy dropped off when he visited. It's very long-winded and boring, but the author, a man called Mr Galton, argues that science can be used to get rid of illness and disability. It reminded me of the broken test tube.'

Cos scoffed. 'Fitzroy isn't a scientist, Pearl. It's probably nothing to worry about. You know the Stains buy anything that they think could make them money – however ridiculous. I think we're on the right track; wait till you hear what we found at the library.'

Cos told the others all about the building plan, the entry about Lord Fitzroy in *Burke's Peerage* and the sketch in the Fitzroy book, and what they'd discovered when they followed Aggie. She wrote everything down and pinned the sketch to the blackboard.

'So Aggie *might* be an outlaw,' Diya concluded with a sigh.

Pearl hugged herself tight, and Cos noticed that today her arms were covered in inked bookshelves and quill pens. 'Those names – her other identities – sound odd.'

Mary shrugged. 'They're probably just random ones she was assigned by her criminal mastermind boss.'

Pearl shook her head. 'Nope, I think they mean something.

Diana Guys, sounds a bit like disguise, if you shorten Diana.'

Miles gasped. 'I knew there was something odd about her fake names! Pearl, you're a genius!'

Pearl blushed. 'Thank you. And I know we say Noone, but if you look at the spelling it reads "no one". "Ignotum" seems to be the odd one out.'

Diya gasped. 'No, it isn't.' She wheeled to the apple crate, rummaging around in it before pulling out one of her pilfered *Inventor's Journals*. She flicked through the pages hurriedly. 'Ancient engineers often wrote in Latin. And look –' she prodded the page she was on, which showed a drawing of a very old and very complicated-looking invention – '*ignotum* means unknown in Latin.'

'So this Miss Noone is playing word games with her fake names?' Miles said. 'That's odd. Even for a criminal.'

Diya's excitement made Cos's mind flash back to the library. 'Diya, do you know what "without issue" means? It was written on Lord Fitzroy's *Burke's Peerage* entry, and I have a suspicion that Aggie looked at it before us.'

To Cos's surprise Diya blushed crimson. She began to fiddle with her shiny swirl of hair in a very Mary-esque way. 'Erm, well, I, er, I think it means children.'

'Huh?' Cos puzzled.

'"Without issue" means no children,' Diya explained. 'Lord Fitzroy doesn't have any.'

Cos scrunched her face up. 'Of course not – he isn't married. But why would Aggie be looking at that?'

Mary fiddled with her sleeves, eyes not meeting Cos. 'Maybe she suspects he has a love child, with someone he wasn't married to. That happens sometimes.'

For one horrifying moment fear spiralled through Cos. Was there an outside possibility that Fitzroy could be her father? Heart thumping and throat clogged, Cos reasoned with herself – of course there wasn't. The initials on her handkerchief read *M. F.* and Fitzroy's first name was Francis. Her panic subsided, but Cos's thoughts still swirled.

'Forget about Fitzroy.' Diya's brows were deeply furrowed. 'What is The Institute doing? You said that the records show it's an improving guild?'

Cos and Mary nodded.

'But what would an improving guild want with disabled children?' Cos wondered out loud, a shiver creeping up her spine.

'I still think the answer lies with that broken test tube,' Pearl said, as she fiddled with the cuffs of her dress. 'Diya *did* say test tubes are scientific instruments, used to improve medicines and chemical mixtures.'

Cos swallowed away a scoff. 'Yes, but, Pearl, a broken test tube at an exhibition with hundreds of new inventions, contraptions and innovations isn't out of the ordinary.'

Out of the corner of her eye Cos saw Pearl's face fall, and there was a tug of guilt in her stomach.

An uneasy silence settled over the dormitory.

'I'm sorry, Pearl. I didn't mean to snap,' Cos said, as she handed Mary the chalk. 'Write it down on the blackboard. It could be useful later. And update how long we've got till Fitzroy comes to collect us. Two more days!' She turned to the others. 'How did your day go?'

'I've finished the jewels and am almost done painting the tiara.' Pearl held up a clutch of sparkling wonders.

Diya grabbed her spanner from her tool belt and began tightening what looked like a metal tube to a kettle. 'And I've made progress on the tools we need. I'm making Luminous Headlamps that will attach to our heads.'

Cos noticed that Diya's eyebrows were half singed. Mary and Pearl were huddled together on Mary's bed, Pearl frantically sketching out what looked like a building plan from Mary's memory.

'Brilliant,' breathed Cos. 'So we're almost kitted out, Pearl is drawing up a map of the Empire Exhibition, and we even have an address for the headquarters of The Institute: 1 Callender Road, South Kensington.'

Cos's plan for the rest of the day was simple if overambitious: she and Miles would sneak back out, heading firstly to the

187

address for The Institute that Cos had memorised from the library, and then to the Empire Exhibition to make a wax mould of the key to the safe in the Jewel Gallery that hung from Lord Fitzroy's belt. It would have been difficult for anybody, but for Cos it was doubly so.

Diya took one look at Cos's discomfort before ordering her into her Wonderful Wheelchair – a Diya-invented contraption adapted from the far bulkier wheelchairs the Stains provided. She and Mary fetched the chair from the cobweb-covered cupboard.

'I didn't know you used a wheelchair,' Miles said, as Cos cupped ice that had frozen on the windowsill on to her sore joints, momentarily numbing the pain.

Cos shrugged. 'My disability is a bit like a zigzag. Sometimes I walk fine. A lot of the time, when I'm in pain, I have a walking stick. And at other times I use a wheelchair.'

'But how are we going to get out of the window?' Miles asked.

'Don't you worry about that,' Cos replied. 'Diya's got a solution for everything.'

Diya had named her solution the Perfect Rappelling Perambulator. It was a brand-new invention made from a bedsheet pilfered from the Stains. At either end of the sheet Pearl had sewn in two extra-long lengths of rope. These ropes then attached to the Wondrous Winch. The idea was that Cos could sit in the comfort and safety of the sheet whilst Diya, Mary and Pearl carefully lowered her towards the ground.

Diya folded up Cos's chair and handed it over to Miles, who hefted it on to his shoulder. He saluted at the girls before climbing down the extendable ladder to the ground below and hiding himself out of sight of the Stains behind the boundary wall.

Cos took a steadying breath as Mary and Pearl bundled the Perfect Rappelling Perambulator out of the window. She took a shaky step forward, sat on the windowsill and swung her legs out, before bum-shuffling into the bedsheet.

The ground stretched out far beneath her, and Diya's invention squeaked in protest as she lay down. It shifted under her weight, and Cos felt as though she were riding a cloud – one liable to drop her at any moment.

The first part of her journey downwards was rather peaceful, and the rest for her legs was much needed. Her friends cranked the handle of the Wondrous Winch, lowering Cos in fits and starts. But then the perambulator shuddered to a stop. Cos frowned, confused, as she pushed herself on to her elbows to see what the matter was. It was then she heard the slam of a door and two sets of hurried footsteps. One look at the horrified faces of her friends told her that the Stains had popped outside for one of their semi-regular pipe breaks. The putrid tang of tobacco smoke filled Cos's nose and hit the

back of her throat, and she willed herself not to cough.

'He wants one early,' Miss Stain hissed. 'He's moving the meeting forward.'

'Then give him one,' her brother grunted in reply.

The Stains were in the middle of a gritted-teeth argument.

Above her, Cos could see the strain of holding her perfectly still weigh heavily on her friends. Sweat beaded on their faces and their arms shuddered with the effort.

'We can't – everything rides on this.'

'Then don't give him one.'

'You know what he has on us. We'd be ruined.'

Even in the midst of her terror of being discovered, panic settled heavily on Cos's chest. Fitzroy wanted one of them sooner than they had planned, which meant that the heist had to happen as soon as possible. Just as Cos thought she was seconds away from plummeting on to the Stains' heads, the siblings finished their pipes and retreated inside.

With a breath of relief the perambulator and Cos finally reached the safety of the ground. Miles helped her scramble to her feet and into her Wonderful Wheelchair.

Cos's breath puffed out in a cloud. She wheeled herself away from the home as fast as she could, into the safety of the bustling street.

CHAPTER FIFTEEN

C os led Miles through a labyrinth of back streets and alleyways a few minutes away from the home, following the directions Mary had written up. Now she was in her Wonderful Wheelchair, Cos found navigating the cobbled roads tricky. She bumped uncomfortably onwards, teeth gritted, as she squeezed past carts and wagons and disgruntled folk.

The Institute's address was imprinted on to her brain. She curled round a corner and found herself in a square of red-bricked houses. A leafy green park stood in the very centre, a natural balm against the London gloom. They were in a rare quiet spot in the city; the rumble of the factories seemed very far away and the air here seemed less soupy and throat-clogging. A horrified governess chivvied her charges away from Cos and Miles, a pinched look on her face. Cos's heart sank; the very sight of a girl in a wheelchair scared them.

As the children and the governess scurried off in the opposite direction, Cos and Miles surveyed the street ahead. Wrought-iron fences separated grand houses. Each was identical, except for one.

Ivy curled round the fence posts of the nearest house, and as Cos wheeled closer to peer through the railings, she saw that the garden within was unruly and overgrown. The house beyond didn't look much better; spidery cracks spread across windows and paint peeled from the front door.

'Is this the place?' Miles thumbed towards the dilapidated building.

Cos pointed through the fence at a wonky 'number one' hanging by the front door. '1 Callender Road,' she said, as she wheeled herself towards the gate. 'It's the address written in The Institute's file at the library.'

'Wait.'

Cos froze. Miles ducked down and pretended to tie his shoelaces as a familiar-looking man rounded the corner of the house.

Mr Bashum. The security guard from the Empire Exhibition.

Cos drew in a breath as she let a curtain of unruly hair fall across her face. She hoped the security guard wouldn't recognise her – after all, she was at a distance, and using her wheelchair.

Mr Bashum marched across the face of the house, coming to a stop at the near side. There he joined a couple of other men, dressed in identical navy uniforms, who were playing cards at a table.

'Guards?' Cos hissed. 'Why would there be guards at a house like this?' It was all very odd – a dilapidated mansion in amongst the splendour of a posh part of London. It was a strange place to be the headquarters of a shadowy organisation.

Miles narrowed his eyes at Mr Bashum and his companions. 'There are guards because there's something in that house worth guarding. Which means your hunch was right, Cos. Fitzroy's hiding something in there.'

Want burned through Cos. She was a creaky gate and a couple of spoke turns away from the front door. She groaned. 'We're *so* close.'

'Don't give up yet,' Miles said with a wink. He handed Cos his matchbox. 'I have an idea. Stay here and out of sight until I give the signal – when I ask them to pick a card.'

Cos reversed her wheelchair and stooped under the cover of the brick section of the wrought-iron fence as Miles slipped through the gate, which gave an ominous creak as he yanked it open.

'OI!' growled the men. 'This is private property.'

'Gentlemen, do you perchance know the direction of Portobello Road Market?' Miles asked confidently.

Cos heard the men grumble in response. She risked a peek over the precipice. Miles was walking, arms wide open, towards the table where Mr Bashum and his colleagues sat. He had left the gate swinging.

'I'm a street conjuror, see,' Miles continued, 'and I heard the market was a good place to ply my trade.'

This time the men sniggered.

'Ah, you're playing cards. Want me to demonstrate my skills, in return for directions?'

There was silence for a moment. Then Cos heard a gruff, 'Go on then'.

The next time Cos looked, she saw that Miles was in the middle of gathering up the cards. He faced her direction, and with a theatrical flick of his wrist, revealed the stack of fanned-out cards in his palm. 'Pick a card, any card, but don't show it to me,' he said to Mr Bashum.

The signal. The guards were all facing away from her, and Miles had their rapt attention. Mr Bashum plucked one of the cards from the deck and pressed it to his chest.

Cos slipped through the open gate and began navigating the gravel path towards the front door.

Miles shuffled the deck, as Mr Bashum took a quick peek at his card. Miles flicked his deck into the air, spinning them into a blur. The cards danced before the men's eyes, twisting and twirling. As she neared the building, Cos held her breath, but she couldn't hear anything coming from inside. She pulled down on the door handle and it came away in her hand; the wood of the door was rotten. It clicked open, and a wave of dusty air hit Cos, tickling her nostrils and making her splutter. Cos closed the door softly behind her, her eyes squinting as she adjusted to the darkness.

She pulled out Miles's matchbox and struck a match. A flickering flame crackled into existence.

A huge room stretched out ahead of her, bookended at either side by two magnificent staircases that curled upwards. There *was* normal household furniture in the home: a ruby-coloured sofa faced a marble-topped table, a bookcase by its side. A teardrop chandelier sparkled far above Cos's head. But what was strange were the things not supposed to be there. The normal furniture had been shunted aside, and in their place were three lab tables packed with test tubes and beakers filled with questionable-looking liquid. Alongside those were other scientific instruments – metal clamps, thermometers and objects Cos suspected only Diya would be able to identify. Cobwebs stretched across the tables and a thick layer of dust had settled like snow, disturbed only by a tangle of footprints that seemed to have been made recently.

She wheeled further into the room. The scurry of frightened paws told Cos a family of rodents had made their home in the abandoned house. Close up, the sofa looked worn and old. A musty smell hung in the air.

She puzzled at the abandoned laboratory. *More strange scientific equipment,* Cos thought. *Maybe Pearl was right to be suspicious.* After all, this old scientific workroom definitely belonged to Lord Fitzroy and whatever The Institute was.

Her explorations were interrupted as Miles tumbled breathlessly into the house through a half-boarded window.

'Goodness,' said Miles, and that was pretty much all Cos was thinking as well.

'What happened?' Cos asked.

'Wowed them with my card trick, they gave me directions, I slipped out of the gate, doubled back and sneaked in through the window.' Miles shrugged, as if it were no big deal. 'Do you want me to check upstairs?'

Cos nodded, and Miles raced up one of the staircases, disappearing from view.

She bent over and flicked one of the test tubes, a *ping* echoing through the room. Cos was certain that Fitzroy's science experiments wouldn't mean anything positive for her and her friends. But still questions gnawed at her. What was he making? And what did it have to do with disabled children?

Miles leaned over the balcony at the top of the stairs. 'Nothing that interesting up here,' he announced. 'Just more old bits of furniture. This used to be a family home, but it doesn't look like it's been lived in for years.' Miles hopped on the handrail and slid down the stairs effortlessly.

Cos nodded as she whirled her spokes forward into the shadowy corridor beyond the living room, past the curling staircases. 'I think it was the Fitzroy family home once.' Her voice echoed, sending shivers down her spine. 'But I don't know how it relates to The Institute.'

Miles followed her, creaking open doors that led to more dusty furniture. Cos was just about to turn back when the final room caught her eye.

Half a photo was tacked wonkily to the door. Cos's heart leaped to her throat as she realised the photo was ripped. She wheeled closer for a better look. Above the photo was a plaque that read *WILLAMINA*.

Cos gasped as she reached up and plucked the photo from the door. It was the bottom half of the one that had fallen from Lord Fitzroy's pocket on the very day that Fitzroy had first visited the Home for Unfortunate Girls. And as Cos peered at the missing half, she realised with a start why Fitzroy had only treasured the top half of the photo.

Willamina was sitting in a wheelchair. Lord Fitzroy's entry in *Burke's Peerage* mentioned that he'd had a sister who'd died. And the pocket watch that Miles had stolen from him had an inscription that read *To Franny, love Mina*. Cos glanced back up at the plaque and the scratched-out name. Mina and Franny were the siblings' nicknames for one another.

'But why is her bedroom on the bottom floor?' Miles asked.

To Cos the answer was obvious. She might only use her Wonderful Wheelchair on occasions, but she knew what a nuisance stairs were. 'Because she used a wheelchair. It would have taken her far too much time and effort to get upstairs.'

'But why did she use a wheelchair?' Miles asked. 'What was wrong with her?'

Cos tried not to let Miles's words sting, but they did. She knew he wasn't trying to be intentionally hurtful, but it needled her. 'Nothing was wrong, she was just different. But I have no idea what condition she had. Maybe polio, like Diya. Or even something like me, where she needed to use a wheelchair just some of the time.'

'Her bedroom might give us some clues,' Miles said, as he creaked the door open.

Like the rest of Fitzroy's house, a thick layer of dust covered Mina's bedroom. Her room was, as Cos expected, much better than the threadbare dormitory she was used to. A thick blanket lay on her bed, and a glamorously mirrored vanity table stood facing a bay window. Mina's empty wheelchair was stored behind the bed. There was a curious contraption sitting on the bedside table. Cos wheeled herself towards it. It looked a bit like a musical instrument. Folded bellows fanned out on one side and on the other there was a tube. Cos pressed down on the bellows and air whooshed from the tube, cooling down the area of the bed where Mina's face would have rested.

A cork board affixed to the wall was cluttered with odds and ends. Cos's gaze wandered over years-old invites to fancy balls and dances, age-curled train stubs, beautiful sketches on scraps of paper, and leaflets with shouting fonts. Cos drew closer to one of the beautiful paintings, a watercolour of a spring-green tree. Cos smiled. Something about the artwork seemed familiar. Mina Fitzroy was an artist, just like Pearl.

Cos moved away and one of the more crumpled leaflets fluttered to the floor. She wheeled forward to grab it. *The British Ladies' Society for Prison Reformation* and *Interview with a Real Prisoner*. Cos was immediately drawn in, especially since her parents might have had a connection to a prison. She read on:

Whilst Britain likes to boast that her criminal system is fair and just, our society has uncovered serious failings with the manner in which both the accused and convicted are housed in our nation. Please join us for a drawing-room meeting on 13th March 1888, when we will be joined by a former prisoner who will testify to the inhumane realities of penitentiary life. Our speaker, E, a tailor's apprentice, was born into poverty, and as such succumbed to petty crime as a necessity for feeding himself and his younger siblings. For this offence he spent a decade in a well-known London lock-up.

Below this were details of how to attend the meeting and

join the ladies' society. But Cos's gaze was drawn by the tiny stars doodled round the letter E. She thought back to her accidentally stolen star clip that had, she realised now, once belonged to Mina.

'Cos, look at this.' Miles's voice dragged her away from her knot of thoughts. He had been rifling through the drawers on Mina's vanity and come across a stack of postcards. 'They're love letters.'

Cos wheeled towards him, scanning the handwriting on the back of a few of the postcards. They made for, in Cos's opinion, pretty toe-curling reading:

Post Card

To my star,
I yearn for your
presence.
Your moon.

My star.
I am undone by news
of your health. I pray
for a speedy recovery.
Love always.
Your moon.

Star.
My love for you is
stronger than the
forces keeping us
apart. I promise you.
Yours.
Moon

'So Mina had a sweetheart before she died,' Miles said, 'and probably a secret one given that she hid the letters under a false bottom in her vanity.'

He flipped the postcard over. On the other side a silver moon was stitched into the card, surrounded by golden stars and a bloom of crimson flowers. Cos's hands automatically went to the map hidden against her neck. Her embroidery was a treasure map from her parents; Mina's had been a love note from a special someone.

Miles placed the stack of postcards neatly back in the drawers. 'Come on, Cos – we've already spent too long here. We'd better hurry to the exhibition.'

Cos nodded, but she tucked the other half of the photograph and the leaflet in her satchel.

As they made their way back through the old Fitzroy residence, Miles picked up a piece of paper from one of the tables that had been half buried by shards of glass; he dusted it off and brandished it at Cos.

Cos frowned as she wheeled herself forward for a closer look. The paper was yellowed and curled, but Cos could clearly see The Institute header and its strange Latin motto below. Under that appeared to be a complicated diagram of test tubes and beakers, scrawled next to words Cos didn't understand and complicated mathematical formulae the Stains hadn't taught her. She squinted at the title: *Experiment #1: Fitzroy's Wonder Elixir.*

An angry red line had been scribbled all over the paper.

Cos and Miles moved to the next table, picking up another paper. This one was scrunched up and crinkled, as if it had been thrown away. It looked like a recipe: one measure of this and a dash of that. But the ingredients were a jumble of random letters rather than words. Scrawled across the top of the paper were the words: *Experiment #37: Fitzroy's Wonder Elixir.*

'He's been working on this elixir thingamabob for ages,' Miles said, as he squinted at the impossible-to-decipher ingredient list. 'Adding new chemicals, using different methods to mix them together.'

Fear swirled round Cos's thoughts. Pearl had been right – the test tube Cos had broken at the exhibition was a clue to The Institute's purpose. She wheeled towards the third table, scattering beakers and metal clamps in her search for another piece of paper. She found it atop a stack of books. This one wasn't covered in red lines or crumpled up. In fact, it seemed to have been written recently and read a little like a newspaper advert:

FITZROY'S WONDER ELIXIR
A modern cure-all for infirmity, degeneracy and illness
Contains a potent mixture of Lachryma papaveris,
diacetylmorphine and arsenic
Guaranteed to heal ALL ailments

Cos frowned at the paper, before carefully folding it and tucking it away in her satchel. 'Let's get going,' she said finally, as she pushed the fear deep down inside.

CHAPTER SIXTEEN

C os couldn't get out of Fitzroy's old home fast enough. The creepy laboratory gave her the shivers, and the old photo of Mina and Francis felt heavy in her satchel. Miles distracted the guards by creating a noisy disturbance at the back of the house, leaving Cos and him free to sneak out of the front door.

It didn't take them long to wind their way to the Empire Exhibition, even with the crowds that still lined the streets outside. Miles and Cos were experts at sneaking around now; they slipped past the guard at the Jaipur Gate, before trundling towards the statue of Britannia.

'The plan?' Cos asked, as they ducked behind the statue to catch their breath.

'Find Fitzroy,' Miles replied with a nod. 'And get the key. I reckon we start to look for him at his office.'

'And then,' Cos finished, 'we need to figure out a way to get the key without him noticing.'

Together Miles dashed and Cos wheeled towards the staff door. They went through and shut the door firmly behind them. Miles stalked down the corridor, pausing every so often when he came across a door. Cos wheeled after him. Finally Miles pointed to a door. 'Here it is!' he whispered.

Cos hurried closer. The door had a glass pane at its centre and was marked with a golden plaque that read *Lord Francis Fitzroy*.

Miles knelt by the door as Cos kept a lookout. Miles withdrew his Diya-made Pilferer Powertool, and in a matter of seconds the door creaked open, and Miles and Cos slipped inside.

Fitzroy's office was much like the man himself: orderly, cold and edged with danger. Miles swept towards the desk, catching his sleeve on a razor-sharp, sword-shaped letter opener that sliced his already ratty shirt. Cos frowned at the desk's clawed feet, a shiver scurrying up her back, as she struggled to navigate her wheelchair closer. *Of course* Lord Fitzroy's office was completely inaccessible for wheelchair users.

Her eyes snagged upon a piece of paper with the word 'SECRET' stamped. Her gaze darted across the paper, taking in the contents. 'Look at this.'

Beneath the now familiar Institute header was a title:

Fitzroy's Wonder Elixir – List of Shareholders. Underneath was a list of names, and next to each name was an amount of money.

She recognised some of the names – Robert Gascoyne-Cecil, the current prime minister, regularly donated, the Princess of Wales had pledged £100. And, right at the bottom, Cos saw two names that filled her with fear and rage: Mr Eustace and Miss Alvira Stain – £5 each, monthly instalments. She ran her finger across the page – the Stains had jointly paid Lord Fitzroy £10 a month for nearly a year. Rage burned through her. That was an extortionate amount – enough to heat the home, feed the girls and educate them properly.

Miles frowned, confused. 'What does that mean?'

'This is why the Stains joined The Institute!' Cos exclaimed. 'They've invested money in this elixir thingy. If it's a success, then Fitzroy will sell it around the world and they'll be rich! But if it fails, then they'll lose everything. They're already in debt – this would ruin them. And look—'

She pointed to another column. In it were additional notes about each of the shareholders. Next to the name of the prime minister was scrawled *conducting an illicit affair with Lord Londonderry's wife,* next to the Princess of Wales *her youngest child isn't her husband's* was written, and next to the Stains *embezzling money meant for degenerate children.*

'He's got dirt on each and every one of the shareholders, so they do exactly what he says. That's why Miss Stain was so scared of him,' Cos realised.

Before Cos could even begin to digest what she'd found, footsteps thundered towards them and a shadow appeared in the glass pane. Miles and Cos shared a horrified look. Cos pocketed the list, before stuffing the rest of the paper back in the drawers.

'Under the desk!' Miles whispered.

Wincing, Cos wheeled herself towards the desk. She creaked herself upwards, as Miles folded down her wheelchair and the two of them hid under the desk. Cos's knee crunched in agony and she bit on her lip to avoid screaming out. She silently rocked back and forth, tears streaming down her face, as footsteps approached.

Fitzroy stood in front of where Miles and Cos hid, just inches away from them. Cos could see his polished shoes, pinstriped trousers and . . . Cos stifled a gasp . . . the glint of the silver key hanging from his belt.

Cos nudged Miles, and he began manipulating the wax in his fingers. They just had to keep Fitzroy exactly where he was for a minute or two longer.

Cos held her breath as Miles, his hand steady, reached up to the key. He shaped the wax round the key, making an impression of it. But just as Miles was about to peel off the wax, Lord Fitzroy stepped backwards, away from his desk.

The key, and the wax mould Miles had wrapped round it, hung tantalisingly close, swinging from Lord Fitzroy's belt. Cos and Miles both tried to grab it but their hands closed on thin air. Suddenly Lord Fitzroy stomped away, the bottom half of his body disappearing from Cos and Miles's view. Cos's stomach dropped and she shared a worried look with Miles. How on earth were they going to get the key now?

Fitzroy paced back and forth, the key swinging just out of reach; Pearl did something similar when she was very stressed. Miles tried – once, twice, three times – to grab the key when Fitzroy neared, but it slipped out of his grasp.

Finally Fitzroy's steps came to a stop near the desk again, his snake-skin shoes pointing towards Cos and Miles. There was a smart *rap-rap-rap* on the door.

'Ah,' Fitzroy said, 'Bashum. Come in.'

Cos gripped her knees tightly, willing them to stay in joint even when she was crunched up in an unnatural position. Another set of feet stomped into the room, and with a creak and a click Cos realised that the office door had been shut. They were trapped.

'Have you found anything?' Fitzroy asked hungrily. Cos hated that she recognised the desperation in his voice.

'Unfortunately not, sir,' Bashum replied. 'I've spoken with all the contractors on site the day the trinket disappeared, and all claim to have seen nothing.'

Fitzroy whacked his palm on to the desk, the slam echoing and shaking Cos's and Miles's hiding place.

'It's no mere trinket,' Fitzroy snarled, teeth gritted. 'That clip belonged to my sister. It was her most treasured possession, and I have faithfully kept it since the day she died. Are you sure it wasn't stolen by that busybody? The one who brought those –' Fitzroy paused for a moment, before almost spitting the end of the sentence – '*degenerates* to the exhibition.'

Cos bit down on her lip to stop herself from roaring with anger at the man. *How dare he talk about me and my friends like that?*

Bashum paused. 'You said the tr— *star clip* wasn't worth much, that it was a mere keepsake, sir.'

'It was given to her by one of the ne'er-do-wells she tried to help,' Fitzroy snapped. 'What of it?'

'Well, thieves don't nick stuff that isn't valuable, sir. And I haven't been able to track down that lady engineer. It appears she was using a fake name. Did you notice where the children were from?'

'Of course I did. I handpicked that establishment for a very precise reason,' hissed Fitzroy. 'That woman knows something. Her prying could ruin my project before we've even begun. I want you to keep searching for her. She's probably a newspaper plant.'

'Very well, sir.' Bashum stomped away, creaked open the door and shut it behind him.

Cos tried to brush away the goose pimples creeping up her arm. Fitzroy was *still* searching for Mina's hair clip. *And* he was suspicious of Aggie. But what confused Cos most of all was the fact that Fitzroy had chosen the Home for Unfortunate Girls for a reason. Maybe it was because he knew about the Stains' embezzling, but Cos suspected there was a more sinister reason. She just couldn't put her finger on *what* it was.

As soon as he thought he was alone Fitzroy sighed deeply. The desk creaked, its weight shifting just above their heads. Cos thought that Fitzroy was leaning on it. There was silence for a few moments, then another *click*.

Cos knitted her eyebrows, puzzled. It couldn't be the door, because Fitzroy's shoes were still pointed towards their hiding place, and they hadn't heard any other footsteps.

'I'm so close, Mina,' Fitzroy whispered, and Cos realised that the click had been his pocket watch opening. 'So close to stopping other families going through the pain we went through. So close to wiping the scourge of degeneracy off the face of the earth for ever.'

In the shadows of the desk Cos felt an unwanted ping of sympathy for Fitzroy. He really thought his elixir was going to help disabled people like his sister.

With a sigh Fitzroy stepped away from the desk, his steps fading. The office door opened and closed again.

Cos cursed herself. She'd been distracted by Fitzroy's words and completely forgotten about the wax key hanging from his belt. She turned to Miles to apologise, but a wry smile was plastered upon his face. He held up the wax mould of the key, its teeth sharp in the outline.

'I got it!'

Cos and Miles sneaked from the exhibition in the fading light, the cold chilling Cos's bones and the wax replica key hidden in Miles's pocket. At the home Miles climbed up the extendable ladder and Cos was hoisted up by Diya's Perfect Rappelling Perambulator.

The pain from a day full of exploits overwhelmed Cos as her friends helped her out of the perambulator and back into her wheelchair. But her mood was immediately brightened by three things.

A pile of tools in the shadows of Diya's invention station. Five Luminous Headlamps, a curious grabber instrument, five sets of the Pilferer Powertool and things Cos had never even seen before. A shimmering cluster of jewels, in its centre a golden tiara, sat resplendent on Pearl's bed, and a finished map spread out on the floor, showing a route in and out of the Empire Exhibition.

'You've finished it all!' Cos said breathlessly to the gathered group. Her heart thumped. 'That's it. We'll do the heist tomorrow night.'

'Tomorrow?' Diya questioned. 'But we've got two more days until Fitzroy picks us up!' She wound the blackboard down and jabbed at the chalked 'three'.

Cos wheeled closer and used her elbow to blur the 'two' into a cloud of nothingness. Pearl chucked her some chalk, and Cos wrote ONE on the board.

Her friends gasped.

'Do you remember that argument the Stains were having when you winched me down earlier?'

Four heads nodded back at her.

'Well –' Cos's stomach clenched as she spoke – 'Fitzroy wants one of us early.'

Fear flashed across her friends' faces.

'And that's not all.' Cos swallowed, her tongue rope-dry in her mouth. 'I know what he wants us for.' She turned to Pearl, as she dug around in her satchel and drew out the piece of paper she'd found at The Institute's headquarters. 'You were right, Pearly, the broken test tube *was* important. Fitzroy's been developing an elixir.' She brandished the ingredient list at her friends. 'One he thinks will cure us.'

Pearl hopped off her bed and she and Diya raced towards Cos's outstretched hand.

'That's not possible, is it?' Mary squeaked, her fingers fidgeting.

'Of course not,' Diya said, as she frowned at the paper. 'It's preposterous to think that *one* elixir could "fix" everyone in the world who is ill or disabled. But many of these cure-alls are dangerous – poisonous – to those who take them.'

'Like arsenic,' Pearl pointed out. 'It used to be in paint – to create a more vibrant green. But arsenic made people ill, and some even died. That's why I always mix up my own colours, so I know it's safe.'

A worried gasp escaped Mary's lips.

'Pearl's right,' Diya said, scowling. 'Another name for

diacetylmorphine is heroin. It's sold as pain relief, but I've read disturbing articles in some of Cos's pilfered newspapers — it's addictive and causes lots of health problems. And it's the same story with *Lachryma papaveris*, or opium. Fitzroy's elixir isn't going to help us; in fact, it might even kill us.'

Cos's heart thudded as her friends confirmed her deepest fears. 'We need to do the heist as soon as possible, before the Stains hand one of us over to Fitzroy.'

For once there was no arguing from the others. Instead, Diya clasped hold of Cos's hand, squeezing tight. Mary's clammy palm snaked round Cos's other hand, and a blushing Miles held Mary's. Even Pearl stuck a finger into Miles's outstretched palm.

They were ready.

CHAPTER SEVENTEEN

The day between Cos and Miles's excursion to the Empire Exhibition and the heist was filled with final preparations. Cos yawned into the frosty winter sunlight, seeing that Miles and Diya were already hard at work – they were passionately discussing how best to combine Miles's magician tricks and Diya's inventions.

Before the Stains came to collect them, Cos updated the blackboard with all the things they'd discovered at Fitzroy's house, pinning the prison-reform leaflet to it. Her gaze snagged on the watercolour they'd found in the book on the Fitzroy family at the library. The brushstrokes and colours looked awfully familiar. With a start Cos realised why. The artist who had created this drawing had also done the painting of the tree in Mina's bedroom. *It was probably Mina*, Cos thought. *After all, who else would be looking at a genealogical book on the Fitzroys?*

As she puzzled over yet another mystery, Cos desperately needed to rest and recuperate. Pearl scooped frost from the windowsill so she could ice her sore joints as the girls settled down to another day in the schoolroom, picking ropes until their fingers bled. Upstairs, Miles was busy chipping away at a key he'd borrowed so it would have identical ridges to the mould he'd made in Fitzroy's office.

After being escorted down to the schoolroom, Mary, Pearl, Diya and Cos huddled together in a corner. Whispered words slipped back and forth between them.

'And when I saw Pearl's drawing of the exhibition, I finally figured out how to get into the building – the ventilation shafts!' Mary's rope-picking didn't even slow as she spoke. 'They've become standard in buildings, even temporary ones, since the fire that burned down the Houses of Parliament in 1834.'

Cos had almost tripped over a huge stack of very boring building history books teetering by the side of Mary's bed this morning. It seemed her friend had spent most of the day before researching ventilation shafts.

Diya frowned, as Cos tucked the now-taped-up photo of Mina and Lord Fitzroy back into her pinny pocket. 'Who's Mina again? And why does she matter?'

'She matters,' Cos replied, 'because she was Fitzroy's sister. I think she's the reason he wants to fix us, because he couldn't save her!'

Pearl paused between stitches. 'That's really sad.' She had put aside her rope to create midnight-black disguises so they could sneak through the Empire Exhibition undetected. The satchel hung from her shoulder, ready to hide the disguises if the Stains came snooping. Inky silhouettes were drawn across Pearl's arms: highway robbers holding carriages to ransom and cat burglars tiptoeing towards their target.

Before they could continue their conversation, the door hatch slammed open, and Miss Stain's beady eye peered through. 'More picking, girls,' she growled.

Cos and her friends sped up their work until Miss Stain and her watchful eye retreated to her office. As soon as she disappeared, Diya nudged Cos's shoulder. She'd placed her chunk of rope down and dug out a few copies of her *Inventor's Journal*, which she'd stowed away in a hidden compartment of her wheelchair.

'I've been looking through these for symbols and their meanings, but I think I'm overcomplicating it.' She slammed the journals down. 'What does a heart mean?'

'Love,' said Mary, at the same time as Pearl muttered, 'A muscular organ that pumps blood.'

'Exactly!' said Diya. 'Well, not quite, Pearl. But think about it, Cos – the embroidered map is more than a treasure map, it's a message from your parents to you. And wouldn't they want to tell you about how they met and fell in love?'

An 'Ooh' slipped from Cos's mouth. 'Could it really be that simple?'

'I bet the heart represents somewhere important to their love story – a park perhaps? Or a ballroom?'

Images danced through Cos's mind – of a star-crossed couple who fell in love at first sight, who met in parks and ballrooms so they could keep their love secret. Could Diya be right?

They hunched back over wooden desks, eyes blurry from the effort of peering at rope, and fell into silence. Just as the hunger in Cos's stomach twisted so painfully she thought she could cry, the Stain siblings marched the girls to the dining hall for a measly lunchtime portion of gruel. Then they were returned to their desks until the sky darkened to ink. Finally the door slammed open, and the Stain siblings marched the yawning girls back up to the dormitory. Cos hobbled up the stairs and her knees – although heavy and pain-filled – didn't crunch with every step or feel as if they would fall out of place at a moment's notice. She would use her stick on the heist and leave her wheelchair behind. As she laid down on her pillow she headbutted something pointy. Cos scowled as she pulled out the star clip – *Mina's* star clip. Even in the darkness of the dormitory, it seemed to sparkle. Rebelliousness kindled deep within her. Tonight, she and her friends would pull off the most impressive heist London had ever seen, and all for a good cause. Who cared what the Stains, or Fitzroy, or anyone else thought? Cos pinned the star clip into her fringe. It had been a precious keepsake for Mina; Cos hoped it would be the same for her.

The London smog blotted out the constellations in the sky above, as they slipped out of the dormitory window using Diya's rope ladder. Cos tucked Mina's star clip under the Luminous Lamp headband handed to her by Diya and sucked in a deep breath of teeth-chatteringly cold London air. The next few hours could change everything.

In the dark the streets seemed edged with danger. The glow of the gaslights didn't chase away the huddled slumps of sleeping figures, nor the drunks that leered as Cos and her friends passed. Although the grinding machinery of the factories had quietened for the night, the city still seemed wide awake. Cos could hear the raucous laughter as people spilled out of public houses, and occasionally, more worrying shouts and screams. Miles, Pearl and Mary darted towards the Empire Exhibition, with Diya rounding off the group, her spokes crunching over icy pavements. The satchel, full of fake jewels, swung from Pearl's shoulder. Cos trailed a little bit behind, leaning heavily on her walking stick. Each of them had Diya's portable Luminous Lamp attached to their foreheads, allowing them to see in the gloom.

They arrived at the great building faster this time. *Probably,* Cos thought, *because they had moved as if Miss Stain herself were a hair's breadth behind them.*

The night-time fog obscured the beauty of the Empire Exhibition. Still, as Cos came to a stop safely across the street, she could still make out a hazy figure stationed at the grand Jaipur Gate and another marching round the perimeter of one of the glass spirals. Torchlight sliced through the darkness, jolting randomly about. *Guards.*

'The fog will help us,' Diya said shrewdly. The Great Grabber lay flat across her lap. 'They won't be able to see us as easily. And Pearl's disguises will help us blend in.'

Mary stepped off the pavement into a pool of gaslight. She squinted at the building, her mouth moving silently as she assessed the situation. 'Pearl,' she said, holding out her hand. 'The plan.'

Pearl plonked Mary's pile of papers into her outstretched palm.

'If there's one good thing about growing up in the care of the Stains –' Mary flicked through her papers, not taking her eyes off the guards – 'it's that they taught me all about patrols. Mr Stain marches round the whole home once every ten minutes. Miss Stain sits in her office. It looks like the guards here are doing something similar. See.' She pointed to the guard who was slowly but surely making his way round the spiral, then at the one standing rigidly at the entrance.

With a flourish Mary fished out her map and unfurled it, handing Pearl and Miles the opposite corners to hold taut. 'The ventilation shafts are here, and here.' Mary indicated the points on the map either side of the central nave of the exhibition, the points where the metal beams of the building met the glass walls.

Diya nodded, gripping her spanner as if it were a weapon.

'I think we should go for this one because it's the closest to us, the opposite side of the building to where the guard is heading and nearest the spiral where the Jewel Gallery is. We still need to move fast, though,' Mary continued breathlessly. 'The guard will reach us in about eight minutes.'

Diya spluttered. 'Well then, what are we waiting for?' She wheeled forward, bumping off the pavement.

'Wait!' Mary hissed. 'The guard at the Jaipur Gate, he'll be watching the road like a hawk – like how Miss Stain always keeps one eye on the kitchen. We need a *distraction*.'

'Ah, now you're talking.' Miles let go of his corner of Mary's map and it sprang back into a tight scroll. 'I'm great at distractions!'

He cupped his hands into a tube shape and brought it to his

mouth. All of a sudden a loud squawk sounded at the opposite end of the street, as though an exotic bird had escaped London Zoo and gone for a jolly around the capital. Even from a distance Cos could see the guard at the gate swivel his head, directing his torchlight away from the unfortunates.

'Go!' Cos whispered. Miles, Pearl and Mary darted across the street, Diya racing after them. Cos cringed as she forced one foot after the other.

As they reached the safety of the building's corner, Cos's heart thumped and sweat beaded on her forehead. She peeked round the edge of the metal beam — the front gate guard seemed to be oblivious. She let out a sigh of relief and turned to Miles. 'What was that? It was amazing.'

Even in the darkness, Cos could tell Miles was blushing. 'It's called throwing your voice. It's an old magicians' trick. Good for wowing audiences.'

The ventilation shaft wasn't very impressive to look at. It looked to Cos like a bit of an eyesore in the otherwise flawless glass building. A metal latticework grate covered the entrance to a dark tunnel that was about half Cos's height and triple her width — just big enough for a child to clamber inside. The grate was secured at all four corners by sturdy bolts. Diya grimaced as she hooked her spanner round the first one and began to twirl. She worked and the others hovered, nervously glancing about, half expecting the rumble of approaching footsteps. As the last bolt dropped to the ground with a clang, Miles prised off the cover, enveloping the group in a cloud of stale air.

'Hurry,' Mary whispered, her eyes wide. 'The guard will be here soon.'

They each dimmed their headlamps and clambered inside. Pearl went first. Mary followed. Diya slid from her wheelchair into the tunnel, holding her Great Grabber carefully, and Cos gingerly sat down at the mouth of the tunnel and shuffled in.

Finally Miles folded up Diya's wheelchair and shoved it into the shaft before climbing in, placing the grate back where they'd found it. Cos hoped the patrolling guard wouldn't notice as he passed by.

Cos felt as if the world were closing in around her. There was barely enough room to squeeze forward, and she kept bumping into Diya's back. Ahead of her, she could hear Mary's breaths puff in and out at a frantic rate, and the shake of the leading headlight told her that Pearl really wasn't enjoying being trapped in the ventilation shaft either.

The journey felt laboriously slow – even for Cos, who'd spent a good deal of her life hobbling haltingly. Each shuffle forward ached her to her bones, and every time Miles nicked the edge of the shaft with the wheelchair an echoey clang rang out that made Cos cringe.

'We're at the other side!' Pearl's whisper carried through the shaft like a gentle breeze.

Diya passed up her spanner, and together Pearl and Mary unscrewed the grate, pushing the cover off. It fell noisily to the floor, and Cos held her breath, but no hurried footsteps came. She sighed with relief.

A moment too early.

It was the dog's snarl that first sent a tremor shooting through her ribcage. It seemed to echo round the greenhouse-like building. The girls buzzed with effort: as Mary leaned out of the shaft, grabbed the grate and yanked it back into place, Pearl switched off the light in the lantern. Diya, Cos and Miles surged forward, fingers poking through the latticework of the grate, helping Mary hold it in place. As they all froze, Cos was reminded of the sausages the Stains regularly devoured for dinner – meat squeezed too tightly into a skin. That's how she felt tangled up with her friends, holding desperately on to their hiding place.

Footsteps followed the growl. They were creeping and deliberate steps and sent a shiver up Cos's spine. Torchlight licked up and down the walls, showering the huddled hiders in occasional flashes of light, and Cos caught a glimpse of a familiar face.

Mr Bashum.

He moved closer to them, his torch more focused on the

galleries and their artefacts than the unassuming grate. The dog strained at its lead, slobbering and sniffing.

As Bashum slunk past their hiding place, Cos held her breath. His shadowy figure stretched eerily towards them, like a monster on the hunt. Miles began shuffling around in the darkness, knocking into the others. Then, to Cos's shock, he pushed the button on his Luminous Lantern headlamp, bathing the others in flickering light. Cos clamped her teeth together to stop herself from screeching in anger. Bashum would certainly spot the strange shaft of light. They were seconds away from being discovered.

Instead, Miles carefully let go of the grate lattice and blocked some of the light with his hands, which he curled into the most unusual shape. Cos frowned as she noticed that the combination of the lamp's glow and Miles's hands had projected a shadow cat on the floor of the exhibition.

With an excited whine the dog bolted towards the shadow cat and Bashum let go of the lead. Free from restraint, the dog dashed away, disappearing into the shadows. Bashum swore under his breath as he lumbered after the canine, his light going with him.

Mary and Pearl cautiously lowered the grate cover to the floor and emerged from the shaft, unfolding Diya's wheelchair so she could slip into it.

'What did you do?' Mary asked, pointing at the spot on

the floor where the cat had been as she switched on her own headlamp.

'Shadow magic,' Miles muttered, his gaze darting around as he helped Cos uncurl from the ventilation shaft. 'It's simple really. I thought it might lure the dog, and Bashum, away.'

'Brilliant,' whispered Diya, as Cos and Mary gave Miles a congratulatory hug.

But Pearl wasn't listening. Instead, she was staring at her overstuffed satchel of fake jewels, a coil of rope poking out. 'That's it!' she exclaimed a little too loudly for Cos's liking.

Pearl cringed as she lowered her voice, turning to Mary. 'Mary, what did you say your grandpa was doing at the workhouse?'

Mary's expression contorted in sadness. 'Picking oakum, or rope. Just like we do.'

'Diya, you said they make residents pick rope in almost every workhouse?'

Diya nodded.

Pearl grinned in the light of the flickering lamp. 'Then I've figured out the rope symbol.'

Cos thought for a beat, searching her brain. The answer came quickly. 'The workhouse!' she hissed, untying her scarf.

Five heads pressed together as they stared at the hankie in the light of the headlamp. They had worked out that the bars stood for Wormwood Scrubs and the book for library. Now

Pearl had slotted in another puzzle piece.

Mary clicked her tongue, making a quick note on the paper attached to her clipboard. 'I *think* we'll be able to figure out where X is now, Cos. I can't promise anything, and I can't even think how I'll do it till we get out of here, but as soon as we're safe I'll get started.'

Hope fluttered in Cos's belly, taking root. She was so close to finding her family she wanted to whoop loudly – shout her joy into the world. Instead, she tied her handkerchief back round her neck and had just taken a few shaky steps forward when a gruff voice cut through the darkness.

'Did you hear that, boy?'

Pearl jolted with alarm and the lamp fell from her head. It hit the floor, its glass case smashing. As Pearl scrambled to extinguish the flame, the rope tiara fell from her bag and on to it, erupting into fire.

Pearl shrieked as she smothered the tiara.

In the distance the dog's snarls exploded into barks.

'We're done for,' said Mary.

Cos could hear approaching footsteps. Warning prickled up her back, but then an idea hit her like a sharp slap from Miss Stain. 'No, we're not. Follow me and hold on to each other's hands.' She grabbed Mary's hand and, in the darkness, felt blindly for the nearest glass wall. As soon as her fingertips brushed the chill of metal and she heard a quiet *brr* of nearby machinery, Cos knew she was close to the Gallery of Inventions. She followed the metal, leading her friends, until she felt a space of air and slipped inside.

'Mary, turn on your headlamp,' she instructed.

With shaking fingers Mary switched her light on, allowing Cos to survey the damage. Diya's Great Grabber was bent at an odd angle – it had obviously got a bit squashed in the ventilation shaft. Diya frowned as she laid the rod across her lap and yanked a spanner from her tool belt. Pearl pulled at her anxious face as she stared at the burnt end of the tiara, now blackened with soot.

Cos tried to work out how to fix her impossibly broken plan as Mary's whole body began to tremble. 'Cos,' she said squeakily, turning her map round and round. 'I can't work this out. I think we're lost.'

Cos tried to swallow her own panic away as Bashum's footsteps and his snarling dog got ever closer. Soon he'd come across the broken glass of their lantern and discover that intruders were in the building. Cos felt rooted to the ground, unable to think up a solution.

Miles elbowed her, nodding towards the exhibits. Huge contraptions were dotted across the floor. He pointed to a particularly big machine squatting in the corner. 'If we can wedge ourselves behind one of the pipes, we can hide out there until he's finished searching this bit of the building.'

They dashed towards the nearest machine, Cos's heart thudding erratically. She watched as the others tucked themselves behind the pipes, and Mary switched off her Luminous Headlamp, plunging them again into darkness.

CHAPTER EIGHTEEN

But the darkness, Cos realised, wasn't complete.

Although the Gallery of Inventions was full of shadows, from her hiding place Cos could see pinpricks of light on the other side of the exhibition that were moving steadily towards the centre of the opposite spiral – beyond the greenery and the statue of Britannia. Miss Stain's lumpy gruel from earlier that evening churned in the pit of her stomach. An occasional murmur of sound drifted across the lit-up building.

Cos crouched down lower as Mr Bashum's torchlight searched the dark crevices of the exhibition, his dog whining and sniffing by his feet. She peered at the guard through the slits in between the pipes.

He paused at the grate, his heavy boots crunching on the broken glass of Pearl's headlamp. Cos's heart was in her throat.

This was it. Bashum would sweep in amongst the inventions and find them. But instead Bashum tutted, kicked the glass away and continued walking, as if the broken glass were but a minor inconvenience.

Diya fiddled with her Luminous Headlamp, as Cos tried to quell her panic – they hadn't even got to the Jewel Gallery yet and everything that could've gone wrong had.

The lantern hissed as the wick caught and a flickering flame allowed Cos to see again. Pearl cradled the golden tiara; one half of the crown was still dazzlingly golden but the other was blackened and charred. Diya scowled at the bent end of her Grabber, her trusty spanner in her hand.

'Diya, can you fix the Grabber?' Cos whispered.

Diya didn't reply; she was already unscrewing a bolt.

Cos turned to Pearl. 'And the tiara?'

'On it.' Pearl had already taken her paintbrush out from behind her ear.

They worked in silence. It only took a few minutes, but Cos swore time tick-tocked away faster than usual. She paced back and forth, each step an agony, but she couldn't stop. Then Diya gave her Grabber a final once-over and tested its lever – it worked perfectly.

She nodded businesslike at Cos. 'Ready.'

'Me too.' Pearl had repainted the burnt edge of the golden tiara, and, although not quite up to the standard of her usual creations, Cos was sure no one would notice it was fake.

They crept onwards, past the dazzling glow of the Light Stadium and the shadows and silence of the art display. Cos tiptoed towards the curtained tent of the Jewel Gallery and noticed something peculiar. As she moved round the spiral, her eyes picked out smudges – on the glass cases containing artworks and treasures from far-away countries and on the bulbs of electricity. At first Cos thought it was simply a result of moving all the exhibits into the Empire Exhibition so quickly. But then, as she noticed more and more smudges, Cos realised that they looked like . . . fingerprints.

Cos peered closely at the nearest suspicious-looking smudges – five prints on a glass case. The tug in her stomach twisted painfully. This complicated matters.

'Cos,' hissed Diya, a look of outrage on her face, 'what are you doing? We need to move fast.'

Cos turned, a thousand thoughts tangled in her brain. 'Aggie's here,' she said, glaring at the shadows, as if the mysterious engineer might jump out of the darkness at any given second. 'These are fingerprints. The only person I've ever met who *always* has ink-stained fingertips is Aggie.'

Diya rolled her eyes but Pearl and Mary stepped closer, examining the ridges and curves of Cos's discovery carefully. Miles continued onwards, closing in on the jewels.

'You've only met a handful of people, Cos,' Diya said, her

disbelief evident. 'I bet plenty of people, writers or printers perhaps, often have ink on their hands. And even if they are Aggie's, she's an exhibitor. Those fingerprints could've been left on one of her visits here. It doesn't mean she's here right now.'

'It *could*,' Cos spluttered. 'After all, we know Aggie's investigating Fitzroy and likes sneaking around.'

'Cos, we have to concentrate on the matter at hand.'

As usual, Diya's sensibility deflated Cos's wild theories. She stepped forward, linking her arm through Cos's. 'Now come on.' She gently pulled her onwards, and they slipped through the velvet curtains of the Jewel Gallery.

The gallery thrummed, or maybe that was just Cos's frayed nerves. Ahead of them a huge iron-barred cage held jewels pinched from across the empire, and a golden tiara with a diamond centrepiece that Fitzroy had had made from one of them. She pushed the strange lights and maybe-Aggie's ink fingerprints from her mind.

A shiver prickled across Cos's skin as Miles knelt next to the keyhole of the iron cage. This was it; it was actually happening. He slotted his key copy in and twisted it. The iron cage clicked open, and Pearl heaved it backwards on its hinges, exposing the glass cabinet underneath. Cos almost forgot to breathe out. They were now just a single clear barrier away from the jewels.

Diya wheeled her chair back and Pearl took a huge step

away, both wary of accidentally brushing the glass and triggering the alarm. Cos did the same, but as she did so she wobbled dangerously close to the glass cabinet. Muttering curses, Cos righted herself and managed to stay upright.

'Phew,' Mary whispered.

'That was close,' Diya added. 'You all right?'

Cos shrugged noncommittally, not wanting to add to her friends' worries.She tried to fix a cheery expression on her face. 'Go on, Diya.'

Diya stuck her tongue out, glowering at the glass cabinet and brandishing her Grabber like a sword. She adjusted her wheelchair position, making sure she was facing the jewels square on, and applied the brake. Cos tried to calm her thundering heart as Pearl gathered her rope-jewels in one arm, her ever-present paintbrush still adding final touches to her creations.

Diya was singularly focused, her hands as steady as a rock as she hovered her grabber just above either side of the glass cabinet. Ever so carefully she edged it lower, and in a single swooping movement had grabbed and lifted the glass cabinet without the glass breaking.

Cos held her breath and counted as the seconds ticked by. The jewels remained still, not dropping below into the safe.

'GO!' hissed Diya through gritted teeth as she held up the cabinet.

Pearl rushed forward, taking the jewels from their velvet cushions and handing them to Cos before replacing them with her rope fakeries. Cos cradled each of the jewels like a baby, before placing them in the well-worn satchel.

Finally Pearl passed over the heavy golden tiara, with its centrepiece: the Star Diamond. The diamond sparkled, glinting in the light of Cos's Luminous Lantern and reflecting her own face back at her in a kaleidoscope of Coses. Storm-cloud eye bags, tangled hair and determined gazes all appeared in the angled ridges of the diamond. It was beautiful. For one moment staring at the gleaming jewel took Cos's mind off the heist and the Fitzroy problem. She sort of understood why men fought over diamonds and ladies adorned themselves with them.

Cos dragged her gaze away and instead gazed up at the glass ceiling of the Empire Exhibition. The London smog had cleared and Cos could see constellations scattered across the sky. *The world,* she thought, *is so much more than the Home for Unfortunate Girls, and I want to see it.*

The others concentrated on carefully lowering the glass cabinet, locking the iron cage and making sure that no trace of them remained in the Jewel Gallery, whilst Cos felt her thoughts drift as she placed the tiara safely into the satchel.

Cos had always liked her name, firstly because Miss Stain despised its unusualness, and secondly because it was the only thing that was all hers. When Aggie told her that 'Cosima' came from the word 'cosmos', which meant the universe, the night sky became Cos's favourite part of it all.

Her thoughts returned to the hankie and the star symbol they hadn't managed to unravel. She found herself untying it, unfurling the cloth in her palm and staring at it for what could've been the billionth time that week.

The star symbol was only a few streets over from the book symbol that Mary had worked out meant library. If it *was* Kensington Library, the star represented something close to the home.

'Cos?'

Cos barely heard Diya say her name.

'Come on, we've got to go.'

'It's me!' Cos exclaimed far too loudly for a midnight heist. 'The star is me.'

'What?' Pearl asked.

But Cos couldn't drag her eyes from the hankie. 'Cosima, which comes from the word "cosmos", of which a major part is the sky. The star marks the location of the Home for Unfortunate Girls!'

Jaws dropped and hands clapped on Cos's shoulders. Cos felt frozen in place —the hankie *was* meant for her. Her parents had cared enough about her to ensure she had a path back to them one day. They also knew where she'd grow up: the Home for Unfortunate Girls.

Mary tugged on Cos's sleeve. 'Great discovery, Cos, but we need to leave.'

Cos helped Pearl hook the now rather heavy satchel on to her shoulders, and almost as fast as they'd sneaked in, the unfortunates departed, winding their way back past the artworks and the glowing lights, towards the central nave and freedom.

CHAPTER NINETEEN

They were mere steps from freedom. But as they entered the central nave Cos's excitement at figuring out the final symbol on the hankie had been extinguished. The tug in her stomach was ever more insistent. She hung back from the others, even though her heart pumped out the constant urge for her to *get out get out get out.*

'Hurry up, Cos,' insisted Diya.

But Cos couldn't – or wouldn't.

She was so consumed by what she was about to do that she almost tripped over a frozen Pearl.

'Someone's coming,' Pearl whispered.

'Quick,' Mary hissed, nodding at the door that led to the staff corridor. 'We can hide in there.'

They dashed across the exhibition, Miles unpicking the

lock in seconds, and slipped inside, just as Mr Bashum emerged from the Empire Pavilions spiral.

Cos opened the door a crack, peering through it as Mr Bashum greeted a group of top-hatted gentlemen at the Jaipur Gate.

'Cos,' Diya said sharply, 'what are you doing? Close the door, you might be spotted.'

Cos summoned up all her courage. This was her chance – her one chance – to bring Fitzroy down once and for all.

'I'm so sorry,' Cos whispered. 'But I *have* to be spotted.'

Her friends blinked, aghast.

'What?' Diya hissed.

'I have to be caught, so Fitzroy can test his elixir on me, and we can *prove* he's a charlatan.'

Mary's eyes filled with tears. 'Cos, you can't. You mustn't.' She pulled her trusty clipboard from the satchel. 'It's not part of the plan.'

Guilt weighed heavily on Cos's chest as she spluttered out her next words. 'It's part of my plan. It always has been.'

Betrayal was etched upon each of her friends' faces.

Miles moved forward to grab hold of Cos's hand. 'Cos, this could ruin everything. It could kill you!'

Cos pulled her hand back. 'Don't you see? It's not enough to steal Fitzroy's jewels. We have to ruin him. Otherwise he'll just do this again to another group of disabled children.

He won't stop – ever.'

For half a second Cos thought her friends might understand. Frowns and scowls gave way to thoughtful expressions. Pearl even let out a hopeful 'Hmm'. The tension in the air slackened ever so slightly. Hope beat in Cos's chest.

But a 'Tsk' from Diya sent those hopes plummeting. 'This is the same thing you do every time,' she said bitterly. Diya's words stung like Miss Stain's stiff leather strap, but Cos knew they were true. 'We trusted you, but you keep things from us. It isn't fair to put us all in danger.'

'The only way to really bring Fitzroy and The Institute down is to catch them red-handed doing something illegal,' Cos insisted. 'If one of you fetches the police, we can—'

'The police?!' Miles exclaimed. 'We've got a satchel full of stolen jewels!'

'Please,' Cos begged. 'Just bring one constable to stop the demonstration.'

'This is ridiculous.' Diya scowled at Cos.

Pearl didn't say anything, but the sadness in her eyes made it impossible for Cos to meet her gaze.

Before she could say anything else to try to convince her friends, Mary pointed a shaking hand past the just-open door, towards the Jaipur Gate. There, mid-argument, stood the Stains. Cos bit back a gasp, a wave of nausea rising in her chest.

The Stains were dressed in their fanciest attire. A moth-eaten fur stole sat across Miss Stain's shoulders; her pouting lips were coloured berry-red. She wore a shimmering black dress and tottered about in too-high heels. Her brother wore his best suit, mismatched patches covering up the most worn fabric. Mr Bashum and his dog stood awkwardly beside the arguing siblings, dutifully guarding the entrance gate. Cos's stomach lurched, but she was relieved to see that the Stains were alone and didn't have a girl in tow. Scowling, his stubby finger jabbing towards his sister, Mr Stain retreated through the Jaipur Gate.

Cos had to move now or she'd for ever lose her chance. She turned back to her friends, opening her mouth to say something – anything – to make it a little better. But no sound came out. So she pulled open the door and stepped away from her friends into the central nave. If Miss Stain turned, she would spot her immediately. She'd be spitting mad, of course, to see her out of bed and away from the home, but it was the only way. Cos would make the perfect experiment subject.

And then, as swiftly as Miss Stain downed a glass of gin, Cos was yanked backwards, a hand clamped over her mouth, and the door firmly closed in front of her.

'Don't make a sound,' whispered someone.

Cos wriggled and turned to see Aggie's bespectacled, determined face. The lady engineer was dressed all in black, her leather bag bulging at the seams.

'Why did you stop me?' Tears blurred Cos's vision as she broke free of Aggie's grasp. 'And why are you here?'

She turned to her friends, all of whom were still pressed against the wall of the corridor, shock etched across their faces. Further down the shadowed corridor, Cos could see Fitzroy's office door splayed open wide. Aggie must've stormed past them to stop Cos from stepping into the central nave.

Pearl came forward, her shock replaced by anger. And that anger, to Cos's surprise, was directed at Aggie.

'We know you're not really an engineer,' Pearl whispered. 'And Agatha Noone isn't your name. It's a *pew-sew-dim*.'

'Pseudonym,' corrected Aggie, one of her eyebrows raised in a very Diya-like fashion. 'How'd you figure out my name was fake?'

'It was simple really,' Mary muttered, arms crossed over her body. 'We overheard that librarian list your other names – Di Guys, Mrs Ignotum.'

'You were at the library?' Aggie breathed. 'How did you get out of the home tonight without that pinch-faced Miss Stain catching you?'

'I've been inventing things to make our life better since I arrived at the home,' Diya said. 'Cos, Miles and Mary used my Phenomenal Protractible Ladder to climb out of the dormitory window whilst the other girls distracted the Stains.'

A quiet 'Ha' fell out of Aggie's mouth, but unlike the Stains her laugh didn't sound harsh or mean but impressed. 'You know, the whole of London has been speculating about my true identity for a while now, but you and your friends are the only ones to even get close to the truth.'

Cos frowned at her friends, whose bewildered expressions matched her own. 'The whole of London?' What had she missed?

Aggie nodded. 'No "respectable" lady would ever choose to work for a living, you see. Women are expected to marry well and have lots of children. But stories have been my currency since I was a little girl.'

A hazy memory tugged on Cos. 'At the library,' she said under her breath, 'the librarian mentioned that as Lady Guys, you were investigating the harmful effects of pesticides, and when you were Mrs Ignotum, you were looking into the mistreatment of matchmakers . . .'

Aggie held up a finger for silence before inching open the door. When she was satisfied that Mr Bashum was none the wiser to their presence, she plucked a folded-up newspaper from her bag, unfurling it and passing it to Cos. The others gathered in close, heads jostling close to see better. It was the same edition Cos had stolen from Miss Stain only a few days before. She flicked to the front page, and her eyes caught on an article:

MISS DOE STRIKES AGAIN – LIES OF A FACTORY BOSS

London's pluckiest and most mysterious girl reporter has
once again proved that energy rightly applied and directed
will accomplish anything. The young Miss Doe has used her
derring-do to expose the shoddy treatment of matchbox makers,
and secure better wages and treatment for the women.
Read the full story only in next week's Gazette.

'"Doe" is just another name that means unknown,' explained Aggie ruefully. 'My real name is far too memorable. Agatha de la Dulce. I'd be discovered immediately.'

Cos joined the dots in her head. 'You're a reporter.'

Mary let out a gasp. Pearl and Miles exchanged a raised-eyebrow look. Diya scoffed, as though she'd known all along.

Everything started to make more sense. On their trip to the Empire Exhibition Aggie had mentioned that Lord Fitzroy had banned the press until the grand opening. She had been caught searching Miss Stain's office and done research into The Institute in the library because she was investigating Lord Fitzroy.

'I specialise in undercover investigations,' Aggie explained.

'I've exposed the awful effects of pesticides and the downright dangerous practices of factory owners. When I learned about rumours that Lord Fitzroy had acquired many of the artefacts through theft, I had to find out the truth.'

'And what is the truth?' Miles asked.

'Lord Fitzroy is the most prolific burglar I have ever come across,' Aggie said bluntly. 'He stole almost every single exhibit from people in the colonies, knowing that he could get away with it because he was a rich lord.' Aggie spat those last few words out bitterly.

'But that wasn't all I found out,' she added. 'When I began digging into his past, I stumbled across a missing baby and a mysterious organisation.'

'A baby?' Pearl rasped out.

Aggie nodded. 'I believe that Lord Fitzroy may have had a child around twelve years ago. Former servants swore to me that they had seen a baby swathed in blankets at the Fitzroy residence. When I saw him visit the home, I thought that maybe—'

'One of us was his child?' Cos finished. Her tongue was heavy in her mouth, and she felt like she was on the cusp of something important, but she couldn't quite work out what it was.

'Yes,' Aggie continued. 'But something didn't fit. There was no trail of money for the paying-off of servants, like there

246

normally is with illegitimate babies. It was strange . . . But enough of all that. I've explained why I'm snooping here after hours, why are you here?'

Cos opened her mouth to speak another half-truth and a scream erupted from beyond the closed door. Aggie frowned and silently cracked the door wider.

Cos and her friends craned their necks to peer into the central nave.

In the distance, next to the Jaipur Gate, Mr Stain had returned. He was holding tightly on to the elbow of a squirming, crying Dolly.

'Please, Mr Stain,' Dolly screeched, tears spilling down her cheeks. 'I want to go back to bed.'

Cos's throat clogged with fear. This couldn't be happening; this wasn't part of the plan. She felt as if she were being ripped apart from the inside out as she watched, helplessly, whilst Dolly was dragged, kicking and screaming, into the spiral of the Empire Pavilions. All thoughts of her secret plan fell away, and panic raced through her. 'No,' she squeaked a little too loudly.

The others held their breath as Mr Bashum frowned in their general direction, his dog straining at its leash. He made to walk towards their hiding place, but then another dressed-up couple of ladies appeared, distracting him. Mr Bashum led the ladies towards the Empire Pavilions, disappearing into the spiral.

Cos looked back at her friends. Tears streaked down Diya's face, Mary rocked back and forth on her tiptoes, face covered by a tangle of her golden hair, and Miles was pale, his mouth a grim line. Despair gripped Cos.

'We *have* to rescue Dolly before Fitzroy gives her the elixir,' Diya said fiercely.

Aggie frowned. 'The elixir?'

'It's a sort of tonic,' Mary squeaked. 'A cure.'

It was Aggie's turn to frown. 'A cure for what?'

Pearl's voice came out all squeaky. 'For us. For kids like us. You know – *defectives*.'

The look of horror on Aggie's face was somehow comforting. 'Oh my goodness.'

Cos nodded. 'But he needs to prove it works, so that The Institute investors will give him more money.'

Aggie took a step back. 'So that's why I saw him at the Home for Unfortunate Girls. He was looking for –' Aggie's expression contorted into disgust – 'subjects.'

'And he's got one. *Dolly*,' Cos said.

Aggie's jaw hardened. She thought for a moment, tapping her fingers on her chin. 'Cos, if I'm correct, your plan was to get caught by the Stains so *you'd* be Fitzroy's experimental subject?'

Cos snorted away her tears and nodded. 'I thought that the only way to really stop Fitzroy was to catch him red-handed.

I was hoping that the others could alert the police, catch Fitzroy in the act, stop him doing . . .' Cos's words drifted off into nothingness as she realised how silly her scheme was.

'Well, now I've got proof that Fitzroy stole many of the exhibits,' Aggie said, pulling a handful of official-looking papers from her bag. 'I'm sure the police will be very interested in both his international thievery and the illegal experiments he is planning to conduct upon children.' Aggie quirked an eyebrow. 'And they'd be far more likely to believe an adult . . .'

'Aggie's right,' Mary said quickly. 'You didn't think this all the way through, Cos.'

'Police *never* believe kids,' Miles confirmed with a scowl.

'And they definitely won't believe a bunch of unfortunate kids,' added Pearl.

'We need a grown-up for this to work,' agreed Diya grudgingly.

Cos drew in a breath, a slightly adjusted plan coming together in her head. She turned to her friends, wiping her cheeks dry of tears and squaring her shoulders. 'What if I told you that I still think my plan will work – with a few adjustments, of course – and we could go one better? With Aggie's help we can rescue Dolly, stop the experiment, expose Fitzroy and his fraudulent elixir *and* prove that he's stolen all his exhibits.'

The girls, Miles and Aggie gathered closer to Cos.

Despite everything, she grinned into the shadows of the corridor. 'Here's the plan.'

CHAPTER TWENTY

They arrived at the Demonstration Hall red-faced and out of breath. They'd hurried round the spiral, passing the deserted and shadowed Empire Pavilions. Luckily Mr Bashum hadn't reappeared – Cos suspected that he was in charge of guarding Dolly. Aggie had slipped through the Jaipur Gate, wishing them luck as she disappeared into the inky night. They were on their own.

Cos peered through the crack in the door to the hall. It was packed with people. A smartly dressed audience sat on rows upon rows of seats, facing a man who was spotlighted on a stage. A man wearing a ruby-red suit and a twirly moustache.

Lord Fitzroy.

Fitzroy's arms were open in welcome, his mouth moving into the shape of words. But Cos wasn't listening. Instead, her gaze fixed upon the laboratory set up behind him. It looked like a modern dust-free version of what Miles and Cos had seen at Fitzroy's old house – strange instruments sat atop tables that stretched across the back of the stage. Test tubes and beakers were filled with dark green-coloured gloop, and at the far side of the stage there was a huge metal vat that almost overflowed with liquid that bubbled and spat.

Cos tried to swallow away her fears as she refocused on Fitzroy. He was grinning widely, all his teeth on display, as the audience politely applauded him. Cos peered past top hats and elegantly feathered brims as Lord Fitzroy quieted his guests with a single finger.

'Ladies and gentlemen,' he began, his booming voice echoing around the hall, 'I have invited you here tonight so that you may be the very first to see a medical development that will revolutionise society. As esteemed members of The Institute, you have demonstrated your commitment to the eradication of degeneracy by investing in this tonic. I am honoured to announce, after rigorous testing and much research, that I have created Fitzroy's Wonder Elixir.'

This time there was no clapping, just a reverent hush. Cos felt as though her skin was being peeled off piece by piece, as though her very being was being torn to shreds.

'The elixir is the cure-all we've all been waiting for,' said Fitzroy, as he paced the length of the stage. 'It will fix those suffering with all forms of disability, whether physical or mental. In doing so it will transform them into useful and able members of society. England will no longer need institutions to care for these defectives – *because they will no longer exist.'*

He paused again for another round of applause.

'Of course, this may sound like heady stuff, scientifically impossible even. Learned minds around the globe have criticised my ideas, but tonight – once and for all – I will prove them all wrong.'

Even from a distance Cos could see the hyper-focused look in Fitzroy's eyes. To her horror Cos noticed a banner that had been strung up, which read *Fitzroy's Wonder Elixir – a Cure for Infirmity and Feeblemindedness.*

'And I will do that through that age-old method of innovation: a demonstration.' Fitzroy threw his arms back with a flourish, as the crimson curtains creaked open at the back of the stage, revealing two figures. Mr Bashum heaved a small wriggling girl round the laboratory apparatus towards the front of the stage.

Dolly.

Cos tried to push away her fear as she nodded at her friends.

Diya's gaze was already focused on the lights, Mary was frantically scribbling down a plan, and Miles plucked one of his magician's tricks from his many-pocketed coat.

Cos swallowed, hands shaking and heart thudding, when a small hand laced through hers.

Pearl offered one of her rare, encouraging grins that made Cos think of sunshine. 'You can do it,' she whispered.

Cos surged through the door, clanking her walking stick loudly on the floor so that audience members twizzled round to see what the commotion was all about. Up on the stage, Fitzroy's fake smile shrivelled away.

'Cos, COS!' Dolly yelled, waving frantically at her.

Cos limped onwards, through the walkway that separated the audience, all the way to the base of the stage. Cos's ears prickled as the audience tutted their distain. As she reached the front row, Miss and Mr Stain sprang up, faces purple with rage.

Miss Stain swiped Cos's wrist, gripping her so tightly that her nails drew blood. 'What is the meaning of this, number one?' Miss Stain hissed, shaking Cos as though she were a rag doll.

There were gasps of shock from the audience, and Miss Stain's grip loosened. Even people who believed that disability and illness could be cured didn't like seeing children being hurt. The matron's cheeks coloured slightly, and she cleared her throat, and said ever more gently: 'You are supposed to be in bed.'

It was time for Cos to put the plan into motion. Everyone's eyes were on her, and nobody but her saw the shadows of four children creep into the Demonstration Hall.

'I . . . I saw you take Dolly, and I wanted to know why,' Cos said, as sweet as the cakes she'd stolen recently. 'So I followed you. And when I heard Lord Fitzroy talking about his amazing elixir, I knew I *had* to be the one to try it first.'

A lady in the second row clutched her necklace, eyes brimming with tears. A man a couple of rows behind her half smiled. There was even a faint flutter of claps. Only the Stains and Fitzroy seemed unmoved.

Fitzroy shook his head, jaw clenched. 'This subject has been specially chosen – the effect of a change of this gravity on the demonstration could be catastrophic—'

'ARGHHHH,' squealed Bashum. Dolly hung from his forearm; her jaw clamped round his wrist.

He shook the small girl off and Dolly darted towards Cos, hugging her tightly.

Bashum rubbed the reddening bitemark, face creased in pain. 'I'm not going anywhere near that monster again, sir,' he protested. 'Can't we use the older one?'

Fitzroy huffed out an angry breath. 'Fine,' he said, spittle flying everywhere. 'Let's get on with it.' He stomped to the laboratory tables at the back of the stage and picked up a huge syringe with a nasty-looking needle at one end.

Cos's courage wobbled. Fear rose like bile in her throat. Under her breath she told Dolly to go and wait outside the

Demonstration Hall as Fitzroy strode towards the vat of bubbling chemicals, dipping the syringe into the liquid. She could feel the gaze of the whole audience bore into the back of her head as she held on tightly to the handle of her walking stick.

Fitzroy clicked impatiently at Bashum, who hurried towards Cos and grabbed her roughly, pulling her up the steps on to the stage.

'And now, ladies and gentlemen, we will proceed with tonight's demonstration of Fitzroy's Wonder Elixir.'

He pulled up Cos's sleeve and yanked her arm straight so that the crook of her elbow faced him. The needle hovered a few inches away from Cos's skin, and she tried her best to forget about all the horrible ingredients in his concoction. Cos squeezed her eyes tightly shut and hoped beyond hope that her plan would succeed.

CHAPTER TWENTY-ONE

When, after a few seconds, there was no sharp pain in her arm, and a chorus of gasps had erupted from the audience, Cos cracked one eye open and blinked as she adjusted to the sudden inky darkness.

Every single light in the Demonstration Hall, from the incandescent lamps that lined the room's perimeter, to the spotlight pointed towards Lord Fitzroy, had fizzled out. All Cos could see were the fuzzy outlines of members of the audience shuffling awkwardly in their seats. She grinned into the shadows. *Go, Diya*, she thought, making a mental note to tell Diya just how smart she was as soon as they were out of danger.

'Don't worry, don't worry,' Fitzroy said placatingly, and Cos's chest felt less tight as she heard his footsteps creak away from her. Even Mr Bashum let go of her shoulder and followed him away. Cos was frozen still in the very centre of the darkened stage. For now she was safe from the needle and the elixir.

But as the Demonstration Hall remained cloaked in darkness a disgruntled murmur spread through the crowd. A familiar-sounding boo rang out, and Cos thought immediately of Miles and his throwing-voice trick.

At the near side of the stage Fitzroy conferred with Bashum and other members of the exhibition staff. The audience's hum of discontent grew louder.

'I said, BE QUIET,' snapped Fitzroy, his words echoing round the room. An awkward silence followed. Fitzroy's next words seemed to be softer, less angry. 'We're merely having a spot of trouble with our electricity supply, which we will sort momentarily.'

Cos stifled a snort. Diya had used her inventing know-how to short the whole circuit and plunge the entire Exhibition into darkness.

'In the meantime,' continued Fitzroy, 'my staff will fetch some alternative lighting, and we will proceed with the demonstration shortly.'

The sound of receding footsteps told Cos that the search had already began. Goose pimples prickled up her arm; her tongue was heavy in the base of her mouth. Diya's knowledge of the latest in lighting technology had definitely disrupted The Institute's meeting, but Cos didn't think it would remain disrupted for long.

A short while later candles flickered, bathing the Demonstration Hall in a warm glow. Mr Bashum and his associates had only managed to procure a few, given the limited time, and so – to Cos's relief – there were still plenty of shadows for her friends to hide within. Cos wrapped her arms round herself, her clammy palms holding her elbows close. Mr Bashum nodded at Lord Fitzroy and resumed his grip upon her shoulder.

Fitzroy stepped carefully over the melting wax of the candles that stood at the very front of the stage, the needle held in his hand like a dagger. He was all smiles and charms again now, his cheerful disposition restored.

'Apologies for that slight inconvenience,' he said, as he neared Cos. 'The demonstration will now begin.'

Despite herself, and the plan she'd thought up, Cos wriggled under Bashum's grasp. The cold sharp promise of the needle sent uncontrollable terror running through her.

'None of that now,' Fitzroy sneered, as he grabbed hold of Cos's wrist for the second time and yanked her arm straight. 'You'll barely feel a thing.'

An ear-splitting scream pulled his attention away from

Cos. A feather-hatted lady sprang from her seat, screeching and flapping her skirts around her.

Cos yanked her hand free.

Fitzroy's needle arm dropped to his side. 'What now?' he hissed.

'A beast,' she shrieked in between sobs. 'A horrid, fearsome beast. It skittered round my ankles and, and—'

Before she could finish, her eyes rolled back and she drooped on to the laps of the people sitting beside her.

Just as the lady's companion hovered a bag of smelling salts below her nose, there was a bellow on the opposite side of the audience. 'I felt something as well,' shouted a pinched-nosed gentleman, hopping almost comically on one leg. 'It tried to go up my trousers!'

The switch from shock to pandemonium occurred almost instantaneously. Shrieks filled the Demonstration Hall as ladies hopped on to their chairs and gentlemen stamped furiously. Cos listened closely, not to the shouts and screams, but to the timid yet firm voice that every now and again whispered 'Now' and 'Go, Pearl, go'.

'There must be rats in here,' thundered an important-looking man. From Cos's position she could see the gold buttons holding his waistcoat together strain as he puffed out his chest and glared up his hooked nose at Fitzroy. 'I know you've spent a lot of time in the colonies, Fitzroy, but this is Great Britain.' The man's jowls wobbled with rage. 'We are England's elite. These conditions are unacceptable.'

A vein bulged in Fitzroy's neck, his jaw twitched, and his cheeks flushed crimson. 'I can assure you, ladies and gentlemen,' he said, words creeping out from between clenched teeth, 'that the Empire Exhibition is built to the highest and most modern standards. There are no rats in this building.'

A roar of outrage rose from the audience. One couple shouldered their coats and stalked away, leaving the Demonstration Hall in a fit of huffs. Cos didn't allow herself to feel any relief. Aggie *still* wasn't here. Cos and her friends *still* weren't safe.

Fitzroy tried his best to calm the crowd, but The Institute members weren't happy. A chorus of scoffs sounded out round the Demonstration Hall.

'This is an insult,' said one.

'It's BALDERDASH,' rumbled another.

'It ain't a rat!' Mr Stain stood up rod straight from his seat on the front row, holding something that made Cos's stomach drop. 'It's just a bit of rope on a wire that the girls from our home have put together.'

He raised Pearl's creation so that the whole audience could stare at it. Like everything Pearl made, it was beautiful. She'd transformed the picked-apart rope into a glittering onyx spider, its eight legs dangling.

His sister stood up to join him. 'Which means,' she snarled, 'that more of them are here. They're probably doing one of their pranks.' Her beady eyes glared round the hall, searching for her charges.

Cos's blood ran ice cold, and she could've sworn her heart stopped dead. They were going to be undone at the final hurdle. Silence stretched across the hall, as audience members began to discuss the Stains' assertions.

Ideas hurtled around Cos's head at a hundred miles an hour. What could she do to distract them? Maybe if she let Fitzroy inject her, that would do the trick? Fear gripped her as she willed herself to say something – anything – to stop the inevitable.

But then Fitzroy spluttered, a wolfish smile on his face. 'Don't be ridiculous, my dear Stains. Defective children such as yours can't fathom such mischief.'

Another pregnant pause settled over the Demonstration Hall as the Stains, red-faced and shamed, sank back into their seats.

'But thank you, Mr Stain,' Fitzroy continued, 'for disproving the rumour of rats in my Treasure Palace. It is only fluff. Now the excitement has abated, can we continue?'

Ladies were helped down from their chairs and gentlemen smoothed their suits. The Institute members were soon seated, their attention back on the stage.

Calm was restored. Fitzroy huffed and stepped towards Cos. But before he could reach her, a series of loud and sudden 'pops' erupted across the hall, followed by flashes of light that illuminated the whole hall for a moment or two. Cries filled the room, as audience members cowered beneath their hats.

Masked by the roar of the audience, Cos let out a shaky laugh.

On their way to the Demonstration Hall Miles had excitedly told her about something called flash paper. It was the trick he'd done when he'd first tumbled into their dormitory – a small burst of flame that left no trace.

But as the final flame flickered into nothingness the electric lights switched back on. Fitzroy's jaw twitched, and instead of apologising to his audience for a third time he strode pointedly towards Cos, wielding his syringe like a weapon.

There was a strangled 'NO,' as Cos's friends surged from the four corners of the Demonstration Hall, hurtling towards the stage. But their 'rescue' barely lasted a few seconds.

Miles made it through the audience and up on to the stage,

within touching distance of Cos, before being caught by Mr Bashum.

The stairs up to the stage made it impossible for Diya to get to her, but that didn't stop her trying. To Cos's shock and disgust one of the guards grabbed hold of her wheelchair's handles, sending Diya screeching to a halt. Then he lifted Diya and her wheelchair up with his bear-like arms, heaving her on to the stage.

Pearl's face was scrunched up, her eyes squeezed almost shut and her fists in balls, as she and Mary ran towards Lord Fitzroy. Seeing her friend like that made Cos want to weep.

'We're coming, Cos,' Mary promised.

But guards slammed into Pearl's side, tipping her and Mary off balance. They gathered up the two girls, leading them on to the stage. Fitzroy pinned Cos's arms behind her. Diya, Mary, Pearl and Miles were huddled together, surrounded by guards to Cos's left.

Fitzroy raised his needle, pointing it at her arm. Cos writhed under his grip, struggling to free herself. The pain was all-consuming; she felt as though she were on fire.

'I apologise, Mr and Miss Stain,' Fitzroy grunted through gritted teeth. 'You were right; it *was* your defectives causing havoc. At least now we know that there will be no more interruptions.'

CHAPTER TWENTY-TWO

There was a smattering of light applause as Lord Fitzroy's piercing gaze fixated on Cos. He bent down and whispered so only she could hear.

'I knew you'd be a troublemaker from the moment I met you,' he spat, looming over her. 'But you are no match for me.' He plucked the hankie that was tied round her neck and let go of Cos. She froze at her sudden freedom, not wanting to leave her friends, or the one clue to her parents, to Fitzroy's mercy.

'Did you know that, for centuries, parents have left tokens for their children when forced to give them up?' Fitzroy asked.

Cos's eyes swivelled unbidden towards the handkerchief held tightly in Fitzroy's fist. Her heart squeezed painfully, and she swallowed away the sudden hope that had bloomed in her chest.

Fitzroy paused, his hands resting almost reverently over the corner of her handkerchief. Cos frowned, confused. Then his fingers began digging into the embroidery and stretching the adornment apart so that threads began to fall from it, curling towards the floor like snowflakes. A cry escaped Cos's throat. All her carefully worked-out clues, gone in an instant.

Fitzroy peered under the yanked-out thread, searching for something – *but what?* 'These tokens were often the only link to the children's past. Knowing that orphanages and children's homes would strip their child of their former identity, parents sometimes left clues hidden in their final gift.'

This time the sound that escaped Cos's mouth was more guttural. She lunged head-first for her hankie. Fitzroy hadn't uncovered the clue – he'd destroyed it. Rage seared through Cos. She was one clue away from unravelling the map's mysteries, and now she never would.

Fitzroy jerked back, holding the hankie out of Cos's reach. He panted out a frustrated breath as he began to rip it apart, unwinding the yarn threads. Cos couldn't hold back her tears now – they tracked down her cheeks as she watched Fitzroy destroy her hankie.

Fitzroy let out a triumphant cry as he reached the very centre of the hankie and a scrap of paper fell slowly to the floor. He snatched it up, eyes scanning it hungrily. Cos hated the grin that played on his lips.

'Interesting. Information I am sure you're desperate to know. Your father's name, for instance.'

Her mouth felt as dry as sandpaper. Everything she'd ever wanted was in the hands of a man who hated everything about her.

'Now –' Lord Fitzroy folded the scrap of paper, tucking it into his suit pocket, and Cos's whole body tingled – 'of all the unfortunates your disability is the most . . . acceptable.'

Cos frowned, shifting her weight. 'I . . . don't . . . understand.'

'You walk with a stick, yes, but other than that, you look *normal*. Not like the others. You'd know they were different with a single glance or a snippet of conversation.' He waved a dismissive hand towards them, and Cos noticed that Mary and Diya shrank back in fear. 'You're almost invisible,' he said happily.

For the first time Cos couldn't think of anything to say. The silence stretched out between them.

'So –' Fitzroy withdrew the paper scrap from his pocket – 'I want to give you an out. You have very kindly brought me four more unfortunates upon whom I can demonstrate my elixir. You can leave now, walk away, and have this piece of paper that will tell you who you are. Or you can stay with your so-called friends, and I will destroy your last chance to find your father.'

Cos sucked in a surprised breath; her heart *ba-boomed* in

her chest. The piece of paper was so close. She could almost reach out and grab it. Then she'd have all she ever wanted, and what Diya, Mary and Pearl already had – a real family. Her fingers twitched involuntarily. This was it: everything she'd ever dreamed of.

But guilt crept through her as soon as she'd thought that. She couldn't leave her friends with this man.

She set her jaw. 'No. No matter what, I'm not abandoning my friends. Not for anything – even that.'

Lord Fitzroy frowned. 'Fine.' He stepped forward, yanking Cos's Luminous Headlamp from her forehead. Then, curiously, he froze. The only movement Fitzroy made was the heaving of his chest and a twitch in his bloodshot left eye. Even in her terror Cos was confused, and the audience noticed. They began muttering amongst themselves and shifting in their seats. With a jolt Cos realised that he wasn't staring at her but at the uncovered star clip hanging in her tangled mane.

Cos's heart pounded. Why wasn't he screaming 'Thief' at her? Why wasn't he snatching his sister's clip? Why wasn't he telling his audience that degenerates like her inevitably became criminals? It didn't make sense. It was almost as if the sight of the star scared him.

Before Cos could try to answer any of the questions running through her head, Fitzroy switched the Luminous

Headlamp on, smashed the glass case and held a corner of the paper above the flickering flame.

Cos bit her lip to stop herself from shouting out, all thoughts of Fitzroy's strange reaction disappearing in a cloud of smoke. She wanted that information more than anything, but she wouldn't give up her friends for it. Mary slipped her tied-up hands into Cos's as Fitzroy dipped the paper into the fire, and flames licked the side of her last chance to find out where she came from.

Snotty sobs tore from her throat as she watched the paper blacken and curl, and the flames reach Fitzroy's fingertips. He dropped it to the floor; it was now no more than ashes.

'I gave you the choice,' Fitzroy said, but Cos detected something other than the usual entitlement in his voice. Doubt maybe? Regret?

Even as a void crept into Cos's stomach, even as despair engulfed her, she couldn't stop her whirring thoughts from finally connecting the dots.

Fitzroy had seen the star clip in her hair. His sister's star clip. But he'd said nothing. Surely that was the perfect opportunity to reiterate his point about so-called degenerates.

But he hadn't. He'd stayed silent, frozen to the spot. Just like Cos did when she was caught in a difficult position.

And how had he known about tokens being hidden in children's keepsakes at homes for unfortunates? Or that the scarf tied round her neck was actually a handkerchief? And why had he paused before he'd ripped it apart?

Everything came back to Mina. She was the answer to Cos's questions.

Fitzroy knew. And now Cos did too. She and Fitzroy were connected.

'You didn't give me a choice because my disability is acceptable,' Cos said, panic rising in her chest. 'You did it because I'm family.'

The audience looked aghast. Cos's friends gasped. Lord Fitzroy scoffed.

'The Fitzroy pedigree is impeccable. How *dare* you suggest we are connected to someone like you.'

'You are, though.' Cos smiled as fear crossed Fitzroy's face. 'Your sister, Mina, was like me. *An invalid.* And when she died, unmarried and with a baby who was also disabled, you had to hide me.'

Fitzroy stiffened. 'Be quiet,' he said, his moustache twitching with rage.

'That's why you developed this elixir,' Cos continued. 'But you still aren't sure it works. And deep down, past all the hatred of people like me, there is a part of you that cares for your sister's daughter. *That's* why you gave me a choice. Not because my disability is more acceptable, but because you're worried your elixir might do more damage than good.'

Fitzroy turned away from her, his expression shadowed.

Cos felt herself tremble as she stared out at the gawping audience, who peered at her and her friends as if they were failed science experiments. 'Are you all going to sit there and watch him hurt us?' she asked, tears pricking at her eyes.

Some of the audience had the decency to look away, somewhat ashamed, but others seemed affronted that Cos had dared to question them. In the first row Miss Stain looked as though she was seething. She was wearing a truly ugly hat, a stuffed peacock perched askew, its iridescent feathers turquoise, blue and green. Beside her, Mr Stain glowered, his meaty hands pulled tight into fists.

Diya wheeled forward. 'This elixir won't work,' she told the audience. 'It has no basis in science or logic. Disabilities like ours cannot be cured. I had polio, which paralysed my legs. Whatever Fitzroy has put in this concoction, it won't "fix" my paralysis or stop Cos's joints from dislocating. Science and medicine don't work like that.'

Mary was shaking so much her teeth chattered. 'If anything, injecting me with an untested substance is going to make my neurosis *worse*.'

Pearl spoke quietly, but every word she muttered was important. 'We're not worth less just because we're different. We shouldn't be shut away and only let out to be cured.'

'Exactly.' Cos was galvanised by her friends' support. They

271

may have failed to rescue themselves from Fitzroy's nefarious plans, but surely *some* members of The Institute would listen to reason. They were, after all, a learned group.

'This is ridiculous.' Miss Stain stood, her lips thin and the dead peacock on her head quivering. 'You are a drain on society.'

A small flutter of claps greeted Miss Stain's words. Cos's stomach dropped. 'You exist only to be hidden away and looked after,' she continued, a cruel grin spreading across her face.

The chorus of claps was louder this time, echoing in Cos's ear.

'This is a chance for you all to be transformed, to make history,' Miss Stain said triumphantly. The applause was deafening, and Cos heard shouts of 'Hear, hear' greet the matron's words.

Cos scoffed. 'No, it isn't. It's a chance for all of you to make money and to stop Fitzroy from telling the world your darkest secrets.'

A grip clamped on Cos's shoulder. Fear shivered through her.

'I promise you, this will change your life,' Fitzroy whispered through gritted teeth. 'You can be normal – someone worthy of the Fitzroy name.'

The needle hovered above her arm again, elixir spitting from its razor-sharp point. This time Cos didn't close her eyes – she refused to. She stared right at her uncle as he arced the syringe towards her arm.

Fitzroy froze, frowning. The shouting to-and-fro between him, Miss Stain and Cos had masked the sound of approaching footsteps. His gaze shifted away from Cos.

A determined lady burst through the door, corkscrew curls bursting from her fashionable hat.

Aggie.

The reporter was shouldered on both sides by a team of burly police officers, who stomped into the hall. Aggie pointed straight at Lord Fitzroy. 'That's the man you're looking for.'

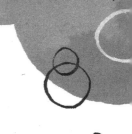

CHAPTER TWENTY-THREE

Fitzroy's expression shifted from anger to fear as the police officers swept into the Demonstration Hall. He stumbled backwards, away from Cos, and placed his syringe on the lab table. The audience was plunged into disarray as the police marched through them towards the stage.

'Officers, please,' Fitzroy said, his voice squeaking up an octave. 'This is a legitimate scientific endeavour.'

Cos's body shook from head to toe and she leaned heavily on her walking stick for support, her breaths coming out in pants. She barely even noticed Fitzroy dart towards a test tube of what looked like small white chunks of salt. Before the police officers could make it up the stairs to the stage, Fitzroy had run to the bubbling vat of chemicals at the side of the stage and emptied the test tube into the liquid.

The reaction began at once. A plume of smoke curled into the air and Fitzroy dived away from the vat, a hand covering his spluttering mouth. Fitzroy's elixir fizzed and hissed as it bubbled over, spilling on to the stage. Over the ear-splitting shouts of the audience something sounded in the distance, but all Cos could focus on was the all-consuming bubble of the elixir.

It took a few moments for Cos to realise that her name was being called. That phrase – *You can be normal* – echoed inside her head. People like Fitzroy, and there were a lot of them, would never accept her as she was.

'Cosima!' Mary screeched for maybe the tenth time.

Cos's gaze swivelled to meet her friend's. Mary's face was blotchy and red, and tears ran down her cheeks. She looked almost as frenzied as when a panic whirlwind struck.

'Listen to me,' Mary insisted. 'Think of a calm place, and count to ten.'

Cos sucked in a lungful of air. She tried to do as Mary said, but she couldn't for the life of her think of a place that was calm.

'One, two, three,' Cos muttered under her breath.

Cos's earliest memories were of the Home for Unfortunate Girls, where it was never calm – not even when the Stains had drunk so much Skullsplitter's they'd passed out. It always felt chaotic, on a knife edge, and Cos never really relaxed. And now that was all Cos would ever have. Lord Fitzroy had ruined any chance of her ever finding out who her father was.

Out of the corner of her eye Cos watched Diya and Pearl move bravely towards the vat of chemicals, hands covering their noses. Pearl was digging in the satchel, pulling out ingredients usually used for her crafting.

'Four, five, six,' Cos continued.

The Empire Exhibition was full of wonders and marvels, but it wasn't calm – and not *just* because of Cos's current predicament. It was full of stolen artefacts – stolen from people under the thumb of the British Empire.

As her friends' figures were obscured by smoke, Aggie leaped on to the stage. 'I did a stint as a laboratory assistant in a factory,' she said breathlessly to Diya. 'Maybe I can help?'

'Seven, eight, nine.'

Mary and Miles raced down the stage stairs and began to lead members of the audience through the smoky hall towards the door.

In fact, Cos couldn't remember ever being in a place that was calm – not once in her life.

The inventor, reporter and the crafter tried various items to calm the vat, with Pearl and Aggie dashing to and from Fitzroy's laboratory tables.

Cos soothed herself as the hissing quietened, the bubbling ceased and the plume of smoke dissipated into nothingness. 'Ten,' she finished, closing her eyes. She may not be able to remember a calm, safe place, but she *could* imagine one. A home that really felt like a home. A kind matron, who cared and hugged and listened. A life full of love, rather than fear.

Diya wiped beads of sweat from her forehead. 'It was simple really,' she said between breaths, as Aggie clapped her on the back. 'We just had to reduce the heat – *fast*.'

Out of the corner of her eye Cos saw the velvet stage curtains twitch. A moustachioed face peered out, focused on the abandoned syringe on the table. She glanced around – the police, Mary and Miles were still too busy escorting the audience to safety, and Aggie, Diya and Pearl had just stopped a vat of elixir from exploding. Fitzroy was hiding! Could he be planning to grab the final syringe of his elixir before embarking on a daring escape?

This is it, Cos thought, as a bitter charcoal taste settled in her throat. He was far closer than she was, and there was no way she could reach the syringe *and* stop Fitzroy escaping all on her own.

It would be impossible.

The word 'impossible' niggled at her. It felt a bit like a challenge. Impossible wasn't a word Cos understood. She huffed out an impatient breath, and with a final burst of energy she stepped towards the syringe, just as Fitzroy scuttled from the cover of the curtains in a most unlordlike manner, hand outstretched.

Cos couldn't move as fast as Fitzroy, but she did have one thing he didn't: a walking stick. She skidded to a halt, walking stick lifted horizontally to ankle height. Fitzroy tripped over it and faceplanted on to the floor. Breathing heavily, Cos stepped over a groaning Fitzroy, picked up the syringe and emptied it on to the floor – destroying the last remnants of the elixir. If being worthy of the Fitzroy family meant putting her friends in danger, Cos wanted no part of it.

The pounding in Cos's head had barely faded. Every sinew of her body was taut, and as Aggie tapped her smartly on the shoulders, she flinched automatically. It hadn't been long since the police officers had marched Lord Fitzroy off for questioning.

'Only me!' she said brightly. 'I'd thought you'd like to know that you are all free to go. The police say they don't need to question you.'

Cos saw the relief in her friends. Pearl squeezed herself tightly, Miles puffed out a 'Phew' and Mary and Diya shared a quick hug. But wariness lay heavy on Cos. She glared across the gallery floor at the cluster of police officers. They were all men, she noticed, and all wore a frown. Every now and again one of them would glance uneasily at the group of disabled girls. Cos sighed. Despite everything – all she and her friends had proved they could do – people were still underestimating them. Dolly had recovered quickly from her torment at the hands of Fitzroy and was now happily skipping round the empty chairs.

'The Stains have been arrested,' Aggie continued, as she scribbled in her ever-present notebook. Cos wondered how on earth she hadn't worked out Aggie's true profession sooner.

It was all over her, from her ink-stained hands to her constant questions. 'I passed on to the police what I'd found out in the course of my investigation into Lord Fitzroy, that there were discrepancies in the books at the home, and they were taken into custody as they fled from Fitzroy's demonstration.'

A bloom of hope sparked in Cos. *No more Stains!* She glanced round at her friends, grins spread wide on all their faces.

'But who's going to look after us?' Pearl asked. 'Will we go back home to our families?' she added hopefully.

An uneasy silence settled over the group. 'Probably not, Pearly,' Cos said, her voice scratchy with sadness. 'The authorities won't let us live with our families full-time. We'll probably either get a new matron, or else be put into other homes for . . . *unfortunate girls.*'

'Why can't *you* be our matron?' Pearl asked, her gaze fixed on Aggie.

For the first time Aggie's collected and confident demeanour disappeared. She sputtered, 'Me?'

Cos's heart pounded with possibility. It wasn't something she'd ever considered – the slightly untrustworthy Miss Noone becoming a more permanent fixture in their lives. But as she thought it over, it didn't seem silly at all. Aggie was smart, a professional woman, and she didn't ever see only the disability but the girl behind it. She noticed that everyone had turned to gaze at Aggie, hope in every face.

'Girls, you deserve a matron who is trained and knows how to care for you properly,' Aggie muttered. 'I'm a reporter; I don't have those sorts of skills.'

Cos felt her hope shrivel into nothingness.

'But –' Aggie's expression was inscrutable, her fingertips tapping against her chin – 'I might know someone who *is* experienced. I met her whilst I was undercover at a governess-training college. I exposed the college as a scam, but Miss Meriton went on to train at the most respectable establishment.'

Hope bloomed again. Happy 'ohs' of surprise broke across her friends faces.

Aggie scrunched up her face. 'A matron of that calibre, though, would cost a *lot* of money.'

'What if we already—' Miles question faltered. He looked at Cos, who gave him a nod. She hadn't trusted Aggie one bit, but that suspicion had been blown away. She wouldn't turn them in.

'What if *we* already had the money?' Miles continued.

Aggie's expression crinkled into a frown. 'I admire you all so much, and you have shown that you are all capable of anything, but I also did my research into the Home for Unfortunate Girls. The finances are appalling. The building itself is hanging on by a thread. Do you really expect me to believe –' Aggie paused, checked that none of the police officers were listening in and whispered – 'that you're sitting on a fortune?'

'Well, we weren't,' Pearl said matter-of-factly, 'until approximately an hour ago.'

Reverently, and with a furtive glance round to check that no other adults were paying attention, Mary opened up their well-worn satchel. In it, five jewels glinted in the early morning sunlight.

Aggie gasped. 'You stole his jewels?'

The girls nodded.

'But how?'

Cos turned to Pearl, who shrugged as if to say *No big deal.* Aggie's gaze drifted to Pearl's intricately decorated arms, her eyes wide.

'You created fakes,' Aggie realised. 'To steal Fitzroy's jewels.'

'Well,' Diya said after a tut, 'we stole them *back*. Fitzroy took all these from countries without permission.'

Aggie's jaw hung loose. 'And what are you going to do with them?'

Diya's jaw was set with determination, her fist clenched tightly. 'Send them home. To their people. Where they belong.'

Cos and the other girls nodded. To their surprise, after a moment of thought, a grin broke out on Aggie's face. 'That sounds more than fair,' she pronounced. 'But then how are you going to make your fortune?'

Mary grinned, pushing the jewels to the side to reveal the golden tiara.

'Fitzroy is a horrible, despicable thief, and we reckoned that he was probably enabled to make this tiara through dodgy dealings or by making life worse for other disabled kids, so really–' Cos's words had tumbled out so fast that she sucked in a huge breath – 'it can't be wrong if we use it to make our lives, and the lives of all the girls in the home, a little better.'

Aggie's expression had been unreadable for the entire time Cos was speaking, but now it cracked into a wide, slightly devious smile. 'Brilliant,' she whispered under her breath. 'Simply brilliant. I didn't think you could surprise me any more, but . . . wow. I have one question, though.'

'What's that?' Mary piped up.

'Well, you can't sell it, that's for sure. Even if the replica tiara remains undiscovered, suspicions will be raised if an identical crown goes on sale.'

Pearl raised an eyebrow. 'You're forgetting about Diya.'

Diya puffed out her chest. 'I'm going to melt down the tiara and turn it into bullion – that's easier to sell – and then we can give the diamond back to India.'

They collected Dolly and returned to the Home for Unfortunate Girls in a blaze of energy, waking the other girls with the news that the Stains weren't coming back. Whoops of joy raced through the home as the girls scavenged the final items Diya needed for her smelter.

Free from fear of Miss Stain's cruel punishments, the girls gathered bits and pieces from the Stains' past get-rich-quick schemes, putting the smelter together in the foyer.

Cos scrabbled through the apple crate in the dormitory, returning to the foyer with a Diya-made tweezer. Pearl held out the golden tiara, and Cos used the tweezer to dislodge the Star Diamond from its mount. It was held tightly, and every yank sent a wave of pain through Cos, but she didn't give up, and with a pop the jewel was free.

Diya wiped sweat from her forehead. Her eyebrows had been half singed off. She was frantically using a spanner to attach what looked like a metal tube to a kettle. 'I'm almost done with construction of the two blow lamps.' Diya put down her spanner and twizzled a knob. The mechanism whirred into life. She puffed into the tube and a blue flame shot from the kettle spout, narrowly missing Cos's knot of hair.

Diya worked and Cos and the other girls carefully packaged up the stolen jewels. Dolly had pinched stamps and labels from Miss Stain's office, and together they wrapped up each precious gem in brown paper and tied it securely with lengths of picked-apart rope. Mary pored through books, trying to find who best to send the jewels to. Then, in her best handwriting, Pearl wrote five separate destinations:

The League of Indigenous Australians, Sydney, Australia
The Matabele People, Mashonaland
The Cape Khoi People, Cape of Good Hope
The Indian National Association, Calcutta, India
The Egyptian Independence Alliance, Cairo, Egypt

Miles placed each package in the satchel before heading off to the post office. He arrived back twenty minutes later, a smile cracked wide on his face, just as Diya switched off her machine, and the heat fizzled down to nothing.

'Now I just need to pad out my crucible,' she said.

'Here you go.' Aggie handed Diya some glass fibre – Aggie's time as an undercover engineer meant she had some crucial engineering components on hand.

Diya, tongue out for concentration purposes, placed the gold tiara into the crucible. Even Cos, who felt sick to her stomach with nerves, was as spellbound as the others as the tiara slowly lost its shape, sinking into a golden sludge. Diya used a kitchen ladle to scoop out the bits that rose to the top, then finally, after the tiara had completely melted, Diya poured the liquid gold into a bullion cast one of the girls had found in an alchemy kit the Stains had once purchased.

Then came the waiting. As the newly minted gold bullion cooled, there was a short, sharp rap at the door. Simultaneously everyone in the hall sucked in a nervous breath. Instinctively the girls at the home shuffled in front of the smelter, blocking it from view, as Aggie and Cos approached the front door and pulled it open.

'Hello.' The man at the door spoke in a nasal voice, not taking his eyes off the clipboard he carried. 'I am required, by the laws of this land, to collect the defective children resident in this home, and transport them to more suitable accommodation and supervision.'

He finally looked up, blinking as the girls sniffled and wiped away tears and held each other tightly. Bile rose up in Cos, clogging her throat. She opened her mouth, trying to turn her racing thoughts into words, to stop this man somehow. But no sound came out.

Aggie swept in front of her, holding out a firm hand. 'Miss Agatha de la Dulce, sir. Reporter for the *Gazette* and professional woman. Your intervention is unneeded sir; a new matron has already been appointed. Miss Meriton has impeccable qualifications. She trained at Norwood College, and most recently was engaged in looking after Lady Blunt's children.'

Cos tried and failed to calm the excited pitter-patter in her chest.

The man snorted. 'This is most peculiar,' he insisted, watery eyes flicking from the paper on his clipboard to Aggie's determined gaze. We have not vetted the candidate; the building seems to be unsatisfactory to say the least.' He blinked at the paint-peeled front door.

'How closely did you *vet* the previous matron?' Aggie questioned, colour rising in her cheeks. 'The girls have informed me that authority inspectors drank alcohol with the Stains.'

The man's blinking intensified. His Adam's apple bobbed nervously. 'Er, well, I cannot comment on—'

Aggie interrupted him. 'Besides, the home has very recently been endowed with a very generous donation from an anonymous benefactor, which has provided enough funds to both look after the girls *and* fix this building up and make it suitable for children to live in.'

Aggie stepped to the side, just as Diya rolled up, the gold bullion sitting in her lap. Gold reflected in the man's eyes.

He cleared his throat. 'Aha, I see.' He paused, scribbling something down on his clipboard. 'Well, I'm sure we can come to some arrangement.'

THE LONDON GAZETTE

20th November 1899   *Price 2d*

FRAUD FITZROY'S MULTIPLE THEFTS EXPOSED

*Lord Francis Fitzroy has admitted that all exhibits in the
Empire Pavilion section of the Empire Exhibition were stolen
unwillingly from their countries of origin. Many of his so-called
inventions were also shamelessly plagiarised. Fitzroy remains
in custody, and a plethora of creditors are demanding his
repayment of loans immediately. His criminal exploits were
discovered by the Gazette's very own dynamic reporter
Miss Agatha de la Dulce, who has decided to forgo
pseudonyms and publish under her true name.*

SIBLINGS ARRESTED: A STAIN ON SOCIETY

*Miss Alvira and Mr Eustace Stain, forty and forty-two
respectively, were arrested after certain discrepancies
were brought to light in their management of a home for girls.
It is alleged that the duo misappropriated funds meant for
the children's wellbeing. They are being held in
Kensington Jail until their trial begins.*

COLONIES ANNOUNCE DISCOVERY OF JEWELS

*Five British colonies have declared that they have found precious
stones long thought lost. The Midjal has been discovered by the
Aboriginal Australians, the Kutinhira uncovered by the people of
Mashonaland, and the Olwandle, the Agrayodhi and the Muntasaf
Allavl jewels have been tracked down in their countries of origin.*

THE INSTITUTE DISBANDED
WITH IMMEDIATE EFFECT

*Administrators agreed to wind up the assets and effects of
the guild . . .*

EPILOGUE
One month later

The home had been decorated especially for the occasion. Tinsel covered every inch of the walls, toys had been cleared away from the foyer and Cos was midway through hanging a welcome banner over the rickety staircase. Laughter floated down the corridors and excitement hung in the air. An over-ornamented wonky Christmas tree stood in the middle of the entrance.

Their new matron, Miss Meriton, paced back and forth, checking the clock every few seconds. She paused and looked up at the banner. 'That looks stupendous, Cos. But maybe let the left side down a little.'

Cos nodded and unknotted her side of the banner, loosening it a little. She was crouched at the top of the staircase. 'How's that?'

'Perfect!' Miss Meriton rushed over to the doorway and

called down the corridor to the schoolroom. 'Everyone, come and see Pearl's banner!'

Cos grabbed her walking stick and, holding on to the banister, made her way down the stairs, just as a gaggle of girls hurtled into the foyer, wheelchairs and walking aids in tow. Cos joined Miss Meriton and the others and stared up at the banner.

WELCOME TO THE STAR DIAMOND HOME FOR CHILDREN. WE'RE EXCITED TO WELCOME YOU TO OUR FAMILY VISIT DAY!

Patron: Miss Agatha de la Dulce, Star Reporter at the Gazette

'*It's beautiful,*' signed one of the girls.

'Your best yet!' Miles grinned at Pearl.

'A true masterpiece.' Miss Meriton nodded. She turned to her charges, her face taut with nervous excitement. She swallowed. 'Are we all ready?'

They were interrupted by the door slamming open, a vicious gust of wind sweeping into the warmth of the foyer.

'Sorry I'm late,' Aggie said, as she bustled inside, a pile of folders and papers tucked underarm. 'I got caught up in preparations for my next assignment!'

'Who are you going undercover as this time?' Miles asked, eyes focused on his brand-new Pearl-made deck of magician's cards that jumped between his palms.

Aggie shook a shudder from her shoulders. Cos could tell the reporter was beset with nerves. 'Myself,' Aggie said. 'I'm to accompany a gentleman as he embarks on a trip round the world, sending regular dispatches back to the *Gazette*.'

There was a chorus of wows and oohs as one of the girls signed: *'Will you write to us?'* Miles clapped Aggie on the back, and Dolly enveloped her in one of her bone-crushing hugs.

'Of course I'll write!' Aggie said, squeezing Dolly back and planting a kiss on her forehead. 'I'll miss you children most of all. And no matter where in the world I am, I will always be proud to be patron of this home.'

Before anyone else could speak, there was a knock at the front door. Miss Meriton and Aggie exchanged an excited smile, then the new matron took a moment to compose herself before striding towards the huge wooden doors. She pulled them open, and Cos saw that a crowd had gathered.

Mary burst into floods of tears as she threw a hug round a wizened gentleman.

Diya wheeled down the door ramp (which she'd only just built), and towards her ma, a respectable-looking lady wrapped in a wool shawl. As she reached her, a grin stretched across her face, a slight Asian man stepped into view.

'Dad!' Diya exclaimed. 'You're back from sea.'

Pearl shuffled past the other girls, heading straight for a small girl and a rather severe-looking older lady. She immediately began to compare heights with the girl, and, satisfied that she was still taller, smiled widely at her sister.

The rest of the girls rushed towards their families, enveloping them in hugs and kisses. Miles threw himself at a grinning lady. In a few seconds laughter and kind words filled the air. Only Cos and Aggie remained at the door. Cos scanned the crowd, hoping against hope to see a person that looked a little like her. Wild hair perhaps? Or misbehaving joints? Blue eyes?

But as the rest of the girls greeted their loved ones, Cos realised that there was no one spare, no one waiting for a chance to meet their long-lost daughter. Her breath hitched in her throat, eyes blurred with tears, as she watched her friends burst with happiness.

Aggie found her hand and gave it a squeeze, a small sad smile on her face. She nodded at Cos, who stepped forward and cleared her throat.

'Come in, everyone! We have freshly baked mince pies, expertly made by Dolly, and piping-hot tea, of course.'

Wintery sunlight streamed into the home as the visitors stepped inside.

Later that day, as the final family member waved their goodbyes, Cos slumped into a comfy chair in Miss Meriton's office.

The relatives had been treated to a grand tour of the new and improved home, which Miss Meriton had snapped up at a bargain price when the previous owners needed to raise funds for their legal fees.

The relatives oohed and aahed at the handsome tome-stuffed library, walked carefully through the paint-splattered art studio, and jumped as Diya demonstrated her latest (and very noisy) contraption in her invention lab. As they'd retired to the dining hall for a well-deserved cup of tea, Pearl's pinched-lipped aunt had tapped Miss Meriton smartly on the shoulder.

'My dear, this is all very well, and it's lovely to see my niece so happy, but how on earth are you affording all this?'

Miss Meriton's eyes twinkled, and she'd shot a wink at Cos. 'Don't you worry about that. I have some very talented and generous friends at my disposal.'

Back in the present, Cos was exhausted. She'd spent the entire day making sure that all the kids had an amazing time with their families. Seeing the grins on everyone's faces made the tiredness worth it, though – it almost made the ache in her chest of having no one visit *her* subside.

She stared up at the board upon which she'd tacked all the clues and theories she'd collected about the possible identity of her father. Mina's drawings, the embroidered hankie, the prison-reform leaflet and Aggie's investigative prowess had narrowed down the identity of the mysterious E, Cos's father.

In the past month Aggie and Cos had interviewed some members of the British Ladies' Association for Prison Reformation. They told Cos all about Mina, her passion and drive for improving the lot of others, her kindness and her love of chocolate bonbons. Cos hung on their anecdotes desperately, every scrap of information a precious connection to her mother. A few of the women *did* remember a speaker – a former prisoner – but none recalled his name. None could tell Cos anything else about her father, other than that he was tall and had brown hair. Frustration bubbled in Cos's belly. E was remaining stubbornly mysterious, like one of Mina's half-finished sketches.

Then Aggie used her contacts in the press to get them into Wormwood Scrubs prison. The red-brick building was tall and imposing and struck fear into Cos's chest. In the prison library Cos and Aggie had searched the records for inmates who had been released in early 1888, having served ten years for a petty crime, with the first initial of E.

Five men fitted the criteria.

Cos had sent out five letters, explaining who she was, asking if they had once known a Willamina Fitzroy, and if so, inviting them to the Christmas visitors' day at the Star Diamond Home.

One had been returned unopened, marked *RECIPIENT DECEASED*.

Three replies had been received, all explaining that they did not know and had never known a Willamina Fitzroy.

A solitary letter remained unanswered.

But none of her potential fathers had come.

Aggie swept towards Cos. 'Are you all right?'

Miss Meriton sat at her desk, sticking stamps on to Christmas cards yet to be posted. 'How are your joints?'

'Sore,' Cos said truthfully. 'But I don't mind. Today was amazing.'

Aggie placed a kiss on Cos's forehead. 'I'm so sorry our E didn't turn up today. But, I promise you, I'll never give up trying to find him for you. For all we know our trawl of prison records could've missed something crucial.'

Cos tore herself away from the clue board, nodding. 'I know, Aggie. And I'll never give up either,' she said, as she rubbed the photo of Mina that she kept in her chest pocket for luck. 'One day I'll find him. But for now I want us to have a cup of tea and closely examine that photograph of the yeti to see if we can prove it's just a malicious scam. Then I want to go and see how Pearl's sculpture is coming along. And check if Diya's ironed out the kinks in her hovering umbrella invention. And—'

'Miss Meriton!' Mary's face appeared round the door. 'I've finally decided on the autumn education curriculum.' She thrust her plans into the matron's hands as she yanked Miles into the office. 'And Miles fixed the stove!'

'Brilliant!' Miss Meriton clapped her hands together.

A loud blast reverberated through the building and the smell of smoke filled Cos's nostrils. There was a screech of wheels and Diya, hair frazzled and ash-covered, and Pearl, clutching a half-painted model of a butterfly, appeared in the doorway.

'Something happened.' Diya's eyes were wide with a mix of panic and excitement. 'There *may* be a teeny fire in the invention lab.'

Miss Meriton grabbed the fire extinguisher (an *essential* household tool when Diya was perfecting her inventions) and rushed from the office. She was followed swiftly by Mary, who was yelling something about following the fire protocol, and Pearl, who was already inking images of flames upon her arm. Cos and Aggie sniggered at each other.

Miles huffed as he yanked off his oven-stained gloves. 'Am

I going to have to fix another broken thing? I thought being an apprentice handyman would be much more exciting than this.' He hurried after the others, muttering under his breath.

Diya paused at the doorway. 'You two coming?'

Cos and Aggie nodded, and Diya gave them a grin before disappearing.

All thoughts of long-lost fathers and mysterious matters fell away as Aggie helped Cos up and they began following the others. Here, right now, in what was once a home for unfortunate girls, Cos felt more content than ever before. Whatever happened, Cos already had her family. It may not be completely conventional, but it was hers.

As she limped towards the office exit, Cos was struck by an unusual silence that had fallen on the home. It was never quiet, not now Miss Meriton was in charge. Laughter and delighted shrieks and explosions (from Diya's inventions) almost always filled the air. Uneasiness crept into Cos as she neared the doorway, and she prepared herself for bad news.

But as she stepped lopsidedly on to the creaking floorboards of the foyer, Cos felt her heart pitter-patter so fast she thought her chest might burst.

An unfamiliar man stood in the shadows of the doorway. His face was craggy and bearded, his hand clutched a crumpled envelope, and, as he removed his cap, Cos saw that his hair was wildly messy. He grinned at Cos, and his dimples matched hers.

Miss Meriton and the children were hugging at the base of the rickety staircase. Diya, Miles, Pearl and Mary were at the very front, grinning at her through their tears.

Cos opened and closed her mouth, goose pimples rising all over her body, Aggie gave her shoulder a comforting squeeze.

When Cos regained control of herself, her voice came out all squeaky and odd-sounding. 'You got my letter?'

Before the man could respond, Cos walked slowly towards him, leaning heavily on her stick. The man's eyes didn't flicker with disgust towards her limp. They twinkled instead, his smile wide and kindly. With two massive strides he closed the space between them, enveloping Cos in a bear hug.

Cos grinned into his shoulder. Thousands of questions burned inside her, but she had plenty of time for answers. Right now, she had twelve years of dad hugs to make up for.

Acknowledgements

This book is in your hands right now because of a whole group of incredible people who have worked so hard and to whom I owe so much.

Firstly, my superstar of an agent, Lydia Silver, for her keen editorial insight and endless enthusiasm. You have been my champion from the very beginning, and I am so grateful to you and the entire team at the Darley Anderson Children's Book Agency.

Thank you to the entire team at HarperCollins *Children's Books* – you have made this experience truly magical and welcomed me so wholeheartedly. My editor, Michelle Misra, who got the story I was trying to tell so perfectly! You have helped Cos sparkle and have been an absolute joy to work with. To Jess Dean, who has been a guiding light. Elisa Offord – thank you for your excellent marketing plans. Cos was brought to life by the talented Flavia Sorrentino, and I still get chills every time I see the cover. Thank you to the cover designer, Matt Kelly, and interiors designer, Elorine Grant.

Writing can get lonely sometimes, but I have been blessed with the best community of fellow writers. *WriteMentor* is where it all began for me. Thank you to Stuart White and the entire team for taking a chance on me when I felt at my lowest. My mentors Maz Evans and Jonathan Eyers were instrumental in shaping my story and providing stellar advice. My fellow 2023 debuts have been so kind and supportive. Natasha Hastings and Amy at *GoldenBooksGirl* are my closest online friends – thank you both so much. Shana Targosz and Christina Dwivedi are my incredibly talented critique partners – I adore your stories and thank you for making mine infinitely better!

Friendship is at the heart of this book, and I don't think I could have written it without the love and support of mine, both far and near. Jasmin Coughtrey, my soul sister and the funniest person alive. Charlotte Chatwin, I can't remember life without you, and I'm so grateful for that. Hannah Gladwell, who got me through university and is always there at a moment's notice. Georgette McLoughlin (please know I still have to double-check the spelling of your surname), Ross Duncan and Mika Duncan – you are all my favourites and I love you all. Cain, Holly, Archie and Cody Giblett – the strongest and most beautiful family. My friends and colleagues at The Devil's Porridge Museum who celebrated with me as I got the news I was going to be published – thank you, Emma, Arna, Desray, Monica and Ellie.

The people of Potton, my hometown, have been an incredible support. I'm so glad I grew up in such a lovely community.

My family are my world. Mum and Dad – this book is dedicated to you both. Words cannot express my appreciation for everything you do for your kids and all you stand for. Tom, my best friend since I was two, and Jayden, our baby brother and the inspiration for Pearl – you both are the bravest, smartest and kindest, and I'm so glad I get to be your sister. My grandparents, Sheila and David, who have been my steadfast supporters since day one. My aunts, uncles, and cousins – I'm sorry I can't fit your names in, but I adore you all. And my new family. Beth – my sister (there's no in-law in my eyes). Nikki Papprill and Al Massie, thank you for your support. Rod Milligan (and Rocky!) – my fellow history buff! My two cats, Scout and Sunny, who only care about fish sticks and chin scratches. Thank you for making me smile every day.

Finally: thank you, Connor, the love of my life. You have picked up the pieces when I thought I couldn't go on and cheered and whooped at my successes. Now you've got a book dedication, so I think you're on washing-up duty for the foreseeable . . .